GEMMA

ALSO BY MEG TILLY

Singing Songs

Porcupine

GEMMA

Meg Tilly

ST. MARTIN'S GRIFFIN

NEW YORK

GEMMA. Copyright 2006, 2010 by Meg Tilly. All rights reserved. Printed in the United States of America. For information, address St. Martin's Press, 175 Fifth Avenue, New York, N.Y. 10010.

www.stmartins.com

Library of Congress Cataloging-in-Publication Data

Tilly, Meg.
   Gemma / Meg Tilly.—1st St. Martin's Griffin ed.
      p. cm.
   ISBN 978-0-312-60529-2
   1. Kidnapping victims—Fiction.   2. Sexually abused girls—Fiction.   3. Child sexual abuse—Fiction.   4. Psychological fiction.   I. Title.
   PS3570.I434G46 2010b
   813'.54—dc22

                                                                              2009040003

First published in slightly different form in the United States by Syren Book Company

First St. Martin's Griffin Edition: February 2010

10   9   8   7   6   5   4   3   2   1

For Charlotte Sheedy
If it weren't for you, *Gemma* would still be a short
story languishing in the top drawer of my desk.

ACKNOWLEDGMENTS

My heartfelt thanks to the *"Gemma* Team" at St. Martin's Press for discovering my orphaned novel that nobody wanted. Not only did they bring Gemma in out of the rain and take her into their hearts, but even more miraculous, they decided to give her a home. The partners in crime are: Sally Richardson, Lisa Senz and Sarah Goldstein, Matthew Shear, Kim Ludlum, Nancy Trypuc, Christine Jaeger, Rob Renzler, Brain Heller, and my wonderful editor, Dori Weintraub, who took the time and made the effort to read a copy of *Gemma* that had been torn up to make Xeroxes and was held together with a rubber band. Thank you, Dori, for dreaming big when I didn't dare to, and for believing in me and this novel I wrote. And thanks to Sophia Dembling for her careful and meticulous copy editing.

My deep gratitude to Laura Langlie, who is everything I ever dreamed an agent could be, and more. I'd also like to thank Charlotte Sheedy for her past support and belief in this book, and Ken Freeman for being one of my first readers, and for his knowledge and insight on the legal and prison protocol side of things. And last, but not least, thanks go to my family and friends for their help and encouragement throughout the writing process and when things got scary. I'd especially like to thank my daughter, Emily Zinnemann, and my husband, Don, for their excellent feedback and suggestions throughout the many stages of this book.

GEMMA

ONE

Buddy, my mama's boyfriend, was waiting for me after school. Waiting in his old rusty blue pickup truck. Almost didn't see him. Almost walked right by, on account of nobody ever picking me up at school before. "Hey, Gemma . . ." he called, and tooted his horn a bit. *Boop . . . boop . . .* Like that.

"Hey, Gemma . . ." And I'm looking around, trying to figure out who's calling my name. Doesn't sound like no kid from school. So I'm looking around, can't see him because the sun's reflecting on his dirty windshield and, yeah, I know his truck. I mean, if somebody said, "I want you to pick out Buddy's truck," if they had a car lineup or something, I'd be able to pick it out fine. Bam. No problem. "That's his truck right there," I'd say.

The thing is, I wasn't expecting him. It was out of *context*. That's why I didn't recognize it.

Pretty good, huh? The way I slipped that in. *Context.* And I think I used it right. I try to work my spelling words into my regular conversation.

That's what my teacher, Mrs. Watson, says we got to do. "Make friends with the words," she says. "Use them, feel them on your tongue, taste them. Let these new words I give you enhance your way of speaking."

Some of the kids laugh at her behind her back. They think she's weird, but I like listening to her talk so passionate and earnest, her cheeks and the sides of her neck getting all flushed and red. "Language will set you free," she says, in ringing tones, like she's a minister standing at the front of the church, preaching hell and redemption. "Language will set you free." She says it ferocious, like it's real important, a life-and-death matter to her that we understand. Like it'll save us from gangs, and no money, and no food in the house because our moms are out boozing again.

It's one of Mrs. Watson's favorite sayings. "Language will set you free." Says it maybe five times a day. Arm out, gesturing, hand all smudgy from the chalkboard. Or sometimes she pounds the desk when she says it, or a book she's holding in her hand. And she really seems to believe it, so I don't know. Maybe it will, maybe it won't, but just in case she's right, I work on my language, my spelling words, my vocabulary. I work on them hard, because I wouldn't mind being free.

And that's another thing. She gives us real weird writing assignments. Take today, for instance. She comes waltzing into the room. "Good morning, class." Nobody answers, never does, not even me. I would, because I like her. Like and feel sorry for her all at the same time, because to be honest, we aren't that great of a class. But even I didn't answer her, because I'm kind of cool. Not real cool, like "lots of friends cool." I'm more like "loner cool." People don't mess with me too much, because if they did, they'd get a face full of fist. I'm a wild card, so people leave me alone, let me fly under the radar screen, like a stealth bomber, and I don't want to mess with that, so I don't say hi, or good morning. I didn't want to look like a goody two-shoes, and just shuffled my feet with the rest of the kids, like I was real bored or something.

Even though I was actually kind of interested to see what she was going to come up with today.

Didn't let on though, just mumbled a little bit of a good morning, that's about all I could get away with, and to be honest, it's pretty respectful, considering what some of the other kids do. I mean, at least I was sitting in my seat, not screwing around in the back of the class, throwing things, swaggering around, pants half falling off my ass, pretending not to see the teacher come in. At least I wasn't doing that.

Now maybe I don't say it loud and clear, in a TV sitcom voice, but at least I say something. At least I mumble "good morning," because it's more than most people do.

Besides, it's not honest to say "good morning," when for most of us, most of the time, it isn't a very good morning at all. I'm not complaining, mornings are generally better than evenings. That's usually when the shit hits the fan. In the morning, I've got the whole day stretching out before me, shimmering like a promise, like maybe today something fun's going to happen, something good, something exciting. I like morning—the way it smells, the way it looks, like it just woke up and maybe today things are going to be okay.

But this custom of saying "good morning" every morning, well it's just not truthful.

"The . . . Topic . . . is . . ." Mrs. Watson read each word out loud as she wrote it, "Love. . . ." When she'd finished writing the words out on the blackboard, she underlined them so emphatically that a little bit of powder fell, like a puff of smoke, from her stick of chalk.

Then she turned around and faced the class, and the expression on her face was almost like a dare. I like this about her, that she's so into what she does. I look forward to it, because most teachers, they're too tired to care anymore, too beaten down. I can see it in their faces sometimes, when all the kids are acting out, screwing around. I can see the weariness, see them wondering why the hell they took this job. Tired out, pissed off, going through the motions like they're underwater swimming.

3

Sometimes, I get worried that Mrs. Watson's going to get like that too, all tired out, sharp edged, and bitter. I try to be nice to her on the sly, so she won't give up, lose hope, and think we're all lost causes.

"The topic is love," she said again, just in case we didn't hear her the first time, hear the whole thing properly.

"We're going to try something new today: *Free association*. I want you to pick up your pen and write. Don't worry about punctuation, or spelling, or telling a story. I want you to write whatever comes into your mind, whatever pops into your head, write it down. The topic is love. You have twenty minutes, start writing."

She turned to her desk, like that was all that needed to be said, but nobody was writing, we were all staring at her like she was a freak show. Because she's come up with some weird assignments, but this one's a doozy. And to be honest, I'm trying to encourage her and all, but even I had no idea what to do.

"Love . . . ," Billy Robinson mimicked in a mamsey-pamsey voice. He started gagging, and his cronies were snickering, and then it's like his face all of a sudden gets mad, like Mrs. Watson assigned this exercise for the sole purpose of pissing him off. "What the hell kind of *shit* is that?"

"Exactly," Mrs. Watson said. She's not scared of him, like some of the other teachers. She just beamed at him and nodded her head, like he'd been real insightful, like he wasn't being a smart ass. Smiled at him like he was joining in for once, and she was taking his question seriously. "Exactly." Then she looked at the rest of the class, acting as if we were having a philosophical discussion. "What *is* love? What does it mean to you? How does love, or the lack thereof, manifest itself in your life?" She nodded encouragingly. "Just pick up your pen and write. There is no right or wrong in this exercise. As long as you have written something on your paper, you'll get a good mark."

So I picked up my pen. She's the teacher after all.

The topic is love, I wrote. I underlined it. And then, that was it. I just sat there, staring at those words at the top of my page, stuck, couldn't think of anything to write.

"The topic is love," I said under my breath, testing the words on my tongue. "The . . . topic . . . is . . . love."

My pen wasn't writing, but my brain, my brain was flipping through memories, all of my mom, none of my dad, but that's probably because I don't know him, never met him. Otherwise, he probably would have been in there too.

And these images of my mom, they're not whole stories spun out. It's not like they made sense. It was more like I was looking into one of those kaleidoscope toys, but I wasn't holding it. Somebody else was, and they were turning it so the images were tumbling, morphing, changing shape too fast and I couldn't catch the tail of them. Just short little memories flying past, little flashes of them. Short flashes, like a strobe light in the dark. And my brain, trying to catch up, flipping through them and discarding. Nope, can't write about that, or that, ho, ho . . . definitely not that! Bits and snatches of her, flying past, like I'm riffling through one of those little plastic recipe holders that normal households have, with recipes written down on index cards. Normal households that have a mother and a father, and the mother cooks, and the children have cookies and cupcakes and things when they come home from school. Normal households with moms who have pretty beauty-shop hairdos, and they drive their kids to piano lessons and skating lessons and things.

Like Angela McCauley, she had a home like that. We were best friends for part of fifth grade, but that's neither here nor there. I'm not bemoaning the fact that we aren't friends now, could care less. That's not what I'm talking about. The point of all this, what I'm getting at is, she had a mother like that. Her mom had a pink recipe holder. It wasn't a pale pink, but it wasn't real bright like hot pink or neon colored or anything tacky like that either. It was more like the color of double bubble gum after it's been chewed for a while. Sort of like that color.

Angela's mother let me look at it once. Took it down from the shelf over the stove and let me hold it.

She had all kinds of recipes in there, some of them she'd tried and some she hadn't yet. There were recipes her friends had given her, ones she had clipped from the *Good Housekeeping* magazines she kept on her coffee table. She liked *Good Housekeeping* magazines. That's the kind of mother Angela's mom was. She liked doing motherly, homey things. When me and Angela were friends, Angela would invite me home for lunch. I'd leave my soggy peanut-butter sandwich in my desk and walk with her to her house. Rain or shine, it didn't matter to me if we got soaking wet, didn't matter one bit, because I knew what would be waiting for us.

Angela's clean-smelling mom would meet us at the door, and on rainy days, when we'd come in, all dripping wet and laughing, she'd fuss and worry that Angela wasn't wearing her coat done up, hadn't used her umbrella, things like that.

She noticed when Angela's hair was wet, for instance. And she'd give us towels to dry off, and we'd stand there in her hallway and we'd rub our heads and I'd pretend like I was familiar with this, like my mom met me at the door and gave me towels too. Angela would roll her eyes at me and I'd roll my eyes back at her as if to say, "Moms, what are you going to do?" But I'd be savoring it. The fresh-washed towel, all soft and fluffy. Thick too. Not all scratchy and thin and mildewy smelling like ours. Not rancid with underarm smell and yesterday's throw up.

No, these towels were thick and soft and fluffy. And I'd rub my hair and my face, bury my nose and breathe in the smell, the softness, and all that love, and pretend that this was me, my life. That I'd woken up in the middle of a Beverly Cleary novel.

I'd rub my hair as long as I could, and then when we were done drying off, we'd head into the living room and sit cross-legged on the floor and play Scrabble on their wood-and-glass coffee table. I'd be real careful not to touch the glass part and leave fingerprints, so her mother wouldn't think me coming over was a whole pile of work. I'd make sure to only let my hands rest on the wood rim that held the glass in place, that and the Scrabble board. It was cozy playing Scrabble while her mom bustled around the kitchen, making us piping-hot Kraft macaroni and cheese.

I'd always say, "yes, please," and "no, thank you," to her mom. Try and behave real good, so her mama would like me and ask me back.

So that was all good. The problem was at night. That was the problem. Because I'd lie in bed, and I'd think about the day. For the first couple of months, I was happy. I liked being Angela's friend, it was real comforting. I'd think about her house, and her mom, and everything, and it made me happy. It was like a real good bedtime story. Made me feel all cozy, and I'd go to sleep with a smile on my face.

But then one night, it flipped on me. I was running through my images, my memories, the scent of her mom, the house, the lemony smell of Pledge, the polished surfaces, the tick of the brass-and-glass clock on their mantel. I'd think about her mom in the kitchen with her yellow terry-cloth slippers making a *shush . . . shush . . .* sound on the linoleum. I could almost taste that macaroni and cheese, and then, the damned thing flipped on me. It's like this little voice dropped down into my head from nowhere, and it said, "Yes, well, that's all fine and good, but be honest, Gemma, do you really like her?"

And me, my heart started racing. "What?" Cheeks getting hot, stomach gripping up, getting all embarrassed, even though no one could see me. "Who?"

"Angela." And this voice is acting as if it thinks I'm the lowest of low. "What do you *like* about her, other than her mother and her life?"

"What are you talking about?"

"Stop playing dumb! You find her *boring* and you know it. You're just using her."

"What?" Me, acting indignant, but I know it's true.

"Borrowing her life, stealing little snatches, pretending they're yours . . ."

And that was that. I had to stop being her friend because it really wasn't fair, Angela thinking it was her I liked. I had to stop, it wasn't right, fooling her like that.

It was real difficult, but I stopped accepting her invitations, stopped going over. Think I hurt her feelings, but I felt like too bad a person the other way, using her good nature like that.

So that's when I became a loner, not because I'm a loser. I'm a loner because I choose to be. Better than being a using, lying *hypocrite.* Ahem . . . spelling word.

It was hard at first, eating my sandwiches by myself, sitting on top of the jungle gym. Pretending I didn't care. Acting like I didn't notice when Angela and her new best friend, stupid Patty Tomas, would walk past me, noses in the air, with their permission slips to leave school property clutched in their hands. Walk out of the playground, laughing and talking, to go to Angela's house for her warm mother and hot meals. It was hard at first, but now, no problem. Doesn't bother me at all.

Anyway, back to my mama. She doesn't do the kind of things Angela's mom does. Not that my mom doesn't love me, she does. She just doesn't have time to show it, is all. I mean, it's hard raising a kid, and I'm no walk in the park. I try to be good, but I don't know, seem to always be messing up somehow, making her mad. And then there's work. She's got to work. How else are the bills going to get paid? How else is she going to keep a roof over our heads? So she's got to work.

Used to be a cocktail waitress at Shooters. Tips were good, but she got too old. "They like their flesh firm over there at Shooters," she says. "They like them young. Young and stupid." That's what my mama says, face all twisted up. "They don't want a washed-up hag like me hanging around, ruining people's appetites. Assholes."

"Mama," I try to tell her. "You're pretty." Because when she's not drinking, she's real pretty. But she doesn't listen to me, just takes another slug of Jack Daniels and threatens to, "go on over there, give them them what-for."

8

Anyway, she got another job, down at Joe's diner. But she's got to work harder, longer hours and tips aren't so good. Apparently, the people that eat at Joe's are cheap, cheap, cheap.

I try to be in my bedroom, with my door closed, when she gets home from work. Try to stay out of her way because by closing time, she's usually in a bad mood.

Now, if my mama had a nicer life, an easier one, she'd have lots of time to be loving and cozy. She's busy is all, worked to the bone. If there was something real, real important, she'd make the time, and that's the truth.

I remember once, in second grade, I had a bad fever. Real bad. Apparently I fainted in the lunchroom and they called my mama. She dropped work and everything. Drove to the school straightaway and took me to the doctor. And I guess what he told her was pretty bad, because she let me sleep in her bed. I was sick, real sick, and no matter what they did, the fever wouldn't break. Gave me medicine, fed me Popsicles, even gave me a shot in my butt. But nothing was working, and the doctor was worried they were going to lose me. And my mama, she stayed home from work and watched over me, soothed my forehead with her cool hands. Had her metal mixing bowl and a washcloth with water and ice cubes in it, and when the huge black spiders, bigger than my fist, would be crawling all over the place, up the walls, and I was the only one who could see them, she'd wring out the washcloth, sponge bathe me, and make them go away. The water so cold that my body would shake and shake and I'd have to grit my teeth to stop their clattering. My head all fuzzy. I didn't tell my mama that I wasn't in the mood for those Popsicles she kept trying to feed me, because she'd already bought them, and Popsicles are expensive, cost good money. So I'd eat them, even though they were weighing heavy in my hand, and it was so hard to sit up. I'd eat them for her, because she was trying so hard.

She let me sleep in her bed for eleven days. Stayed home from work. Eleven whole days. Wish I could remember them better. Kind of passed in a blur. I try to force my brain to remember more. But it doesn't work. . . . Just clutching at images, bits and pieces, like the memories were scattered, torn by a windstorm.

But I do remember she let me sleep in her bed once. I do remember that.

And all of this was flashing through my head, and I still hadn't written a damned word. I heard the other kids writing. Heard their pens dragging across the paper. Heard Billy Robinson saunter across the room. Didn't even have to look up. Knew it was him, his footsteps.

"Where are you going?" Mrs. Watson said.

"The crapper." All innocent as can be. "Got a bad case of the runs." His sidekicks giggled like he was God or something, because everyone knows he doesn't have the runs. Isn't going to come back for a good fifteen, twenty minutes. Going to go sneak a smoke out back, behind the gym.

He shuffled out, because what could she say? "You can't go to the bathroom . . . ?"

And there I was, still staring at the page. Time was running out. Didn't want to get an "F." Had to write something.

So I wrote "Love is pretty good at my house, the quality of it." And I wrote about going home for lunch, and Kraft macaroni, and warm, soft, sweet-smelling towels.

I wrote about it like it was me. Like it was my mom. And I've got to say, it was fun, really lost myself in it. Almost believed what I was writing there for a moment. Got this excited feeling in my belly, like maybe, when I got home, it would be true. Like maybe, in the writing of it, it was a reminder to God or something. Like maybe he didn't realize, didn't remember that he'd made a mistake.

Anyway, Mrs. Watson's class was the first class of the day and crazy as it may seem, all day long, on and off, I'd get excited all over again. Wanting to get home. Knowing the story I wrote wasn't true, but the wishing part of me wanting to get home, just in case.

So I went through my day with a little tickle of anticipation dancing in my belly. Not a big excitement, more like the feeling when I find an old piece of candy in my pocket that I forgot I had, and my mouth is watering, waiting for recess. It's more like that level of excitement.

I mean, come on. I'm not a baby. I know magic isn't true. But sometimes it's fun to pretend.

So anyway, because I had this hope, the day seemed to drag on, go so slow. Finally, when the final buzzer went, I was out of there like a flash. Like, yeah, I got somewhere important to go. Out the front door like a bullet, but by the time I'd reached the bottom of the front steps, I'm like, "Who am I kidding?" And all of a sudden I feel real stupid, like, "Why am I racing home?"

Then, to make matters worse, Buddy was waiting for me. Like what the hell's that about?

And when I said I didn't see Buddy at first, it's not because I have bad eyesight. I didn't see him because I wasn't expecting him or his dumb old truck. There is nothing wrong with my eyes, I saw him fine once he got out.

"Hey sugar. . . ." he calls, with that stupid southern drawl he thinks sounds so smooth. Makes me want to punch him in the face. I hate it when he calls me that. "Sugar. . . ." Hate it. Stupid smirk on his fat face. Stupid asshole.

"Give me some sugar. . . ." he always says, late at night when he creeps into my room, my bed. "I need somah yo' sugar. . . ." Stupid creep. "Your pussy's so sweet. . . ." he says, while he's grunting over me like a filthy, sweaty pig. "I'm addicted to yo' pussy. It's your fault, you know. Your pussy's so sweet, it keeps me coming back for more." Says it like he thinks it's a compliment, like I should be pleased! He knows I don't like it! Hurts like hell and he knows it. Why else would he be holding his stupid greasy hand over my mouth? Why else? I'll tell you why. He don't want my mama to hear me crying, that's why. Don't want my screams waking up the neighbors.

Thought I was going to die the first time he did it. Eight years old. Thought I was going to split in two for sure. Mama was out of town,

11

visiting my granddaddy. Just me and Buddy at home. One afternoon, Buddy, he comes home from work, and he's acting weird, been drinking, smell it on his breath. He puts the music on. Pumps the volume up loud, so loud I could feel the bass pounding right through the soles of my feet. Music, loud, loud, loud. Neighbors couldn't hear, nobody could hear, Buddy, holding me down, doing bad things to me, me crying out, but nobody could hear nothing.

I tried to tell my mama when she got back, but she wasn't up to talking. Sometimes she gets that way after visiting Granddaddy. She went straight to her bedroom with her bottle of Jack Daniels and took a good, long nap. I didn't bother her because I knew she was tired. But later, after she woke up and was rummaging through the refrigerator, trying to find some eats, I tried again, followed her in, but she was still in no mood.

"Jesus Christ," she said, slamming the fridge door, nostrils flaring. "I get so tired of your goddamned whining." Hands fisted on the ledge of her hips.

Thought I was whining and I hadn't even told her the worst of it, any of it really. Hadn't gotten to the bad stuff yet, had just said that I didn't want Buddy to babysit me anymore when she went to visit Granddaddy, that I didn't feel comfortable, didn't feel real safe with him. . . . I wanted to tell her more, everything, but the way she was looking at me stopped me cold. "What am I supposed to do?" she said, mouth twisted. "Who am I supposed to leave you with? You tell me. Hmm? Do you see great mobs of people standing in line, clamoring to take care of you?"

I didn't have no answer.

"Do you?" she demanded, voice rising. She started looking around the room, like she was searching for volunteers. "I don't see anyone," she said. "I don't see anyone saying 'Oh please, let me.'" All sarcastic like. "I don't see a single goddamned living soul. . . . I mean, please, correct me if I'm wrong, maybe I'm not seeing so good. Do you see anyone volunteering?" And of course I didn't, how could I, there was nobody else there. No right way to answer that one, so I shut up, and Buddy stayed my babysitter. And when he heard from my mama that I was complaining, that wasn't good. He got me alone and slammed me up against the wall in the hallway, my feet dangling off the ground, his face up close, bad breath, stinking me out. Told me to shut my yap. Did I want to be thrown in jail? "Yes that's right, thrown in jail, because that's what they do to little girls who seduce grown men. Flaunting your pussy like you do. If they knew about you, they'd lock you up in jail and throw away the key for good."

That's what they do because apparently, what I did with him is against the law and I can't tell anybody. Anybody at all, unless I want to spend the rest of my life rotting away in jail. And I don't want to do that, I'd be scared of jail. I'd be real scared. So it's a good thing, I guess, that I found out in time. Found out before I accidentally spilled the beans and told someone. Good thing I found out about the laws.

Anyway, it's bad enough I have to deal with him at home, but now he's waiting outside my school, sleazing the place up, calling me sugar, people are looking. I hope they don't know what that means. Sugar.

"Hey sugar. . . ." Buddy says, coming round the front of his pickup truck, left thumb slung in the belt loop of his saggy old blue jeans, right arm free, loose, dangling. "How was school?" Like he cares, stupid jerk, coming around here. He's got no right.

I keep walking. Head in the air. Pretend I don't see him. Keep walking past like he's got nothing on me, like he's just a squashed fly on his windshield. Just speed up my steps a bit, move round to the other side of the sidewalk, get a few kids between us. I do it casual, like I just remembered I'm late for something important. But he speeds up too, and catches me by the arm. Laughing like it's a game, but he's got my arm hard.

"Ain't letting you get away as easy as that," he says, and hauls me off to his truck. Nothing I can do about it. Don't want to cause a fuss. Don't want kids looking any more than they already are. Nothing I can do about it but make my feet walk in his direction.

"Bet you're wondering why I picked you up from school," Buddy says, looking over his shoulder, out the back window, stepping on the gas, swinging the truck out into the traffic, when even I—and I'm only twelve, can't drive, no matter—even I can see that there's not enough room. That silver car's coming way too fast. But he swings the truck out, turning the steering wheel hard, causing the silver car to slam on its brakes, lean on its horn. Which pisses Buddy off. "Fuck you!" he yells, sticking his middle finger out the open window. "Fuck you!" Like they were the asshole. Like they were the screwup.

Then, like nothing happened, like he didn't just almost kill us for sure, he turns back to me. "Betcha can't guess!"

I am a bit curious why he picked me up, but I'm not about to give him the satisfaction, because that's the thing about Buddy that I've got to watch out for. He always pretends he's got a special treat for me, something real great, builds up my expectations, when more likely than not, it's going to be a big, steaming slice of crap pie.

I don't say nothing, just look out the window and keep to my side of the truck. Don't get too close to Buddy, because even with that big belly hanging down over his jeans, he can move pretty damned fast.

I feel him looking at me, but I don't turn.

"I got you a job," he says.

"A job?" I keep my voice casual, keep the eagerness out, just in case I heard him wrong, just in case it's a joke or something.

"You got me a job?" I say, and I'm kind of nervous, but, to be honest, this is exciting too. I wouldn't mind a job. Make a little money. The kids at school would be jealous. Don't know anybody my age that's got a job. I thought people had to be fifteen, or sixteen. Which is kind of a dumb rule, because I'm a real hard worker. Shouldn't matter the age, they'd get their money's worth out of me.

"Yeah. . . ." he says. "I got you a job." He looks at me. "And you want to do well at this job right?"

"Yeah," I say. "Yeah!" I smile big, so he'll know I mean it. Don't know why he's being so nice all of a sudden. But a job would be cool. Real cool.

"Don't want to mess up, right?" he says, and I shake my head so he'll know I'm sincere. He keeps talking. "Because if you mess up, I'm going to be real pissed. And you don't want to get me pissed, isn't that right?"

"Uh . . . huh. . . ." I nod my head. I don't know why, but my heart's pounding and my mouth is real dry. I mean, I'm glad to have a job, but I'm kind of scared too. Buddy's not much fun when I mess up. "What . . . what do I got to do?" I ask.

But he doesn't answer me. Not really, just laughs—not a nice laugh, not a friendly one—and says, "Sugar, you just do what you do best." And he's still laughing about that one as he jerks the steering wheel hard, cross two lanes of traffic, and there we are, pulling into a Denny's parking lot. "Oh, Denny's," I think. "Maybe I'm going to get to be a waitress."

I'd like that. That would be nice. Maybe I'd get a uniform and everything!

•   •   •

Hazen is sitting in Denny's restaurant. Got himself a booth in the corner, back against the wall, good vantage point of the door. Hands sweaty, the dregs of his coffee gone cold, got that tie-dye thing going with the sugar, the cream. He swirls it slowly, both hands wrapped around the mug, like it's still hot, drinkable. Sits there, like he has every right. Takes a sip, something to do. Waiting for Buddy, just on the off chance, pretty sure actually, that he's not going to show. But Hazen's waiting, just in case.

The waitress with blue mascara slides by, fresh pot of steaming coffee. He gestures her over. Not that he wants more. Stuff tastes like shit. Badly brewed. Already feeling jittery, drunk two cups of the stuff, but what the hell, he'll give Buddy ten more minutes and then call it a day. What a bullshitter.

15

Just getting ready to leave, the waitress smelling like cheap talcum powder and last night's sex. Settling up his bill, when Buddy waltzes in, thirty minutes late. Hazen had thought he'd been stood up, played for a fool. The fucker was just blowing smoke up his ass. Telling him all about this Gemma chick he was banging. Saying what a great lay she was.

"You've never had it good until you've tried some of this," Buddy'd said. "The kid's twelve, talk about tight, best lay this side of the Rockies, and beautiful too. A regular little Lolita. Insatiable. Can't get enough, begs for the cock, twenty-four/seven." Said it with this satisfied smirk on his face that made Hazen want to call his bluff.

Hazen thought Buddy was just blowing smoke up his ass, but then in he walks, the kid in tow, and she is perfect. Absolutely perfect. Long blond hair, pale blond, the color of summer grass along the highway, and Hazen Wood wonders about her heritage. Swedish ancestors? Danish perhaps? Beautiful blond hair, a natural. Yes sir, she is perfect, just how Buddy described her. High tight ass perched on lanky colt legs, legs not quite filled out. No tits, none visible anyway. Maybe just little buds, little swollen buds hiding beneath her T-shirt, the nipples just starting to swell. Absolutely perfect. Well worth it, the wait, the money.

．　　　．　　　．

"This is Hazen," Buddy says, pushing me forward, giving me a slap on the ass. Like he owns me, like I'm a donkey or something. And this guy, this Hazen guy, is stepping forwards, smiling big for a mouth that looks like it's not used to smiling much.

"Hey there, little girl . . . ," he says, which kind of offends me, because I'm not little, I'm twelve, for Chrissake. Would correct him on his assumption, but I don't want to be rude.

"Hi," I say. I'm feeling funny, don't know why. Don't like the way this Hazen guy is looking at me. Looking at me all greasy, oily-like. Freaking me out.

16

"Well, what do you think?" Buddy asks, me standing there, just standing there.

"Good. She'll do, she'll do real nice," says Hazen, smiling. Runs his forefinger down my arm. He does it slow, like he's branding me. I don't like it. Try to step back, but there's nowhere to go. Buddy's stepped in right behind me, right up close, crowding me in. Nowhere to go, and I kind of suffer from claustrophobia, sort of like panic spells when people crowd me too close. I get dizzy, everything kind of slows down, rushes by, blurry-like. Standing there in Denny's, Buddy pressing up against my back, this Hazen guy right in front, table, chairs, cutting out my air. I can hear the kitchen noises, dishes, cutlery clinking loud. Real loud, like they're amplified, and yet voices, muffled, foggy, like they're talking through a vacuum hose. And Buddy and Hazen, they both laugh, tunnel laugh. Then Hazen takes his wallet out of his back pocket and starts counting out money. "Twenty . . . forty . . . sixty . . . eighty . . . and . . . one-hundred dollars." Gives the money, the hundred dollars to Buddy. And I'm wondering what this has to do with my waitressing job. But Buddy doesn't explain. Just pockets the money, gives my ass a feel, then stuffs my hand into this Hazen guy's sweaty, clammy one. His soft, pulpy, soggy hand, that feels like mashed, spit-out bananas. "She's all yours, man," Buddy says, smiling still. Smiling big. Then he makes a noise like a train whistle. "Whoohoo!" he says, pumping his fist up and down in the air. "Go to town."

While Hazen's putting away his wallet, Buddy leans over me, smile gone. No smile now, eyes like ice picks, drill right through me. "You be good," he says, hand slid under my hair, squeezing the back of my neck. Squeezing it hard, real hard, making my eyes fill up. "Hazen's boss now, you hear? You do whatever he says, you hear? Whatever he says. He'll bring you home when you're done, and I don't want to hear about you giving him any flak. You hear me?"

And I'm trying to keep my head upright, trying not to let on how much it's hurting. How humiliating it is, for him to be doing this kind of thing in public. "You hear?" Gives me a shake, speaking low, through his teeth, nobody but me, me and Hazen can hear him.

"I hear you," I say. "I hear you." He gives me one last shake for emphasis, then lets me go, and his friend Hazen is laughing, shaking his head. "You got her trained good," he says admiringly, like I'm a dog or something. "You got her trained real good."

Next thing I know, Buddy's gone. Didn't fill out no application for no waitressing job. Don't know how to get home from here. Got no idea. Stuck here with Hazen, not sure why. Not sure, but I got a feeling. I got a sick kind of feeling in my belly. Stuck here with this Hazen guy, but I'll be damned if I'm going to cry.

TWO

He knew she wasn't a virgin. Hell, Buddy had told him so. He'd had her. And according to Buddy, he probably wasn't her first either.

Hazen knew she wasn't a virgin, but he couldn't help the brief stab of disappointment when he entered her. It's like his head knew that she wasn't, but the rest of him refused to believe it. She was warm, tight, small, real small, kind of dry, but spit had helped that along. Not much hair, just a little bit of peach fuzz, hell, her only being twelve and all. But he wasn't her first. And the sensation that was missing, the resistance, her gasp of pain, surprise, pleasure as he first forced his way into her, his keen disappointment made his penis go soft, flaccid. And his dick doesn't care how nice she feels, his dick is annoyed with him and his goddamned fairytale promises and starts sliding, oozing out of her.

"Shit!" he yells. "Shit!" He rolls onto his back, yanks the covers up over his waist, arms crossed, gripping them to him, trying to get his breathing under control.

"Paid a hundred bucks. A hundred lousy bucks, and you can't even make me keep it up," he says, glaring at the ceiling.

"I . . . I'm sorry . . . ," she whimpers, face puffy, tear-streaked. Hasn't stopped crying since she got to his apartment and received the bad news. Apparently Buddy hadn't told her what she was there for, what the deal was.

"No . . . no . . . no . . . ," she kept saying. "You don't understand. . . ." She was babbling on about some waitressing job at Denny's. Clutching at her clothes, like she had half a chance. Trying to keep her clothes on, trying to scramble out the door. Not that that bothered Hazen, the chase. Kind of funny, actually, how scared she was. No, that didn't bother him. It was the fact that she didn't feel quite how he imagined. That was the thing that made him get soft and shrivel up like a snail doused in salt.

He glares at the ceiling, doesn't look at her, doesn't want to feel guilty, wishes she would stop her goddamned crying and enter into the fun a bit. Tries not to look at her face, but he can see it hovering in the periphery of his sight line, her long, blond hair swinging forward, falling, obscuring her like a curtain, her naked body wrapped around itself, legs and arms all tucked in, small, like she's trying to disappear. Tucked up so small he could easily fit her in the half-size oven he has in the kitchenette. Bake her up for dinner. He has to laugh at that. Might have lost his hard-on, but he still has a sense of humor.

Her body is rocking slightly. "Can I go home now?" she's whispering, voice coming out all scratchy. "Can I go home?"

He doesn't answer, stupid bitch, little cock-teasing whore.

"Ask me nice," he finally says, not that he has any intention, paid a hundred bucks for Chrissake, but he's interested to see what she'll do.

He can feel her thinking, holding her breath.

"Ask . . . me . . . nice." His voice slow, measured.

There's a slight pause.

She takes the bait.

"P . . . please . . . can . . . can . . . I go h . . . home now?" Her head

20

tips up slightly from her knees, and he can tell that she is peeking at him from behind her hair. Sussing him out. It's a chess game now, pure and simple. And Hazen, all modesty aside, is a damned good chess player.

"P . . . please?" she's saying. This is good, the pleading thing, the dick likes this.

"Nicer than that," he says. "You got to ask me way nicer than that if you want to get home. Push your hair away from your face. I want to see your face." Feels good to boss her, to be the boss for a change. Feels goddamned good.

Her hand, shivering, shaking slightly, pushes her hair back from her face. "That's better," he says. "Now ask me again, and make it good."

"Pl . . . please . . . can . . ." But he cuts her off, smacks her across the side of the face. Not hard, just enough to snap her head back a little, jerk it up, snatch her breath in.

"Words! That's it? Goddamned words? That all you got to offer? That all you got, you little slut! You stupid whore! He hits her again, harder this time, full fist, full dynamite force. The power of him sends her flying off the bed and smashing into the wall like a comic book character. Smashing into the wall, crumpling to the floor.

Then everything's still, like even the clocks have stopped.

"Little slut . . ." he says. But he says it kindly, more like a joke, anger gone. He can afford to be more compassionate now. She's learned her lesson. It's not her fault she likes getting laid so much. Some kids are born that way, come out of the womb craving the cock. Some kids are born to be whores.

"Come here . . . ," he says. She comes to him pale, shaky legged. "Sit." He pats the bed, and she sits down beside him, too scared to cry, just shaking, whole body shaking. "I'm not going to hurt you," he says, stroking her long, blond, sunlight hair. "You don't have to be afraid. I'm not going to hurt you, baby, I just want you to show me a good time is all. It's only fair." Her hair is so silky and soft. "I paid my money for a good time, that's your job, it's only fair. You're supposed to make it good for me, see? You're supposed to make it the best for me. That's what you whores do."

He pauses.

"I tell you what, you make it good for me, and I'll take you home. Plain and simple, that's the deal. You fuck me nice, and you can go home, okay?"

She doesn't answer. Needs a little more persuading, the gentle kind. She's in the palm of his hand now, she's listening now, no need to play rough. "Listen Gemma, that's why I paid all that money. I paid a hundred goddamned dollars. That's a lot of money. I don't have that kind of money floating around. It doesn't grow on trees. I had to work hard, damned hard, for that money. Now I've paid that money, it's gone. I've given it to Buddy. Not that I mind. The minute I saw you, I knew you were worth it. But Gemma, we're talking about a hundred dollars here, and a hundred dollars should buy a man a pretty damned good time. A fucking amazing time, as a matter of fact. Anything less is a rip-off. Anything else is a cheat." He takes his time, lets what he's said sink in.

"Now . . . ," he says, all friendly—after all, he's a reasonable man, this is just business. A simple business transaction. "Gemma, sweetheart, you wouldn't want to cheat me, would you? I'd get pissed off if you were trying to cheat me."

She shakes her head, breath all catchy.

"Do you have the hundred dollars? If you have the hundred dollars you can pay me back and go home right now." She doesn't answer, just looks down at her hands, which she is twisting in her lap. Her hands, he notices, are disproportionate to her wrists, like they don't fit her body, like he tried to fuck her just before a growth spurt or something.

"Do you have the hundred dollars?" She shakes her head. "You don't?" He makes his voice surprised. "So what are you going to do?" He puts a little impatience in his voice, a little pressure, a little snap, and it works. He can feel the sting of it stiffen her body. Her hands shake, twisting, like she's wringing out a dirty dishrag. Face is twisted too, contorted, already starting to swell up, discolor where he smacked her.

"Well?"

A small moan comes out of her lips. Face like a moving picture show, all the color drained out. "I . . . I'll . . . ," she whispers, head tipping down, like it is just too heavy for her neck to hold up anymore. "I'll . . ." She starts sobbing in earnest, but her fingertips reach out, she hesitates slightly, a shudder runs through her skinny frame, rattles through her and then she does it. She touches his cock. The tips of her fingers icy, on his hot skin, like she's been gripping a cold vodka on the rocks for the last half hour.

"That's good," he says. "That's more like it. . . ."

And they go to it. He gives it to her good, the little whore. And it's amazing. Better than his dreams. It's a wild, crazy night. She lets him do everything. Doesn't stop crying, but she lets him do everything. Everything, everywhere. She doesn't want to let him and cries out big time, screaming, has to slam his hand over her mouth. Guess Buddy never got around to that last place. She was a virgin there. Buddy never got around to there, but Hazen does. Hazen is thorough.

He does her hard. Doesn't let up until she is bloody and ragged. He drives it in, hard and deep, shows her no mercy, and he cums. Oh God, does he cum. Cums like a goddamned Fourth-of-July rocket.

*   *   *

Couldn't sleep after he drove her home. Dropped her off half a block from her house. Watched her climb stiff legged up the front steps and disappear through the door.

Couldn't sleep. Was too revved up. Just drove and drove and drove. Windows open, music blasting. Felt like howling at the moon. It was after four in the morning when he finally got some shut-eye.

*   *   *

Buddy looked real worried when he saw my face. Never hits me in the face, just places where it don't show. Going out the door for school when he grabbed me by the arm, said he'd thought about it and decided it

23

was only fair that we split the profits. After all, he said, we were partners in this. Business partners. Took out his wallet and counted out
fifty bucks, gave it to me, slipped me a Kit-Kat bar too, finger to his
lips, like we had a secret, him and me. "Shhh . . . ," he said, voice low,
quiet, looking over his shoulder to their bedroom, where my mama
was sleeping.

Then he took me out the front door. Apparently he wasn't done
talking, walked me as far as the telephone pole, yapping at me. Re-
minding me about the police, how I couldn't mention this to anybody.
That if I told anybody what happened, the police would find out. They
have spies everywhere.

"Little slut like you, seducing grown men, corrupting them. Throw
you in jail for sure, before you ruin the rest of the state of California."
He tells me this, face getting all greasy like a fried egg. And hey, it's
not like I didn't know this already. I mean *please*, if he's told me once,
he's told me a thousand times. What does he think I am? Retarded?

I walk to school. It takes longer than usual because my body is sore.
Hope nobody notices my face. I styled my hair over it, because it's all
swollen up like a jack-o'-lantern. I hate that Hazen guy. I really hate
him. Hope I never see again for the rest of my life. Stunk to high
heaven. Really, I'm not joking, he stunk. I had to hold my breath.

It's lucky I know how. It's a skill of mine I developed because my
mom smokes and I don't like the smell. Then one day I discovered that
if I shut my nose in the back of my throat and press my tongue up in
the back and breathe through my mouth, no one can tell that I'm plug-
ging my nose. They just think I'm talking weird because I have a cold
or something. They don't know that they stink. I don't hurt their feelings, and at the same time I protect myself against having to smell
them.

Stinky Hazen. That's what I should have called him. Stinky Hazen.
Should have plugged my nose with my fingers, wiggled my butt at
him, and made farting noises with my mouth. That's what I should
have done. "Suck my cock." "Screw you . . . *ppllllatt.*" That's what I

should have done. That would have been good, would have served him right. Stupid asshole.

My face hurts pretty bad. Has that *waaah . . . waaah . . .* feeling, like my heart left my chest and is pulsing in my cheek and my jaw. My tongue's bad too. It's kind of hard to talk because I accidentally bit it when he whacked me. Other parts hurt too. Hurts more than when Buddy does me, bigger I guess. Hurts bad, but I'm too ladylike to mention them.

"Stupid, mean old dickhead," I should have said. "You nasty, one-eyed snake." Actually, I've heard about one-eyed snakes, but I've never seen one. Bet they're mean, on account of having only one eye. Bet the other snakes laugh at them and beat them up at recess. They do that at my school. Gang up on kids and beat them up. Not me, though. I'm like the one-eyed snake. I'm mean, real mean when I have to be. I got fists, and I know how to use them.

But there's this boy, José—I was going to say friend, but he's not really my friend because we never talk to each other. The boys are always picking on him, making fun of his stutter. They stand around him in a circle, pushing him and laughing their fool, stupid heads off. Flopping their arms around like dead fish, eyes bugging out, pretending to stutter, making big gobs of spit fly all over him. Laughing, thinking they're so cool, but they're not. They're just stupid, ignorant jerks. And then, when they get tired of pushing him around and pretending to stutter, sometimes they let him go, but more often than not, they beat him up. Day after day, week after week, and the yard duty does nothing. Nothing. Just stands there talking.

Grown-ups don't care. That's the fact of the matter. They plain don't care. "Stop pulling my arm, missy," was all the yard-duty supervisor said when I was trying to tell her what was going on with José. "Stop yanking on my arm. Didn't yo mama teach you no manners?"

I feel bad for José, I really do. But the reason I say he's not my friend isn't because I don't like him, because I do. I don't mind his stutter. Think it sounds like a beat-up old car warming up on a cold winter morning. When the ground is covered with a thin layer of frost, so if I squint my eyes, it sort of looks like its snowed. And I get a catch in my breath, even though I know it's not true, I get that catch, like maybe, just maybe, I went to sleep in Oakland, but I woke up in Alaska. Cold winter mornings, everything frozen to the bone, so when my mama turns the car engine on it complains, goes *kachunk . . . kachunk . . .* That's what José's stutter is like. Like a car engine that isn't warm yet. And he's got nice eyes.

The reason I say he's not my friend is because we've only talked once ever since he moved here, and I was the only one talking.

But I have to say, I knew from the minute he walked in the classroom, they were going to pick on him. New kid, hair all in place, neat, clean clothes—and I mean neat. Someone in his house is in love with ironing, because I swear, if he took his pants off, I bet even his underwear would have a nice, neat crease right down the middle of them. A recipe for disaster. Him looking so sweet, like a scared, lost puppy, I knew he was going to get picked on. I mean come on, of course they're going to.

The time I talked to him was about three weeks ago, back in September. What happened is, I got behind him in the hall at after-lunch lineup. They'd pushed him around pretty bad at lunch. His shirt was all stretched out of shape where they had yanked on it. They had gotten some dirt in an old pop bottle and were holding him down by the jungle gym. Had him pinned to the ground, one guy sitting on his chest, a guy on each arm. A bunch of them standing around like it's a rape or an orgy, while Billy Robinson tipped the pop bottle over José and poured a steady stream of dried-out dirt in his face. Standing over him, straddling his face, laughing and pouring dirt just like he was peeing on him, getting it in José's nose, his eyes, his mouth. José's skinny body twisting and turning, trying to get away, trying not to cry, but he was. I could see that even from where I was standing. So I started throwing rocks at them. Hit Billy Robinson in the head. Must of hurt like hell, because he bellowed like a wounded bull and leapt off José and started chasing me. It was real funny, because with him chasing me, everybody else did too, like a big, long, choo-choo train. Follow the leader. There's not an ounce worth of individual thought among the lot of them. And for me, no problem, don't worry about me. I just ran into the girls' bathroom. Waited for them to cool off, and then sauntered out as fine as could be.

I looked all over the playground for José. Didn't know where he went. Couldn't find him, and I'm real good at finding things. When my mama loses something, her wallet, her keys, pack of smokes, whenever she loses something important, she sics me on it. I always find things for her in no second flat. So if I couldn't find José, he wasn't there. Must have left school property. I was worried he'd get in trouble for skipping, because nobody's allowed to skip. But when the lunch bell rang, there he was, trying to slip into the back of the line like a shadow. And, I don't know, I kind of did it wrong. Didn't mean to. I'd been holding onto my Kit-Kat bar all lunch hour. Got out of the line and walked to where José was standing. I was going to give it to him casual, like I wasn't hungry for it. "Hey," I was going to say. "Want my Kit-Kat? I'm full."

Sounded good in my head, sounded just right. But it was a screw up. At first, it was like he didn't hear me, or didn't know I was talking to him or something, so I said it a little bit louder. "Hey, José. Want my Kit-Kat bar?" And I was wishing I didn't have this stupid idea, because he was not looking happy. He looked embarrassed, like he thought I felt sorry for him. He shook his head, just a little twitch like I was a fly he was trying to flick off. And his face got this odd, stiff look, jaw all clenched up, like Kit-Kat bars made him mad or something. But his eyes, they started squeezing up and blinking, as if he was trying to hold back a fresh flood of hurt. "I'm not making fun of you," I said, face getting hot, sweaty. "I mean it. You can have it if you want." I held the candy out to him and I thought he might take it, but apparently stupid Billy Robinson was listening and he started laughing and saying in this mamsey-pamsey voice, "Oh . . . José has

27

a girlfriend?" Real nasty, and they all started making loud smacking, kissing noises. Needless to say, after that fiasco, José avoided me like the plague.

·　　·　　·

Hazen sleeps in. Late to work, Gemma on the brain. Needs to see her. Calls her school during his coffee break. Goes down to the pay phone on the corner. Pretends to be a parent. Little Johnny had forgotten his lunch. When would his lunch hour be?

Hands sweating, the school secretary's voice tinny, faint, barely audible through the traffic noise, through the buzzing in his ears.

"What grade?" she's asking. She sounds impatient, like she's already asked him before.

"What grade?" His palms slippery with sweat. Trying to think.

"What . . . grade . . . ," she is speaking very slowly, enunciating every syllable, "is your . . . boy . . . in?"

"Oh. . . ." His mind scrambles, trying to find a way to answer, to be plausible. She knows. He thinks. She knows. "Uh . . . well, let me think . . . sh . . . he . . . sorry . . . uh . . . he turned twelve in July. Uh, July twenty-third."

There is a brief pause on the other end of the phone followed by a weary sigh. "You men," she says, disapproval prickling. And he can just see her. Some dried-up old gray-haired virgin, lips puckered up like she's sucking sour apples. Never been laid, taking her disappointment out on the world. "You're all the same. You don't know your own child's grade. I bet you don't even know who his teacher is."

And Hazen finds himself standing on the street corner, getting mad. Phone slammed up against his ear. Forefinger stuffed in the other. Finds himself getting incensed, even though his son is fictitious. "How dare you judge me?" he snaps. "What gives you the right? I am a good father." He's yelling now. "A damned good one. And I want to know when my son's class gets out for lunch so I can bring it by the school so he won't starve. What's so goddamn difficult about that?"

His voice, in his outrage, had built to a roar, and the silence that followed was deafening.

"Very well. . . ." There was a long pause. She sniffed. Another pause. "How old is your son?"

"Twelve. He's twelve."

"Then he'd be in the *seventh* grade. Their lunch break is from eleven forty-five to twelve-thirty."

She hangs up without saying good-bye, leaving him with an allover body flush that he had not experienced since he'd peed his pants at school in third grade. An allover body flush, a dead phone clutched to his ear, and a boner the size of Montana.

.   .   .

He gets there early, parks his car across the street from the schoolyard. Feeds the meter a quarter, gets back in the car and waits.

He feels her before he sees her. He was watching the front entrance and then it's like something tapped him on the shoulder, jerked his head around. And there she is, coming out a side door. She is alone. Her shoulders rounded slightly, her hair falling forward, covering her face. She is walking a little bowlegged. That's good, he thinks. Maybe he hadn't been her first, but by the way she's walking, she's not going to forget him anytime soon. And that thought makes him feel good in his gut.

Then just as he felt her, it's like she feels him, because all of a sudden she stops, in the middle of the schoolyard, kids swarming on either side of her. She stops and her gaze leaves the pavement to travel the expanse of the playground, through the iron link fence, and across the street to where his car is parked in front of Jamba Juice. All that way her eyes travel to lock with his. He can see her chest rising up and down, her mouth moving like she's praying. And he can see that her face is slightly bruised from where he hit her, but more than that, he can see, oh sweet Jesus in heaven, he can see that she wants him. Can see that from all the way over in his car. He watches her run away around the back of her school, face pale, hair fluttering behind her like a tattered flag. And in this moment, he knows that he is to save her from the life she is leading, the crooked path she is on. Knows that they are meant to be together, meant to get married. That he is to plant his seed into her again and again, and watch her grow ripe and round with his seed. And he knows that God led him to her, because she is his destiny.

· · ·

That little kids' book *Alexander's Very Bad, Terrible, Horrible No Good Day*—well, that's the kind of day I'm having.

Mrs. Watson didn't believe my story about walking into a door. Which really isn't fair, because poor José gets the crap kicked out of him every day. And nothing. I come to school with one little black eye, a swollen cheek, and it's like she became the frigging FBI. Asked me a bunch of personal questions about stuff which, I have to say, is nobody's business but my own. Then she sent me to the principal's office, and the principal made me talk to Mr. Jamison, the school counselor. Who smelled like old ladies and mothballs and was acting all concerned. Asked me all kinds of sly, sneaky questions. But I didn't tell him a thing. Knew what to say. Buddy has been over this material with me a million times. I didn't switch my story one iota, no way I'm going to jail.

I did tell him my concerns about José, though. Did tell him that what was happening to that poor boy was criminal. Those were my very words. I don't know where they came from. Just popped out of my mouth all articulate-like. It was really cool. It was the kind of sentence I always wished I'd said, when I think about the circumstances later. When I'm lying in bed, late at night, I can think up plenty of good things to say, but it doesn't help me, if I didn't think of it when I had the chance. So that was very satisfying indeed. Mr. Jamison said he'd check into it, and talk to the yard supervisor.

But other than that, this day is turning into a real stinker. Old sicko is at my school. At *my* school! Sitting in his stupid old car, ruining my lunch hour. Just sitting there gawking. Giving me the creeps. I mean who asked him to ruin my lunch hour? Stupid jerk. Trying to freak me out. Stupid old creep. But I'm not going to be scared. Not going to give him the satisfaction. I'm going to stay here behind the school. No problem. He doesn't bother me. I'll just play out here in the back.

·   ·   ·

Hazen can't see her, but he stays, waits in his car, touching himself through the lining of his pants pocket. Stroking himself, squeezing the tip hard when he gets too close to cumming. Watches the playground. The other kids moving and surging, running, playing, legs flashing, arms flailing, soft and succulent necks and cheeks. He watches, but they are more like the background, the rumble of a big crowd before the hockey players take the ice. He watches them, not whole, just pieces Scotch-taped together. An arm, a leg, the curve of the neck, the ass, the color of her hair, the length. He takes bits and pieces and sews them together in his mind to create her. And he wishes he didn't have to do this, but it can't be helped. She is hiding, playing coy, playing hard to get. He knows the game. That's okay, he has time, he can afford to indulge her.

The bell rings, and the children run towards the big double doors, shrieking, laughing, playing tag. A massive movement from all corners of the playground, like a watercolor painting with too much water, all the colors blurring and smearing and running towards the bottom. He watches close, eyes moving fast, because he knows she's there somewhere, knows she's got to go in. And then he finds her, wouldn't have if he wasn't watching carefully. He sees her, sneaking around the side of the building. She is running, head down, her knees slightly bent. Trying to stick to and hide herself in the periphery of a group.

But he spots her, oh yes, he spots her and all his plans of waiting until he can safely jack off in the bathroom at work go flying out of his dick. Because there she is, so skinny and awkward. So beautifully young. There she is with her tight little child's ass that he had the night before, and he can't help himself, he cums right there in broad daylight, right there in his car in front of Jamba Juice.

And it is good.

When he is done, when he has finished pumping a full soggy fistful into his hand, he wishes she were here, so he could force her to taste it, rub it on her cheeks, her forehead, her chin. Not let her wash, make her go back to school with the proof of his love all over her face. And the very thought of it makes his heart start racing and his cock get all riled up again.

But he is late. Very late, so he starts up his car. He has to drive to his apartment first, because there is no way in hell he can go back to work without changing his pants.

Gets home, strips down, wipes his leg off with his underwear. His mouth is tasting rancid and dry, so he sticks his head under the faucet and sucks up a few mouthfuls of water. Then he grabs a new pair of pants, does them up as he sprints to his car.

He tries to slide in late, but the old gorgon is waiting, talons outstretched.

"Sorry, I'm late," he says. But, oh no, that's not good enough for her. Stupid bitch can't let it go, her loud, strident voice screaming out for the whole floor to hear. On and on, she harangues, about how how incompetent he is. How he'd better watch his step. How *inconvenienced* she was. Having to answer her *own* phone for twenty-three minutes!

And he wants to take out his dick and piss on her shiny Gucci pumps. Piss all over them. That would shut her up. But he doesn't. Just stands there, arms dangling, neck and ears hot, eyes lowered. He tunes her out, saying an occasional "Yes ma'am . . . No ma'am." And "It won't happen again, ma'am." Just stands there, trying to keep the smile off his face, thinking about Gemma's hot twat and how good she felt last night.

·   ·   ·

32

He calls after work. "Hi Gemma," he says. "It's me." She doesn't answer, but he knows she's there. He can hear her breathing. "Hazen." He tells her, a mere formality. She knows who he is.

She still doesn't speak, but he's happy to listen to her breath, shaky and rapid.

"I want to see you," he says

She hesitates. "I'm sorry. . . ." Her voice is more high pitched, younger than he remembers. "I'm . . . I'm sorry. I . . . I think you have the wrong number."

"Gemma," he says, "I need to see you."

"I . . . I think you've reached the . . . the public library," she says, her voice small, tentative.

He starts to laugh, ready to reason with her, but she hangs up. The little bitch hangs up. Won't pick up even when he calls back again and again and again.

· · ·

Stupid phone. Ringing all day. Wish I could unplug it, but Mama would get mad. Stupid, asinine phone. Not going to let it bother me though. I'm going to pay it no mind, ignore it, that's what I'm going to do.

Oh hey! I got a brand-new turtle! I bought her with my money. Bought a turtle, an aquarium, a package of turtle food, and some little plastic greenery. Took all my money, but it was worth it. I've been wanting a turtle for a long, long time. What happened was, I was walking home from school, and as usual, I browsed through the pet store, wishing I could have a pet. Walking through the Critters and Fins Pet Store, and then I saw her. *Bah-da-bing.* . . . Love at first sight.

And I was standing there, feeling sorry for myself. "Oh poor me . . . my mom can't afford for me to have a pet. . . ." Whine, whine, whine. And then I realize . . . wait a minute . . . I have fifty whole bucks of my own. Fifty bucks to do whatever I want with. So I talked to the shop lady, and we figured out the whole thing, all the costs, including tax, was forty-eight dollars and fifty-six cents.

It was so cheap because they were having a sale that day on turtles, turtle food, turtle aquariums. They were even having a sale on the special light thingy I needed to keep my turtle warm. "Full-spectrum light." Fancy, huh? It produces special light rays just for them, to keep them healthy and warm and keep their shells hard. I mean wow, I didn't even know turtles needed that. They were having a sale on all this. Which was amazingly lucky for me, because I never would have been able to buy all that stuff otherwise. It was brand-new sale. She hadn't even gotten around to getting the sale sign up, and the whole kit and caboodle was only going to be forty-eight dollars and fifty-six cents.

Well, I took the money out of my pocket, and bought that turtle right there on the spot.

I had to walk careful going home. Had to glide my steps like a roll-erblader in slo-mo, so I wouldn't jostle her. My feet, skimming the ground, didn't care if I looked ridiculous. Sidewalks can be tricky, with all the potholes, red lights, curbs and things. I didn't want to trip. So I walked real slow and smooth. It took me a long time to get home.

At first, my turtle was scared and stayed in her shell. But after a while, she saw how nice I fixed up her new home, that I made her a little swimming pool out of a cereal bowl and got her a rock from out-side and put it in the middle of the pool so she could crawl out of the water and rest between laps. That I moved all the furniture around in my room so that my dresser was out from under the window, because I know how important it is for turtles not to get a draft. That's what the lady at the pet store told me. "Very important, because they could catch cold and die." Interesting, huh? I didn't know turtles could catch cold. Anyway, after my turtle saw what I did to make it nice for her, she came out. First the tippy tip of her head peeked out. I held really still, didn't breathe. So then the rest of her head came out, and then her legs, and her tiny little tail poked out the back. She nosed forward, craning her head this way and that, taking in her fabulous new home. It was funny. Made me laugh.

She's so cute, with her little black button eyes. Fits in the palm of my hand. She's around the size of a silver dollar. I have one of those. My granddaddy gave it to me when I was ten. He pulled it out of the pocket of those old, saggy brown pants he always liked to wear. They were his favorites. It was hard to get them off him to put in the wash.

He gave me his "lucky silver dollar" for helping him roll his cigarettes. His hands were getting too shaky to do it, and he was spraying tobacco all over the table, so I volunteered to help. Then one day, after I'd made a ton of cigarettes, he flipped his lucky silver dollar arcing it up into the air. "Catch," he said, but when I tried to return it, he wouldn't take the dollar back. Said I earned it. Hell, I would have done it for free. I liked rolling his cigarettes. He had this fancy-shmancy cigarette-rolling machine. It was really fun. Made me feel like I had a job. A real job in a cigarette factory, because I had to roll a lot. It was an all-day proposition. My granddaddy liked to smoke. When I think of my granddaddy, I always picture him with a cigarette hanging out of the side of his mouth. Either that, or drooping from his fingers. Even when he didn't have a smoke, the inside of his smoking fingers between the second and third knuckles were permanently stained. Looked like they had been tinted with iodine.

I loved that cigarette machine. I asked if I could have it when he died. Don't know why everybody got so mad. They had asked me if there was anything of his I wanted. No figuring out grown-ups sometimes.

It was fun rolling cigarettes, peaceful. Made me feel good in my belly to able to do something to help him. It's hard work, though. I'd get a crick in my neck, and my eyes would get strained from concentrating so hard. Making good cigarettes is difficult to do. There's a trick to getting it right. Can't just slap the papers and the tobacco in any old way. Got to do it right. Like the cigarette papers—I had to take them out gentle, so I didn't crinkle them. Hold them careful, between my thumb and forefinger. Had to be careful, not get too nervous and grip the papers too tight. Sometimes it felt like I hadn't picked up anything. I had to look down and see my hands to make sure, because the cigarette papers were so delicate and light. Then I placed them in the curving cigarette-shaped indentations. Lay them down like little blankets. Next I got the tobacco can, opened it up and breathed in deep. Not that smelling the tobacco helped make better cigarettes. It was part of the ritual and that first deep breath, as all the tobacco odor *wooshed* out. Smelled so good. By the end of the day, it had given me a headache, but that first smell . . . Well, let me put it this way, it wouldn't feel the same if I hadn't.

Then, I took out the tobacco, had to hold it gentle so I didn't squish it, and pack it in. If I packed it in too tight, my granddad couldn't smoke them, because they'd be impossible to suck the air through. I had to pack it just right, not too fat, not too thin. Just right, that's the way to do it. Nice and even. Then I cranked the handle and, *pshoo, pshoo, pshoo, pshoo* . . . out came four cigarettes. And they looked good. Real good. Just like store bought.

That's how I ended up with Granddaddy's lucky silver dollar. I would have spent it by now. I've been plenty tempted, because it's good, like regular money. Even though it's metal and all, not like an everyday one-dollar paper bill, I can spend it. People in stores will take it. I was having fun planning what kind of candy to buy. I didn't want to do it lickety-split. Was having fun going to the liquor store, rattling my silver dollar around in my pocket, trying to decide if this was the day I was going to blow it. I was trying to decide when my granddaddy up and died. Just like that. Surprised the hell out of everyone. He was having stomach pains creeping up on him, catching him by surprise, doubling him over and stealing his breath.

"Nothing," he used to say, breath wheezing out of him like an old accordion, "a shot of whiskey can't cure." He'd have me run get the whiskey for him and he'd throw it back, his face screwing up real bad when he swallowed, sweat popping out on his forehead. He'd take that shot of whiskey, sucking in between his teeth, like it was burning bad as it went down.

That was my grandpa. Here one day, gone the next. Dead as a door-nail. Cancer, they said. Cancer everywhere. Eating up his stomach, his liver, his lungs. Cancer all over the damn place.

I wonder what it looked like in there, all that cancer. Wonder if that's why he was getting so skinny? Did it make holes in him? Like little train tunnels, or worm tracks? What's cancer look like? And that's another thing I don't get. If the cancer was eating him, then wouldn't the cancer be getting fat? And since the cancer was inside him, wouldn't he have stayed the same weight? Why was he losing weight all the time? I wanted to ask my science teacher, Mr. Stanley, but I was worried he'd think I was macabre. Another spelling word. Macabre. Nice to get a chance to use it. Although honestly, I'd rather not be using it in context to my granddaddy, because I miss him.

Anyway, he died. Here's another thing I haven't told anybody about. Don't want them to make the connection. I feel awful bad, and I worry about it a lot. See, I help my granddaddy. He gives me his lucky silver dollar. I take it. Keep it, because I don't realize how important it is. I keep it, and he dies.

His lucky silver dollar scares me and fascinates me all at the same time. I feel like a moth sometimes, circling around a hot lightbulb, dipping in, out, swooping, singeing my wings, and yet I keep coming back. Keep coming back until it does me in. Scares the hell out of me, but I can't stop looking at it, touching it. Terrified I'm going to lose it, accidentally spend it, and then boom, I'm up there in heaven with Granddaddy. That's me, like a goddamned moth, circling around the lucky silver dollar.

So I save the lucky silver dollar, don't spend it. Keep it safe in my dresser. I could get off my bed right now and walk across my room, pull out the drawer and there it would be, nestling among my under-wear, staring up at me like a frozen eyeball.

Anyway, I was describing my turtle. As I said, she's around the size of a silver dollar, but she is much fatter. If I stacked up three or four dollars on top of each other, that would be around how tall she is. I've decided to call her Boxcar Julie. Boxcar for short, because when she comes out of her shell, it's like she's a little boxcar chugging along on little tiny legs. So determined. She has a hard shell on her back and it keeps her safe. It's hard like a rock, or a super-thick toenail. Like maybe a camel's toenail. Her shell is tough. Camel tough. Which is a very handy thing because all she has to do when she feels danger, or a predator like a lion or something, is *zoomp*. Tuck everything up into her shell in one second flat. *Zoomp.* And everything is safe and sound. Nothing, nobody, diddly-squat can harm her. When she's tucked up like that, someone could probably drive a cement truck over her and she'd be sitting in there laughing. Not that I'd ever do a thing like that. Never. But I bet Billy Robinson would. Do it just for fun.

I sure love Boxcar Julie. She's so cute. Maybe I'll take her to school in my pocket. She's so tiny, no one would even notice her crawling around. It would be like having a little friend in my pocket. She likes me, I can tell. She knows I'm her friend, and that I'll always take care of her, make sure she has food and water and plenty of conversation.

Stupid old stinko keeps calling. Calling and calling, ringing the phone off the hook, in Mama's bedroom; the kitchen too. It's kind of obnoxious. Kind of scary. Wish he'd stop. Wish both of them would. Buddy and Hazen. Stop bugging me. Big fat losers. Buddy trying to sneak into my bedroom when my mom's asleep. Well, I've had it. It hurts when I pee, hurts when I pooh, burns like fire. Got to suck my breath in just like my granddaddy when he was drinking whiskey. So I'm going to tell Buddy if he tries to lay a hand on me, I'll scream the house down. That's what I'm going to tell him, and I mean it too. I'll do it. Now normally, that wouldn't deter him, because my mom can sleep through anything. But that on top of the school counselor wanting to have daily chat sessions with me, the two of those things put together might do the trick.

Damn phone. I wish it would stop ringing. It hurts Boxcar's ears. She doesn't like it.

She's so cute when she walks. Maybe I should call her Choo-choo. That's a good name. I wonder if it would confuse her if I switched her name on her? Nah, better stick with Boxcar.

Wish I had a little house I could carry on my back, tuck myself up when I didn't feel safe. Wish I had a little house on my back. Dumb phone.

Oh . . . Ah . . . There it is . . . stopped ringing.

•　　　•　　　•

Mrs. Moore, the librarian, says I can be her library helper at lunchtime.

I'm really excited about it because I love books, reading them, the smell, the feel. I feel so safe and cozy with a good book in my hand. Especially the hardcover ones. There's something so solid and satisfying about the weight of them, feels sort of like the promise of a good meal. Like I don't have to panic, because I know I'm going to be fed, and it's going to taste good. A book in the hand is a deep kind of contentment. I especially like the ones where the bindings are a little worn. Starting to fray. It makes me think about how many times these books had to be read and enjoyed to get that worn out. Sometimes makes my mind dizzy to think about it. Specially the really old ones, where the pages are all yellowing and soft around the edges, held together with Scotch tape that's discolored and gone brown, like the color of sugar candy, from age. Old, old books, probably from the fifties or something. I feel like I have to read them quick because their time is running out, and they might disappear, disintegrate into nothing, before I get a chance to devour them. These ones I treat extra special. Carry them one at a time, use both hands and watch my step.

I love working at the library. Putting things in alphabetical order. Everything in its place. I love the library, love Mrs. Moore. She smells nice, all homey like. And she smiles at me. A soft, gentle smile, like she really likes me. Kind of like she's the mother chick and I'm the baby chick, except instead of teaching me which bugs taste the best, she teaches me about books and authors, and I don't have to go outside with the other kids and see old sicko waiting in his car. I love Mrs. Moore.

●　　●　　●

Can't sleep, can't eat, Gemma on the brain. Wasted lunch hours spent at the school, combing the playground for her, but he can't find her. She's not there, or if she is, she's not coming out. Staying holed up inside, playing shy. That's what he thought at first. But it's been three days now. Three days of waiting, watching. Three days of nothing. And he doesn't know, maybe she's sick, hurt. Worried. Calls her house five, ten times a day, but no one answers. Calls until six. After that, he can't call. Doesn't want to talk to her mom. Not yet. Not ready for that one yet. But tomorrow's Friday. And he's got this feeling, like time is running out. Got this feeling, like a big, angry rottweiler is ripping hunks out of his gut. Like if he doesn't move quick, God is going to give up on him. Not going to waste his time on him. A wuss with no balls. Have to act quick, decisive. Got to do something strong. Getting sweaty. Getting sweaty. Time is running out.

●　　●　　●

José talked to me today! Said "hi," all shy like. It surprised me, caught me off guard. But I covered well, said "hi" and smiled friendly and encouraging. He didn't say anything else. His cheeks got red and he bent over his social studies book, like he was real interested in it all of a sudden. It was kind of cute. Made me hopeful. Think maybe we'll be friends after all.

And another good thing, Mr. Jamison kept his word about José. I've seen him through the library window, out on the playground during his lunch hour, standing by the swings, walking around the yard. It makes me feel good to see Mr. Jamison out there, because that's one thing I was worried about. With me working in the library, there was no one to look out for José.

I think I'll be a witch for Halloween. Either that or a gypsy woman.

THREE

Mama and Buddy are fighting something fierce. Screaming, yelling, and carrying on. Must have been out on another all-day drinking binge, because this is a doozy.

I'm hungry, but there's no way in hell I'm going out in that kitchen. Got my bedroom door locked, pushed the dresser up against it for good measure. I'm no fool.

Sure am hungry, though. Wish they'd finish, or go out or something, so I can make myself some dinner.

· · ·

Ten o'clock, and they're still at it. Seems to be winding down though. She's not screaming anymore, not throwing things. Crying now. That's what she always does at the end of their fights. Great noisy, heaving sobs. That's what she does, mucus-filled, sloppy-drunk, slobbery sobs. Hope the neighbors can't hear.

Hungry. Really hungry.

Oh shoot. Now they're doing it. I'm never going to get my dinner. My belly's hurting. All squeezed up and angry with me. Maybe I should go to Burger King. It's only three blocks away. Shouldn't go out at night. Not by myself. Not a very safe neighborhood. It's okay in the day, but at night, woohoo. It's only three blocks away, though. I could run. I could bring Boxcar Julie. Then it wouldn't be so scary. Could wrap her in some toilet paper so she won't get cold. She'd probably like to see it. I bet she's never been to Burger King before.

I'll wait five minutes and see. Maybe they'll move into the bedroom.

•   •   •

He waits. He is patient. Drove the last block with his headlights switched off, rolled up outside of her house soft and silent like the Bat-mobile. He sits in his car, engine off. Sits in the darkness, half slid down. Sits low, waits, watches, willing her to come out. Elton John's "Tiny Dancer" running through his brain. Humming it out soft, pads of his thumbs beating out the rhythm on his steering wheel. And he's got an excitement in his gut. Like right before a big date. "Come out, baby . . . ," he whispers. "Come on. . . ."

And she comes. Like he's got a direct line to her brain, she comes. Not out the front door though. She comes out a window, her bedroom window maybe. One leg first, then the other, crouching for a moment on the window sill, then swinging her body out, over, hanging on the ledge, dropping to the ground. Old hat, like she's done this a million times before. And he's glad to see her, but he's pissed too. "Who is she sneaking off to fuck?" he thinks, slinking further down, heart racing, not sure what he's going to do. He can hear her footsteps coming, closer and closer. He's there, bent at the waist, head lying on the seat of his car listening to her shoes reach the pavement, and the next thing he knows he's out of the car, his coat somehow finds its way off his body and over her head, and she is kicking and screaming and scratching, and he doesn't know what to do, but she's making a hell of a lot of noise, so somehow he gets the trunk open, throws her inside, slams the lid down fast. Accidentally bangs her on the head with it. Doesn't mean to, but she's moving so fast, clambering up on her hands and knees. Has to slam it down fast, hell, with all the noise she's making. Slams it down fast. Hops in the car and drives away, heart banging like a red brick in a dryer.

"Now what?" he thinks. "Now what?" But he doesn't know, so he just keeps driving, her making little scrabbling whimpering noises, scuffling around in his trunk.

.   .   .

Julie fell out of my pocket. She must have fallen out when old fuckface here threw me into the trunk, because I can't find her anywhere. Must have fallen out then. Stupid asshole! I knew it was him, even though I couldn't see a damned thing, that stupid stinky coat over my head. Stupid dickface. I knew it! I shouldn't have come out! What am I going to do now? What's Julie going to do? What does she know about city living? I never should have taken her with me. Stupid! Dumb! She didn't need to see Burger King. And now what? Now what Missus Smarty-pants? What's she going to do, crawling around the streets at night? Who's going to feed her? Take care of her? Keep her safe? What if a car runs over her, or a cat eats her? What if Billy Robinson finds her in the morning on his way to school? That would be bad. That would be really bad. . . . I'm not crying because I'm scared. I'm not. I'm not scared at all, and that's a fact. I'm not really crying, it's just . . . it's hard to breathe in here. Dark. Darkest dark. Like I'm drowning in black ink. That's all. It might seem like I'm crying, but I'm not. I'm not scared . . . I'm just . . . It's just that . . . I'm worried about Boxcar, is all. That's what I'm crying about. That's why I'm crying, I'm worried about her. . . . I hope he doesn't kill me. . . . Stupid jerk . . . Hope he just does me and lets me go. . . . Hope that's all he wants. Should have answered that phone. . . .

Better now. Stopped crying. Stopped crying now. It's kind of embarrassing, I let myself go like that, got out of control. Don't usually do that. Not a crybaby. Better now. I've got a plan. A good one! See, I'm being real quiet now so he'll think something happened to me, that I'm dead, asphyxiated from lack of air in this stupid, stinky trunk. I'm being quiet, not moving, barely breathing. He'll think I'm dead or asleep or something. So when he comes to the trunk, he'll be off his guard. When he comes to the back and opens the trunk, at first, I'm going to lie real still, pretend to be asleep. I'm good at that, had lots of practice with Buddy. Sometimes it works, sometimes it doesn't. Sometimes, he wants the pussy and it don't matter if I'm asleep or not. Enough of Buddy. This is what I'm going to do. Hazen opens the trunk. I pretend I'm asleep. Pretend I'm asleep to catch him off guard! Then, when he's least expecting it, I'll jump out of the trunk, quick as a wink, and run! Run fast! Get away! I'm a good runner, see. One of the fastest in my class! I'll get away, see! I'll run like the wind! I'll get away from him. Far, far away!

•   •   •

He runs her down three times, three times before she finally stops running.

Runs her down, hits the ground hard, him on top of her, falling on her body. Falling on her soft, fragile body. Her sweet, tender body. Falling on her, pinning her down with all of his man weight. Pinning her down. Her wanting it so bad that she's panting like a cat in heat. Cute, how she kept trying to get away. Wouldn't stop running, even though she knew, had to have known, he was going to run her down. Made him feel powerful. Made him need to have her. Morning sun just rising, not there yet, but almost. Everything painted in gray. Gray, charcoal, black silhouettes. Everything gray but her, one vivid splotch of

45

color. Cold, can see puffs of steam escaping from her mouth as she gasps for air, chest heaving up and down. Has to fuck her. Dust, grit, grinding into her hair. Has to take her out on this abandoned road, her fighting and cussing. Her screams breaking that waiting, still, silence of the wilderness. So wonderfully isolated. Her cries echoing, reverberating off the rocks, the trees. Bouncing, ricocheting off them, like some kind of wild mating cry, some kind of beautiful love song on a National Geographic show. Primitive, stunning. He fucks her again and again, until she stops fighting him. Stops biting and screaming. Just quiet sobs of relief and acquiescence. Beautiful. He did it right.

• • •

I hate him. I really hate him. I'd kill him if I could. If I knew how to drive, I'd steal the car, grab it when he wasn't looking, and drive over him. No problem. Drive right over his big, fat, stupid head! Squash his brains out, squirt them out like strands of spaghetti, that's what I'd do if I had a car. Kill him. The stupid, snot-eating prick. Hate him.

• • •

I'm so damned happy! Guess what? I FOUND BOXCAR! It's true!

What happened is, I heard this little scrabbling noise. He was at a stoplight or a stop sign or something. Not important, the thing is, the car wasn't moving, and that's how I heard it. It was just a brief stop, the engine idling, me in the trunk, and I heard this *scrabble . . . scrabble . . . scrabble* sound. A faint little noise, like fingernails dancing across the kitchen counter.

The car started going again, and I couldn't hear nothing, thought maybe that scrabbling noise was a figment of my imagination. . . .

But then! *Scrabble . . . scrabble . . . scrabble . . .* I heard it again. And it wasn't until the second time that I recognized the sound, and my heart leapt, it jumped, because I knew it was Boxcar Julie! I became like a person possessed, feeling around, but keeping my body still so

I wouldn't accidentally squish her. I must have looked like a crazy woman, my hands patting, searching every last corner. And when my fingers found her, I started crying like a baby. And I kissed her and kissed her, so happy that she was safe. So happy.

•   •   •

I was so glad to find Boxcar, to not be alone in this dumb old trunk, but I wasn't thinking straight. I'm worried now. Scared for her. See, I don't have her special turtle food. I don't have water in this trunk. Don't have her full-spectrum light to keep her warm. I'm holding her inside my shirt, up against my tummy. Trying to keep her warm. It feels funny when she crawls. Tickles, makes me giggle.

I like having her here, but I'm worried. I need to escape the first chance I get. It was bad enough when it was only me, but now I got her to think of. She counts on me.

I've got to get away. Going to have to be tricky. Going to have to do some real hard thinking and come up with a plan.

"Don't worry," I tell her. "I'm going to get us out of this." I'm not sure what I'm going to do, but I tell her this to keep her calm, so she won't panic. And I think it makes her feel better. But I got to come up with something fast. I mean, this is inhuman. She's been in this trunk for a whole day and a half. No food, no water, no sunshine.

Worried, so worried. Old dickface isn't going to like her. "We got to keep it a secret," I tell Boxcar. I take my sock off and have it ready. I'm going to wrap her in it when the car stops. I'm going to have to move fast, wrap her in it to keep her warm, and put her in my pocket. I'll be quick, so he won't know.

This situation is real bad. I feel sorry for Boxcar, because I don't know what her future is going to be. But even though the situation makes me feel sad, I would be lying if I didn't admit that I'm glad she's here, even though it's selfish. It's nice to have a friend, someone to talk to. Without her, it would be pretty damn lonely in this dumb trunk.

·　　·　　·

He's letting me ride up front with him. This is my opportunity. My chance. Don't want to blow it. I've got to be careful. Got to be fast and decisive. My heart is pounding, throat jammed shut. Keeping my eyes on the lookout for a good spot. I don't have my seat belt on. Am ready to move quick. Mouth dry. Acting normal. "Nice day." That kind of thing, mind jumping, spinning, checking out options. I'm going to do this thing. Don't want to let Boxcar down.

·　　·　　·

Unfortunately, he has to ride with her in the trunk again. Trussed up like a little piglet. Can't share the road, the scenery, conversations. Can't feel her pussy to help pass the time, alleviate the boredom of the road. Can't do that. She wouldn't behave. Kept leaping out of the car at every stop, every light. Had to tussle her to the ground. Damned inconvenient. Draws unnecessary attention.

So, no more front-seat driving for her. It's her own fault she's back in the trunk.

But even that wasn't good enough. She screamed and yelled, banged her feet on the lid of the trunk, making the car bounce slightly. Hazen had to have music. Blaring loud, to cover up her noise, the banging in the trunk.

So that's why he ties her up and gags her. Not because he's an animal. Please. It would be much nicer riding with her up front.

He ties her up because it is a necessity. It is a must-do, for both of their safety.

·　　·　　·

I can't move, can't speak. He's got his stupid, stinking underwear in my mouth. Cut them up slow with his hunting knife, never taking his eyes off of me. It made me nervous. Like maybe he was thinking about using his knife on me. And the idea, the thought of that, made me get real quiet.

I'm not going to say what he did next in the cut-up underpants, it's too disgusting. After he finished, he made me open my mouth. I did what he said, holding my body real still, keeping my eye on the knife.

Him laughing and calling me "sweetheart." Telling me this way I'll behave. Won't be making a big, noisy ruckus no more. This way I won't forget who's the boss.

Tells me he knows I miss him while I'm in the trunk, but at least I'll get to taste him. "Isn't that love?" he said in a sweetie-sweet voice. "Aren't you the lucky one? Now you'll get to taste me the whole live-long day." I would have argued, but he had the knife, so I didn't do anything. He tied his underwear around my head real tight. Jammed it way back in my mouth like it's reins and I'm a horse. Tied it so tight, that my face is stretched out like I'm at the dentist and he needs to get a good look at my teeth. Some of my hair got caught up in the knot. It hurt. "Umm . . . yummy," stupid dickhead said. "Taste good?" he asked. Then he pulled the back of the knot so my head nodded up and down. And that made him bust out laughing all over again.

He took off all my clothes, trying to act all matter of fact. Stripped me stark naked. Even my underwear. Made me stand in the middle of the room at Motel 6. My belly feeling like I'd swallowed a whole bottle of Clorox bleach, because Boxcar made a tiny bump noise when my shirt hit the ground. And I'm praying she didn't hurt her head. Praying to the Almighty that she'll keep her wits about her and won't panic and crawl out.

And him, trying to act all casual, sat down on the sofa, started pretending to read the newspaper. But he didn't fool me. Not one bit. I could see his thing sticking up in his pants like a rolling pin, and I knew what was coming next.

So, here I am, naked as a jaybird. Trapped in this stupid trunk. It's cold. Not that I'm complaining or anything. I mean, I'm grateful he didn't leave my clothes at the motel. He's got them up front with him. So Boxcar's okay, because it's warm, there's heat up there, with him and my clothes. So she's okay for now, just as long as she stays put. But other than that, things are pretty bad. I can't try to get away. I'm all tied up. And even if I wasn't, I'm sure as hell am not going to try to run away without my clothes on.

I hate this gag. All slobbery and gross. Hate it. Hurts my mouth, my jaw is sore and tired. And I have to focus real hard as the taste of him goes down, think of other things so I won't throw up, because that would be dangerous. Real dangerous. There's nowhere for the throw-up to go. It can't go out because the underwear is in the way, so it would have to go back down. I wonder if people have died drowning on throw-up? I try not to think of it. That's the best way. It's important not to cry. I figured that out right quick. When he first tossed me back here, I started to cry, but that was a real dumb thing to do, because everything clogged up, made it hard to suck air in, choking on snot, tears, and cum. Had to calm myself down and think of other things, like Boxcar, and I try to send nice thoughts to her. Peaceful thoughts. I hope she doesn't worry about me, or think I'm mad at her because I'm not playing and talking with her, and putting her on my belly. I try to let her know with my mind that I would play with her if I could, but I can't. I hope she's not too worried.

I send her imagination places that we're going to visit when we get out of this mess. Really beautiful ones. One of my favorites is a lush meadow, all serene and green. And I'm lying on my back, hidden by the tall grasses, face up to the sky, her on my belly. And the wind blows slightly, gently, soothes my face, my warm skin. My eyes are shut, but I know the sun is shining because I can feel the heat of it on my face.

I create these images and send them to her, so we can travel in our minds. Helps me not panic and freak out. Because if I let my mind wander, even for a moment, to this trunk and the hours I spend in here, the darkness, the closeness . . . If I let my mind go to the smell . . .

forget it. It's curtains. I don't allow my mind to settle there. I have to be strict.

When he first puts me in and I know the trunk's going to close, that's when it's the hardest. It isn't shut yet, but I know it's going to. Know I'm going to be trapped. That's the worst. That's when the panic closes in, squeezing the life right out of my throat. That's the most difficult time to keep it together. I have to fight real hard, because it wants to suck me under like a tidal wave. "Be strong," I tell myself. "Don't panic, don't cry out." I pretend I'm in the war, and it is a test, and the safety of my country hangs in the balance. Or I pretend I'm in a movie. I'm the heroine and this whole situation is make-believe and at any moment the director's going to yell, "Cut!" And then he'll come up to me, and kiss me on both cheeks, saying, "Beautiful, darling, beautiful. I knew you had it in you."

That's the crucial time, when the trunk is about to slam shut. That's the time I have to start weaving fast before the darkness closes in on me. I create beautiful places, out in nature, beautiful places in my mind. It's amazing, because if I focus hard enough, I actually feel like I'm there. Really, really there. It's a wonderful skill to have and useful too.

Maybe when I'm grown up, I'll teach people how to do this. I could call it "Gemma Travel." And I'd only charge rich people. I'd teach kids and poor people for free. It would be a good job, because I could help people and support myself too.

And the cool thing is, I can do it with food. I can create whatever I feel like eating. Anything at all. Macaroni, spaghetti, big burgers with everything on them—cheese, bacon, extra ketchup. Then I eat it real slow, and I can actually taste it and smell it too. I can create chocolate milk shakes, hot-fudge banana splits, even Milk Duds, if I concentrate hard enough. It comes in handy, because sometimes he forgets about meals, and me and Boxcar get awfully hungry.

Actually, Boxcar isn't eating so well. I'm worried about her. I tried to give her some of my hamburger last night, but she wouldn't come out of her shell. I left it in my shoe with her in case she wanted to nibble on it during the night. But I don't think she ate much.

•   •   •

I wonder if my mom misses me? If she noticed I'm gone? Has she realized that Boxcar is gone too? Is she trying to find me? Has she told the police? Are they looking for me too?

Wonder if Buddy's going to tell her what he was doing to me. Wonder what she'll say. If she'll be mad at me. Want me to stay gone. I hope he doesn't tell her. Hope he keeps his stupid mouth shut. Wonder if he'll stick around, stay with her, now that I'm not there for his own personal entertainment. Did Buddy tell her about Hazen? That maybe it was Hazen that took me?

I wonder if it's sunny. If the skies are blue. Or maybe there's a storm rolling in. A fierce thunderstorm. With rain and lightning. I love storms. Make me feel all wild, excited. Like a daredevil. No fear. I'd run out, barefoot, no coat, no umbrella. I say that like I got an umbrella. I don't, but if I did, I wouldn't bring it outside. Not in the fierce, raging storms. I'd only use it on the dainty drizzle days. And it would be a beautiful, pomegranate red. And I'd be all elegant, like those prize show horses I see on TV, with the pretty ribbons and braids in their hair. I'd be all graceful and refined and walk like they do, picking my feet up like I was a fine lady. And I'd twirl the handle, not much, just a little so the umbrella would spin, like those fancy ladies in those old-time musicals. That's what I'd do.

But in a dare-you-dance storm, in a wild, midnight, raging storm . . . No umbrella for me. I'd just run out and dance. Dance with the gods. Dare them to take me, make me fly, fly away, on one of their magnificent thunderbolts. I wonder if a storm's rolling in.

I miss the sky. Miss breathing in, long and deep. Miss that. In this trunk before it's light. Only let out when it's night again. He won't even let me out to pee. Gave me a dumb old mayonnaise jar. Now how am I going to use it with my stupid hands tied? It's hard to do. Real hard. Slops on me and everything smells of pee. I hate this trunk. Stupid, stinky, old dickface.

I wonder if it's Halloween yet. Wonder if it was fun. I'm probably going to be too old next year. Depends if I grow. People tend to give kids dirty looks if they trick-or-treat when they are too old. I'm lucky I'm short. Wasn't sure if I could go this year, it was touch and go. I drank a lot of coffee, and it did the job. I was going to be able to squeak one last year out of trick-or-treating. One last year of free loot.

Stupid dickface. Ruining my last chance at Halloween. Stupid pig. Hate him. Really hate him.

Wish I could see the sky.

.   .   .

She'd snuggled up next to him, crying out in her sleep.

Bad dream, another bad dream. And he comforted her. Stroked her, as her body trembled from her night terror.

He held her, his little Gemma, comforted her. Let her know she was safe in his arms.

.   .   .

I saw my mama on the TV, crying. Buddy was holding her hand, looking all sincere. Stupid jerk. His fault I'm in this mess, shopping me out like he did.

I wonder if he told them what he knew. About Hazen and all. Wonder if he told them.

Probably not. Probably just interested in his own skin. Two-faced jerk. Standing there looking *so* concerned.

Saw my mama crying on the TV and the announcer's talking, saying something about "an epidemic," something . . . something . . . "teenage runaways." Not sure, quite, it was the tail end of his sentence. I wanted to watch, but Hazen flipped the channel fast, his ears all red.

One, two, three channels. Then turned it off, paced the room a bit, and *Bam*, no more TV, no more room, didn't even get dinner. He threw me in the trunk again and off we drove.

Had to camp out that night, camp out in the woods. He kept me in the trunk. Gave me his jacket though. That was nice. Gave me his jacket to keep warm.

Camped out in the woods, coyotes howling, circling. Safe in the trunk, knew that, but still I was scared. Scared that somehow they'd find a way to eat me, and I'd never get home. Just end up a pile of old bones. Gnawed clean, all the flesh ripped from them. An unrecognizable pile of bones. And my mama, Mrs. Moore, Mrs. Watson, the kids at school, none of them would ever know what happened to me, Gemma. I'd just be these old bones rattling around until those got chewed up and gone too.

I got sad thinking about this. Got a powerful wave of homesickness. Wanted my mama, my home, my bed. Wanted it so bad.

FOUR

He had to keep on driving, keep moving. Because when he slowed down, when he didn't keep himself, his mind, busy. Allowed himself to think. Sometimes, if he didn't control it, wasn't prepared for it, a wave of panic swept over him. A wave of panic that had him slamming on the brakes and running into the nearest bathroom at hand, be it at a rest stop, a gas station, a bush if he had to. Because when those waves hit, he got the runs bad. Bent him over for a good ten, fifteen minutes. And as he was crapping, running through his head, like a fucking mantra, "How did this happen?" "In too deep now." "No turning back." In those moments, it seemed like, all this just happened to him, like a runaway train. God threw this at him. As a test, maybe. Who the hell knew. No road map, no preparation.

It scared him sometimes, that he didn't recognize his life. It felt as if at any moment, he was going to wake up and be the old Hazen Wood. The one before Gemma.

Always had the feeling that from here on out, the map of his life was going to be divided in two. And he'd look back and see that distinct crossroads, see it as clear as the thumb on his hand, where he veered off, or on, course. Always, those thoughts were careening through his brain, joining the chorus, the full orchestra symphony that had consumed his body. Dancing about, tangoing with, the violence his bowels were inflicting on him.

Motel after motel. It didn't matter. Traveling the country. Never stopping, staying anywhere too long. Didn't give anyone an opportunity to get familiar. Ask questions. Dusty motels, full of grit and disappointment. And there was something about the dirt and the seediness that excited him and depressed him all at the same time. She was like a drug. A bad habit that had sunk him into the depths, made him one of those desperate junkies, living for the next fix, the next stop, when he could feel her body under him again.

·   ·   ·

I used to wonder, wanted to sneak into the trunk of my mama's car. I thought it would be fun, kind of cool to ride around in one. Like in a spy movie.

That was before I knew that people actually did. I thought it was a fun, fanciful thought. A "what if?" thought, like what if magical carpets really could fly. That kind of thought.

I had no idea. And I will never look at cars, car trunks the same way.

I wonder how many other girls are stashed away, trapped in smelly trunks, trying to get away.

It doesn't have to be like this. There's more room in here than I'd imagined, and it wouldn't be so bad, riding around in a trunk, if I didn't have to. If he wasn't making me.

If I was doing the planning . . . If I was the one stealing a kid, and I was going to force them ride in a trunk for a long period of time, I'd fix it up cozy. Like a little fort, and nice soft pillows to lean against, and a little blanket for when it gets chilly. I'd have snacks, and a "little bitty reading light" like they have in fancy catalogues, where the woman

56

clips it to the top of her book and she can read while her husband sleeps beside her with a smile on his face.

I'd get one of those lights and all kinds of books, magic books, adventure, learning books, history. A ton of books, so all this time, riding down the road, I could be learning too.

•   •   •

Every night I wait till he's asleep, snoring softly, with the lower part of his mouth hanging open. Then I creep out of bed, quiet, so quiet, like a ghost, like the fog, silent, so silent. I get Boxcar out of my pocket and we go to the bathroom. I shut the bathroom door, slow and easy, with the knob twisted open so the latch won't snick. When the door is shut, then, carefully, I turn the knob in my hand. Hold my breath because this is the tricky part. Turn the knob just so, and the latch slides silently into place.

Then I turn on the water. Just a thin stream, so the faucet won't make noise. I turn it on gentle, like I'm a heart surgeon, push the plug down and let the water gather in the sink. Boxcar likes it. She usually takes a long drink and then swims a little. Little circles round and round. And I talk to her, soft whispers, keeping one ear open in case he wakes up and notices I'm not in bed with him. He doesn't like it. Gets real mad if he wakes up and I'm not there.

Boxcar's my best friend in the whole wide world. I miss her during the day. Miss her so bad, now that she rides up front with my clothes. We're quiet in the bathroom, Boxcar and me. I whisper, quiet as a dandelion puff. I tell her everything. All about Buddy and my mom. All about José and Mrs. Moore. And I tell her about Hazen and the things he does to me. And she listens and looks at me with these sad, sad eyes. Cocks her head like she's saying, "Yeah . . . yeah . . . I know how you feel . . . I hate him too . . . I'm so sorry. . . ."

But she wouldn't come out of her shell today. I put water in the sink like I always do. Nice and lukewarm, comfy-like. But she wouldn't come out, didn't want to drink, didn't want to swim. I put her in the water, hoping that would cheer her up. Make her poke her head out and swim a little. But she didn't. Just sort of turned upside down, all floppy like. I was worried she'd drown, swimming like that. So I took her out right quick. Dried her off and tucked her back in my sock.

I'm so worried about her. Think maybe she's depressed. Tired of life on the road, riding up front with old stinko. I don't blame her. It probably was more fun in the trunk with me.

·　　·　　·

Tied her hands a little too tight. Was in a hurry, slept in, was almost light outside. Did a sloppy job of it. Hurrying, trying to get her into the trunk before the town woke up. Tied them just a bit too tight. Were all blue and purple when they stopped for the night. Had to rub them for a good hour to get the circulation going.

A near thing. Could have lost her hands. Told her too. "You have to behave," he said. "Have to stop fighting me, for your own good. You could have lost your hands. Could have lost your goddamned hands with this foolishness." Smacked her around a bit to get her to focus. "Could have lost your hands. Would have been a freak. A freak with no hands. . . . How would you have liked that? A freak with no hands, just because of your stubbornness. Just because you think you're too good, too fucking goddamned special to ride up front with me."

And she could have. That's a fact. A fact he drilled into her, fucking her that night. Could have lost her hands like in World War I. In World War I, soldiers were losing their limbs left, center, and right. Get wounded, lose consciousness, and collapse. Would have to get limbs amputated, cut right off, because they'd fallen, passed out, with a leg, an arm twisted up under them. Unconscious, didn't, couldn't move. Had to have body parts cut off with no painkiller, just an old rag to chew on. Lopped off with an ax, a machete, a knife, whatever the hell was handy. Lost circulation, got gangrene, and the limb had to be cut off. And that's the goddamned truth of the matter.

Have to come up with another solution. Another option to their traveling dilemma. Will sleep on it. It'll come to him. He is patient. He will pray tonight and God will tell him. God will tell him what to do.

. . .

"Get your hunting knife." God said. And so he did. Got his hunting knife out. Had to do it. Couldn't be helped.

Have to think of it like a choke chain, a training device, a temporary measure, until she learns, accepts the order of things. "And woman shall submit to man, as man shall submit to Jesus." It's right there, right there in the scripture, right there in the blessed Holy Bible. "Woman shall submit to man," or something like that, can't remember the exact phrasing. But it's there in black and white. Look it up later, maybe tonight, and read it to her. Help her understand her duty. He's not being tough, just teaching, training her. That's why he's taken to holding his hunting knife on her. For her own good. To teach her obedience. Holds the handle against the small of her back, the tip of the blade caressing the soft, sweet flesh just under the ribs. His arm around her waist, so they look like two friendly people on a little outing.

The knife, their sweet, private secret, his knife, his cock.

Sometimes, he nips her with it slightly. A love nip. Just to remind her of his love. He likes it. The knife thing, the way it makes him feel. Her breathing, all shallow, swallowing hard, eyes big. Walking careful, no sudden movements, doesn't want to get nipped. Behaving so well.

And he tells her, reminds her as they drive, how it was her own choice. She'd promised, given her word that she'd behave. And did she? No. Made a scene at that Texaco station outside of Portland. After he had been nice enough to let her out of the trunk. Let her out of the trunk and ride up front like a big girl. She'd given her word of honor. And what did she do? Broke it. Plain and simple. Made a big stinky scene at that Texaco station. He had to forcibly haul her into the car, leave without paying. Had to do that just to keep her safe. And he

59

reminds her of this every time he takes the knife out. Because that incident scared the hell out of him. Too close for comfort. Don't need to be drawing attention to themselves. That's the last thing in the world they need.

So now he does that thing with the knife as a matter of course. Just until he gets her trained.

Has got it down to a science. Holds it, lying flat under the baggy sweatshirt he'd bought for her in Tacoma. Holds it under that, the cool metal up against the heat of her skin. So she knows, can feel, that he is the man now. And she knows that he'd just as soon gut her as make love to her. Gut her like a week-old fawn. Fast and easy, his blade piercing, slicing into her young flesh, her sweet, soft belly that takes his cock in so tenderly. Just as soon kill her as lose her. And he tells her that, so she'll know of his love. And she listens to her man. She behaves. Is very docile now. His sweet, beloved Gemma.

.   .   .

I hold still now. I don't move or he'll cut me. He likes to cut me, but I don't let him know I'm afraid. When his knife comes out my heart starts pounding hard, and it's like the thumping of it forms a stairway, and I follow it up, serene, peaceful. It's like I become my own angel watching me. Watching me behave so good, keeping me safe.

I float up above me, so that even when he cuts me, it's like I don't really feel it. Just heat. Sharp, heat that calls me back and slams me into my body. Slams me back, but only for a second, and then up I drift. Up my staircase to safety.

.   .   .

He likes to brush her beautiful, blond hair. Long, smooth strokes. Has her sit in her pink, see-through, baby-doll pajamas. Size petite. Picked them up at the same sex shop he got her very first vibrator, a gold, sleek one. Likes to use it on her sometimes. Sits on a chair administering it, her sprawled on the bed, he likes to watch it go in and out, slide in and out. Likes that.

Not tonight though. Tonight he's doing the hair-brushing ritual. Wanted to try out his new prop, and it's working good. Got her to hold a fuzzy white teddy bear he'd picked up at the gas station, with a red ribbon around its neck and a red heart with "I love you" written on it in white. He's got her holding it. His very own Lolita.

What a night, what a beautiful night. Very hard to get to a hundred strokes of the hairbrush. A difficult task he's set out for himself, a near impossible task. He has to squeeze his eyes shut so he won't stain her lovely pink nightie with his seed. "Not yet," he says. "Not yet." Wants to draw it out. Has to think disgusting thoughts, wrinkled old women's vaginas, shit like that. Has to think shit like that to keep from cumming.

Keep counting. Fifty-eight . . . Fifty-nine . . . Keep breathing. Remove from his body. Sixty . . . Sixty-one . . . Sixty-two . . . And he's brushing and brushing. But old ladies' wrinkled bits aren't working because there she is, so beautiful. Such a good girl, sitting in front of the mirror. Lollypop face, legs slightly spread, just the way he placed them, so he could get a glimpse of her naked little twat. Her sweet-smelling child's twat he had soaked and scrubbed and washed clean in her nightly bath. Washed clean and pink. Then dusted lightly with a sprinkling of Johnson's baby powder. Keep counting, keep brushing. "Sixty-seven . . . Sixty-eight . . ." Keep brushing with his fine, sterling-silver hairbrush. The one he'd bought on impulse, had to, because she's so damned special. Needed something appropriate for her long, blond hair, corn-silk soft. Her lips are slightly swollen from sucking. . . . Damn! Keep counting, keep counting. "Seventy-four . . . Seventy-five . . ."

She squirms. Just a little, shifts on her seat. Like maybe she's sore from last night, from him. Just a few inches of movement, and he can't wait. He just can't wait any longer.

"How the hell am I . . ." he says. He tries to keep his voice level, keep the excitement out. A simple matter of disobedience and punishment. "You tell me . . . how the fuck am I going to brush your hair, if you keep on fucking squirming?"

He is hard now. Hard as a fucking teak coffee table. But she doesn't answer, never does anymore, just loses her color and looks down at her hands.

He was going to make her walk over to the bed, lie down across it, paddle her behind there. But the whore got him too hot. He yanks her out of the chair and swipes at her butt a few times. She doesn't dance out of the way like she used to. Stands there, mute, head down, staring at the floor, trying to ruin his fun. But it's not going to happen, no way. This whole scenario is way too sweet. Doesn't even need to smack her hard, just enough to get her tushy nice and rosy and then, he bends her over, pushes his cock in. Takes her from behind, bent over the vanity. And he watches in the mirror, watches his big powerful steam engine slam into her, and as he pulls part way out, preparing to thrust again, he notices, on his cock, a little streak of blood shimmering like a promise. And it is good. It is so good, especially with that teddy bear clutched in her hand.

•   •   •

He stopped holding his knife on me. Wears it on his belt, in its leather holding container. His leather knife pouch has a snap around the handle for easy access, and his knife comes out fast. That snap pops right open. He showed me back at that Motel 6, how fast he could get at it. Real fast.

So I don't do nothing. Just smile and act nice. I don't run away. I don't fight him no more. Because if I'm even thinking about it, somehow he knows, and he gives me the backhand across my face and shakes his belt at me to remind me what's hanging on it, how fast he can get at it. I smarten up right quick. I'm not a fool. Although I don't know what's so funny about it. I hate the way he laughs at me after he shakes his belt. Laughs and pinches my cheeks like he thinks I'm so cute. Hate it when he does that. It's so condescending.

That was a spelling word. One of my spelling words right before I was taken. Mrs. Watson always gave me a couple of real hard ones. Gave them to me special, because I'm such a good speller. She'd give out all the spelling words to everybody, write them out up on the blackboard. Then she'd say, "And these two are for Gemma." She'd write out two real tough ones and everyone would say they were glad they weren't me. I'd groan a little and pretend I didn't like it, but I did. I'd always groan real soft so Mrs. Watson wouldn't hear, because I wouldn't want her to get the wrong idea and stop doing it. It made me feel good getting extra work. Like I was smart, special. I liked it a lot and I'd study real hard, so I'd get one hundred percent.

I am building a future for myself. A foundation. That's what I'm doing. Want to go to college. Got big plans.

I'm a little worried, though. I don't know how long Hazen's going to keep me. Am scared I'm getting stupid, behind the class. That I'm going to come back and be the dunce and have to sit in Billy Robinson's group. I'm hoping Hazen will get tired and let me go soon. He's being a little nicer. Lets me ride up front. Still does me at night, but he's put his knife away, so that's something. Maybe if I'm extra good. If I explain how important school is to me and tell him how Mrs. Moore really needs my help in the library, that she's probably getting overwhelmed with returned books that need to be put back in their place. Maybe if I tell him that, he'll let me go home.

·   ·   ·

I'm real worried about Boxcar. I think she's sick. She hasn't wanted to swim, eat, or drink for three days now and I don't know what to do. She's just sleeping all the time. I gave her a gentle shake to see if I could wake her up. Tipped her slightly to the side, trying to look in her shell to see how she was doing. One of her arms, one of her legs, and part of her head fell out. Not out on the floor, just flopped out a bit. Like her muscles were tired of holding them in.

She's starting to smell a bit too. I think she might have the flu. Diarrhea, or something that she can't hold in. And she's too sick to do it out of her little shell house, so she's doing it inside. Poor little Boxcar. She's kind of stinky, but I don't tell her. I don't want to hurt her feelings. She can't help it if she's sick. I just say, "I'm sorry you're not feeling well." "Wish I could get you to a doctor." That kind of thing.

So worried about her. Trying to be strong, but I'm fighting back tears all the time. I don't want her to know how scared I am about her health because then she might start worrying too, and she needs all her strength to get healthy again. I tell her how great things are going to be. How goodness is just around the corner. And if tears overwhelm me, I turn around quick and hum a little happy sounding song, until I can get my emotions back under control, because me being all weepy is the last thing Boxcar needs.

•　　　•　　　•

Fucked her good last night. Real good. Thinks maybe he made her cum, because she was sobbing and shuddering something fierce. Her whole body was convulsing. Moved to tears she was. Good little lay. Not fighting him quite so much now. Getting more used to the fact that he is the man. Getting more adjusted. Doing quite well, his Gemma.

•　　　•　　　•

In Bellingham. Flirting with the idea of crossing the Canadian border to visit the great Northwest. Hazen Wood and the great Canadian Rockies. See the Royal Canadian Mounted Police. Loved them when he was a boy. Visited Victoria with his grandmother when he was seven. Greatest trip of his life. Got to pet one of those great big horses on the nose. The rest of the horse was rough, the hairs short and prickly. But the nose—soft, so soft. It snorted when he was petting it. Shook its head, rattling its reins. Made Hazen jump, and his grandmother and the Mountie had laughed. He laughed too, and then petted it again, its breath warm, fragrant, sweet. Smelled of hay, and grain, and horse. His grandmother took a picture.

Always wanted to be a Mountie. Maybe he'd join. Nothing to stop him from getting a red buttoned-up uniform; great, brass buttons; a big stick. Get himself a fucking big Canadian stallion. Join the RCMP.

"What do you think, Gemma? Think I'd make a good Royal Canadian Mounted Police?" He asks her, smile on his face. Likes the dichotomy of it. Would be fun. Representing justice, the law. He'd be damned good at it, that's for sure.

She doesn't answer. Rarely does. Just looks out the side window, face pale, shut. Hair, falling forward around her face, closing her off from him.

"What do you think, Gemma? Shall we go to Canada?"

There is a pause, an intake of breath, and then she answers in that soft, shy voice of hers. A hesitant skip in it.

"No, I . . . I don . . . don't want to . . . go to Canada. . . ."

Ah, he's got her talking. "Why not?" he says, all jovial. "Aren't you curious?"

"No," she says. That's all. Not a brilliant conversationalist, his Gemma.

"Well, I want to see it. I'm the man. I make the decisions. Because what you want, to be honest, darling, what you want doesn't matter one iota to me."

He swings the car onto Route 5, towards the Canadian border.

"What," she says, so softly he can barely hear her, "are you going to tell them about me? What if they want a passport? I don't have a passport."

"A what?" he says, but he heard her. Forgot about passports. Wonder how other people did it. Other people in his situation. They always seem to end up hiding in Canada or Mexico. Everybody he's ever heard about. On the news and whatnot. They got across.

But then again, she's got a point; they might want a passport, might ask some questions. Things are supposed to be tougher now. Harder since 9/11. What if they ask him a lot of questions? What if they want to talk to her? Probably okay, but sometimes, she's unpredictable. Wouldn't be good. What to do?

His mind starts going through options like a fliporama book— little, short, silent movies playing out. Sorting through all possible scenarios, all possible conclusions that could occur.

"Okay. . . ." He turns the car around. "Okay," he says, like he's making a generous concession. "You don't want to go to Canada, we won't go to Canada."

She snorts through her nose, a small, suppressed, noise. But he decides not to take umbrage, pretends not to hear. Because actually, he's glad she thought of the passport thing. Don't know what the hell he was thinking.

·   ·   ·

Hazen almost took me to Canada. Scared me. I pretended to be calm, but really, honestly, I didn't know what to do. He almost got us to the Canadian border, but luckily I was smart and remembered Mrs. Bird talking about passports in social studies. How she needed her one when she went on her honeymoon to France.

Now, I don't know if Canada needs passports, but I pretended they did. It was lucky I remembered, because if we went to Canada, and he became a police, I'd never stand a chance of getting home. I'd be stuck with him forever. Who'd believe me over a police officer? So, that was a close call.

·   ·   ·

He keeps bugging me, quizzing me on Disneyland. I don't know why. I've never been. So what? Big deal.

But he won't let it go, talks about it all afternoon, all evening, about how great it is, and how much I'd enjoy it.

Well, I know that. I mean, DUH! Who wouldn't like it? Yeah, DUH! I know I've never been. What's it to you? Insensitive jerk.

And I don't know why he keeps mouthing off about my mama. What he doesn't understand is, my mama loves me. She didn't have time, is all. She was busy and Disneyland's expensive. Damned expensive. Not everyone can afford to go to Disneyland. Stupid asshole. I would punch him in the nose if I could. Punch him in the nose to shut him up.

But he's got the knife, so I just sit, nice and sweet. I sit and think my thoughts, watch the sky, and tune him out. Make him like a slow fade on the radio dial. His mouth is moving "Blah . . . blah . . . blah . . ." But I hear nothing.

.   .   .

Couldn't get their conversation out of his head. Never been to Disneyland. Hell, she hadn't lived more than five hours away. Six, tops. And she'd never been. Fucked his stomach up to think about it. Poor kid.

She'd love it. That's for sure. If ever a place had Gemma written all over it, Disneyland was it.

He thought and thought about it. All through their evening bath, the nightly romp. Watched the evening news carefully that night, ABC, CBS, CNN, NBC. Local and national. Flipping the channels carefully, scanning. Watched until the early hours of the morning. No mention of Gemma. Nothing, nada, zip. It was like she never existed. It was like God was handing her over, saying, "You've done good, Hazen, showed me you're worthy. She's all yours."

A good thing too. A damned good thing. From the bits and pieces he'd picked up from the TV over the last few weeks, she had a real bad situation at home. Neighbors talking. "Probably a runaway." "Mother in and out of rehab." Not to mention that lowlife Buddy. Accosting her, raping her at every chance he got. Selling her to every asshole that crossed his path.

Christ, Gemma should be thanking her lucky stars. Thanking sweet Jesus that he picked her up and saved her. Rescued her from that hellhole.

And now she was his. Totally his. And he was going to take his baby doll to goddamned Disneyland. "I'm going to do it," he finds himself saying out loud. Hearing the words fill up that old, rancid motel room. Swelling his heart, blood pumping. Filling his body with that adrenaline rush, like the first step into a boxing ring. That kind of testosterone high. "I'm going to do it!" he yells, pumping his fists in the air.

"Gemma!" he says, shaking her awake. Waking his sweet baby up. Her, all tousled and sleepy eyed. "Gemma!" he says. Happy, so happy. Because this thing he's going to do, it'll do the trick. When she sees the risks he's willing to take to show her a good time . . . When she sees that, she's going to wrap her arms around his neck. She's going to realize just how much she loves him. How much he loves her, because what he's planning to do, it's dangerous. Damned dangerous.

"Baby, wake up. I'm taking you to Disneyland. I'm taking you to fucking Disneyland!"

He watches as she wakes, the confusion, the sleep, the delight, all battle with each other. And she leaps out of bed, dancing around in her little bare feet, arms hugging herself in excitement.

"Really? Really? Disneyland? Disneyland?!" And she's excited. So excited. They both are. He swings her around the room. Just like one of those old-fashioned love stories. And life is good. Real good and getting better.

He can't wait until morning. Too revved up. Got a long way to go. Two state lines to cross. They get in the car. Shivering in the night air. Brought the blanket from the motel. Wrapped her up in it. Let her stay in her baby dolls. No need to get changed. Had her crawl into the back seat to sleep.

Driving to California. The sunshine state. The night sky, stars, moon still out. Headlights sweeping, arcing across his car, his face, his baby tucked away, wrapped up and sleeping in the back seat. Just like in one of those old time movies. And he feels good. Damned good. Driving to California, taking Gemma to Disneyland. Going to show his baby a good time.

.   .   .

"We're going to Disneyland," I tell Boxcar. "Disneyland!" I've always wanted to go. Have heard so much about it. I wish this car had wings. Frigging wings like Chitty Chitty Bang Bang, so it could fly. Wish I had a magic ring that I could turn around my finger three times and we'd be there. So excited.

Hazen's taking me to Disneyland!

I'm being real good. Don't want him to change his mind and turn the car around. I'm doing whatever he wants. Whatever. He's getting no guff from me.

And he's so happy. He's not half bad when he's happy. And he's telling me all about it. How much I'm going to like it. How it's the greatest place on earth. How much fun it is, how exciting, how expensive. . . .

I'm so excited, I can hardly take it. Feel like I have to pee every five minutes. But Hazen doesn't mind. He throws his head back and laughs. Doesn't mind that we keep having to stop at rest stops.

I'm so excited! I get to go to Disneyland. And not only that, there are going to be crowds, lots of people. Maybe after I see everything, I can slip away.

.   .   .

Pulling his car, his locomotion, his charcoal gray Dodge Intrepid right up to the front door of the Disneyland hotel. Not a Motel 6. Not even a Best Western. Uh huh. When Hazen Wood does something, he does it right. Does it with style. Nothing but the best for his baby.

Pulls right up to the goddamned front door.

It's a hot, humid day. Sweaty and sticky, salt on the skin. A great day for cotton candy.

69

Cotton candy and Gemma. It's a fucking beautiful day.

Valets in white uniform with gold trim leap off the curb to open his car door. Because they know, they can feel that he's the man. He looks over at Gemma. Her mouth is hanging open like a trap door someone forgot to close.

"Here we are," he says, striding up to the red carpeted walkway, gesturing expansively. "Here we are. Just for you baby—Disneyland!" She scampers after him, timid as a mouse, smiles up at him. A, "You did it!" kind of smile. An, "Oh my God, I'm so lucky to be with you!" kind of smile. Like she can't believe her good fortune. Like dreams really do come true.

And then, sweet Jesus, without him even asking, she takes his hand. Slips hers in his, first time ever, takes his hand because she wants to. Takes his hand, eyes big, face shy. Half hiding, peeking out from behind him. And they walk like that, hand in hand into the hotel lounge.

.   .   .

The hotel room is fantastic. Seventeenth floor. Can see out over the whole universe. It's fantastic! Huge king-sized bed. All pale and pastels, mirrors everywhere, sliding mirrors on the closet doors, in the elevators, in the bathroom. Free coffee, a coffee machine.

"Can we go? Can we go?" Gemma dancing around, eyes sparkling, beautiful, so beautiful. Mine, he thinks. All mine. And it is satisfying, looking at her. Knowing she belongs to him.

"Come here," he says. She comes. So obedient now. So well trained. "Give me your undies." She hesitates, a flicker of something, but then she slips them down from under her skirt and hands them to him, her gaze on his knees, but she gives them to him. He pats her on the head. "Good girl," he says. He's proud of her. Come a long way, his Gemma. "It's the way of things," he says, teaching her the rituals of Disneyland. "You aren't supposed to wear underwear at Disneyland. Nobody does." She glances up at him quick, eyes searching his, but he doesn't let on. Keeps his expression straight. And her gaze slides away.

"Can we go now?" she asks, voice shy, tentative.

"Not yet. Things we have to do, chores that must be done, preparations that must be made before we can go. You want this to be perfect don't you?" And she nods slowly, face wary.

. . .

He's done her two times, sweet and gentle. Two times he filled her up, slow and tender.

The Disneyland hotel. Expensive as hell, but so worth it. Being with her. Taking his time, her champing at the bit. Wanting to go see Mickey Mouse and Dumbo.

But she has to wait, be patient, has to be good. Has to let him catch his breath, do her one last time. Needs to act like she really wants it, and then he'll take her to catch the tram and see Peter Pan's Flight.

. . .

Kept her underwear, wouldn't let her put them back on. The two of them, walking around Disneyland, hand in hand. Every now and then he likes to squat down, pretend to tie her shoe, take a peek up, look at the goods. And even though she doesn't want to let him tie her shoe again, she does, because he holds all the power. She knows if she causes a scene, if anyone looks at them sideways . . . Boom! No more Disneyland.

So she lets him check her out. Face blushing. He loves it when she blushes, so childlike, so innocent. Cheeks flushed, eyes averted. Lets him check her out. Peek. Sneak a feel.

Pirates of the Caribbean. What a high that is! Dark, all dark, fireflies and crickets. The slap of water against the side of the boat. Gemma and Hazen, snuggled up like two lovers, have the back row of the boat all to themselves. He slides his hand up under her skirt, fondling her. Quick, surreptitious feels. Her body stiff beside him. Not saying a word. Because she's good now, his Gemma. Doesn't say anything. Lets him touch her because she likes it. It gets her hot too. Sexy little whore. Knows how crazy she makes him. Little lollipop slut. Longs for it. He makes her beg for it. And she does. Begs him for it, just like he taught her.

She's well trained, his Gemma. A well-trained little slut.

. . .

I wish he would stop, wouldn't do that. I'm so scared someone's going to see and throw me in jail. Don't like it. It's ruining Disneyland. Wish he wasn't here with his big, meaty hands. His stupid, sweaty, greasy hands. Glazed eyes, doing his heavy, "I'm going to fuck you" breathing. I wish he would stop. One day. That's all. Just give me one day to be normal.

. . .

What a day. What a glorious day. Gemma, what a spark plug. She seems to love roller coasters. The little daredevil. Had never been on one. Never in her whole life, and yet here she is laughing. Head thrown back, skinny arms thrust in the air.

"I can fly!" she's screaming. "I can fly!"

Sunshine. Laughing. Happy, so happy. And for this second, it's like time holds still and all of life is encapsulated in this one moment. The entire point of his existence is wrapped up in her sweet face. And he can't help himself, throws caution to the wind, and kisses her, tongue forcing its way deep into her mouth. Kisses her long and deep, even though she's fighting him, even though they're in public, even though they're trying to pretend, be sneaky. Can't help it, even though they are on the Matterhorn and it's broad daylight. He needs to take her, claim her.

Doesn't want to stop, but she pulls away, clouds filling her eyes, laughter gone.

"What?" he says, but it's too late. Gone too far. Too obvious, too public.

Can't do nothing but watch as she wrenches herself away, arms snapping across her skinny flat chest like a door slamming shut. Yanks away, sitting stiff, squashed up against her side of the ride.

"What?" he says, but he already knows.

"What?" he says voice more belligerent than he feels inside. He grabs her arm and pulls her around. "Look at me when I talk to you!"

Her head snaps towards his, her eyes dark with loathing. And the intensity of her stare makes the hair stand up on the back of his arms, his neck, and his stomach feels like he'd just eaten a bowl of cold lard. And he regrets turning her around. Because he knows, he can see it, just for a flash, before the veil drops down across her eyes, he can see the magnitude of her hatred.

.   .   .

Bad day, getting worse. Hustling her out of the park, and she's resisting, carrying on, doesn't want to leave. Forgetting all the lessons she's learned as of late. Behaving badly. Hanging on to lampposts, bushes, trees. Grabbing hold of anything, screaming. Calling stuff out. Bad stuff that could really cause problems. She's screaming out, freaky, scary stuff. It's like she doesn't care. Just doesn't care. Is pissing on, trying to destroy, this great life he's created for her. And she's smiling. The little bitch is smiling, and laughing, and crying, and screaming. Tearing up the place. And he's trying to get her under control. Trying to shut her up. But people are looking, turning away, listening. Security comes. Spit-and-polish California kids.

"Excuse me, sir . . . We're going to have to ask you to leave."

He tells them they're leaving. Apologizes for her behavior.

"She suffers from severe Tourette's syndrome, poor thing. Acts out. Medications worn off. Was going so well . . . poor dear . . . Wanted so badly to see Disneyland. . . . If you could just help me contain her." He pries her hand off a tree, trying to act light. Trying to keep the sweat from showing. "I'm scared she's going to hurt herself. Poor baby." Keeping his voice calm. "She's not herself in times like this. If you could give me a hand?" Gripping her tight, hanging on to her, don't let her escape. She's wiry, wiggling hard, trying to break free. "Whoopsy daisy. . . ." A laugh here, a little laugh. "Too much child for one man to handle. . . . She's tired. . . . The poor thing."

And they help him. So helpful, these pasty-faced milksops. They help him hold her down, pin her arms and legs, bundle her up, carry her out like a rolled-up carpet.

They help him, eyes averted. Embarrassed for him, the trials of his life. The things he has to put up with. They buy his story, hook, line, and sinker. Buy his story in their pansy little "security" suits. Stupid little twerps.

Help get her all the way to the room. Her fighting, screaming, cursing, biting. Little spitfire.

And she's saying things that have his stomach run cold. But they don't hear. It's like they have inner tubes stuffed in their ears. They only hear him. Hazen Wood. They only hear what he tells them. It's like he's Svengali. They listen, while he spoon-feeds them their portion of Pablum.

They put her on the bed. Hazen sits on her. She's tearing at her face now. Raking huge claw marks across it.

"Is there any thing else, sir?" they say, discomfited by her passion. "Anything else?"

"No. Thank you for your kindness. Thank you so much."

They straighten out their uniforms, file from the room, trying to catch their breath, because even though there were three of them, counting Hazen, four . . . even though there were four of them, Gemma gave them a run for their money.

The door clicks shut behind them. And it's like with the door shutting, all the air, all the fight, leaves her body. Just wooshes out, like a balloon deflating.

But he doesn't care, if she's sorry. He waits. Waits until he can hear them get in the elevator, hears the elevator door ping shut.

Then he beats the crap out of her. Thoroughly and systematically. From top to bottom and back up to the top again. Beats, pummels, whips every inch of her body, using his fists, elbows, knees, feet. Releases his belt from his pants, uses that, both ends, buckle and leather. Covers every inch of her body, so she'll know, remember, never, ever to do that again.

·   ·   ·

Covering a lot of miles these days. The incident at Disneyland appeared to have tipped the authorities off. A few mentions on TV. Not a nightly thing, but enough to be worrisome. The occasional poster. Needs to be careful. Some nosy little busybody said something. So they drive now, not much else to do. Just drive, and drive some more. Gas, so expensive. Goddamned Disneyland took a hunk out of his Visa. Everything getting maxed out. Over the limit. Just a matter of time before it all explodes, implodes, whatever.

Don't think. Keep driving.

Can't stop, rest, settle. Her face is looking too bad. The bruises taking a long time to heal. Belt buckle took a few hunks out of her face. Can't stop. People would ask questions. Looks bad.

Didn't mean to mess her up so thoroughly. She asked for it, but still. Hard on Hazen's stomach to look at her. Makes it hard to do her, when she's lying like a limp rag doll.

And another thing. The little freak was carrying a dead turtle in her pocket. A dead, stinking, rancid, rotting turtle in her pocket. How messed up is that?

The damn thing fell out of her pocket.

"What the hell is this?" Couldn't believe his eyes.

"Wh . . . what?" she stammered. "I . . . I don't . . . know what . . . you're . . ." Trying to cover, the little shit, always trying to cover.

"Why are you," he enunciated clearly, so there could be no mistake, no miscommunication, as to what he was referring to, "carrying . . . a dead turtle . . . in your pocket?"

"She's not dead." Gemma was speaking fast, overlapping, cutting him off.

"The turtle's dead."

"She's NOT dead. She's sleeping! She's SLEEPING! She's JUST SLEEPING!" The kid was yelling. Getting hysterical.

But fact was fact. There's no two ways about it. Not doing her any favors playing make-believe.

"It's dead. The fucking thing's dead. Jesus Christ! You blind or something?"

He whacked her across the face to knock some sense into her. "This turtle's DEAD!" And the ludicrousness of the situation had him bust out laughing. Couldn't believe she'd been carting this dead turtle around for God knows how long. Very unsanitary. Stunk to high heaven. Little freak.

Then, to top it off, when he disposed of it, did her the favor of flushing the damn thing down the toilet, she acted like it was her grandmother, for Chrissake. Plunged her arm into the toilet. Into the goddamned toilet. The thing's gone. Flushed. Out of here. And the little nutcase was on her fucking hands and knees, scrabbling around in the toilet.

Carried on, weeping and wailing well into the night. Wouldn't talk to him all the next day. The silent treatment. She was giving *him* the silent treatment. Jesus Christ, he did her a favor. It's not like he killed it. The thing's eyeballs were half rotted out of its head. It was dead. The stupid thing was dead.

. . .

Don't worry. I've figured out the whole deal. Boxcar wasn't dead. She was pretending because she saw what Hazen had done to me. She was scared of him, so she played dead. She's a good actor, so he believed her, didn't hurt her. Flushed her down the toilet instead.

At first I was real upset. The weird thing is, I took this way harder than when my granddaddy died. And I loved my granddaddy.

It has me a little worried. Like maybe I'm a bad person, that I cried way more when Boxcar got flushed than when my granddaddy passed away. I mean, she just got flushed. He died. Dead. Never to come back. When my granddaddy died, I cried maybe an hour, an hour and a half tops, when I add all the different times together. So what's that say about me?

In my defense, however, I did think Hazen was killing her. I mean, my granddaddy died in his bed. I didn't see nothing.

And to be honest, when Hazen flushed her, I thought he was murdering her. It was like he was the Nazi, and I was the mother, and I was being forced to watch the destruction of my child. Of course I was going to flip out. Who wouldn't?

But after a little while, I figured it out.

Boxcar was pretending. Hazen flushed her. She got a fun ride, like the roller coaster at Disneyland. "Wheeee!" Down the drains into the pipes and plumbing, twisting and turning this way and that. And here is the exciting part . . . Where do the plumbing pipes lead? They have to lead somewhere. And when I thought about that for a moment, I deduced that there was only one possible solution. . . .

They lead to rivers! And the rivers lead to lakes. And lakes are the very best place *in the whole world* for turtles to live. The very best!

Think of it, Boxcar is living in a beautiful lake and has probably met a handsome turtle husband and gotten married. I bet she has lots of happy little baby Boxcars running around and her nice, thoughtful husband helps her find worms and flies and other tasty tidbits. He shows her the ways of the lake and has built her a cozy home.

Boxcar's fine.

Actually, if I'd thought of it, I probably would have flushed her myself.

•   •   •

I got away. Walked out. Just walked right out, calm as can be.

He'd gone next door for coffee at Denny's. He hadn't tied me up or taken my clothes. Went to get himself a coffee and I upped and walked right out of the room. Didn't look left, didn't look right. Didn't want to attract attention to myself, which might seem crazy, because there was no one else in the room. But that's how I felt, like someone was watch-ing me and I had to be very careful, move slow so as not to attract any undue attention. Walked out the door like I had a right to.

Just walked my body out of that door and down the stairs. Not too fast, not too slow. The blood rushing in my ears, like an old washing machine. I glanced down, my hands were shaking. My heart feeling like the stereo, with everything but the bass turned off. It's booming away. Throbbing so hard it's making the front of my blouse jump like this— *Boomp . . . Boomp . . .* —with each beat.

Going down the cement steps to the first floor. It was all enclosed and me, so scared I'd meet him, coming up, carrying his coffee.

Walking careful, breathing soft. No sudden movements, ready to run. Ears on hi-fi stereo sound. Listening, straining to hear the scrap of his slag-stepped feet.

Once I got to the front of the building, I began to run. I ran and ran and ran. Heart pounding, shoulders scrunched down like it was raining and I was a cat not wanting to get wet. I don't know why I was running that way, but I was. Running all weird like I didn't have a right to. Like I half expected a big fist to grab ahold of me by the scruff of my neck and haul me back to him. Running like I had an invisible bungee cord attached around my neck, and I don't see it, don't know it's there, but he does. And he's sitting in the restaurant, laughing and taking his time, drinking his coffee. Just laughing and waiting for the bungee cord to snap me back, yank me off my feet and slam me back, so I am lying, cowering like an worn-out rug at his feet.

.   .   .

Caught her. Caught the little bitch. Drove the streets of Denver for four days. Four wasted days looking for her. Found her in an alley eat-ing pizza out of a Dumpster. Eating fucking garbage! Almost didn't recognize the little slut, almost drove past. Her hair, one big massive tangle, face grimy, clothes torn, filthy. Almost didn't recognize her. She's the one who gave it away. If she hadn't gotten the trapped-in-the-headlights expression, if she hadn't tried to bury herself in the garbage, he would have driven right by. That's how dirty she was.

But she tried to hide, and he found her. That's how he caught the little slut. More trouble than she's worth. Had to get in the stinking Dumpster and drag the bitch out. Her acting like a wild animal. Weird animal sounds, primitive noises, coming out of her. Clawing, scratching, biting.

Got her back in the trunk. Being none too gentle. Roughed her up a bit. More trouble than she's worth. Slammed the trunk door down on her. Stupid little slut. Not about to let her up front. Can't trust her. Besides, she's too disgustingly filthy.

●　　　●　　　●

She's quiet. His Gemma. She's peaceful now.

Had to clean her extra hard, scrub her skin raw. Had to use Clorox, Comet, and a scrub brush in order to clean her good. Get the germs off. Took two hours to comb her hair out.

But she's behaving now. Not fighting him. Is probably relieved he found her. Probably was scared on the streets, poor tyke. Probably glad, grateful to be back in his arms, safe with her Hazen again. Probably understands now, how hard it is to survive on one's own. Survive on the streets. Must have had some scary experiences. Doesn't want to talk about it. Just shakes her head, eyes filling up. Doesn't say anything, but Hazen knows it wasn't good. Knows she's not going to try that again anytime soon.

Took her to bed. Wasn't planning on it. Was still a little shaken, a little mad about her latest escapade. But she seemed to need it, want it, four days without. Gave it to her everywhere, then pulled out, shot it all over her face. Her eyes squeezed shut tight like she was taking holy communion.

Liked seeing it like that, glistening, streaked across her face. He rubbed it in. Massaged it in, small circular movements, like he was an esthetician at some fancy beauty salon. Like he was giving her the treat of some priceless face cream. Actually, it's probably damned good for the complexion, full of protein.

Yeah, they stayed up late. Did her well into the morning. Felt the need to be thorough. Just in case the little slut sold out while she was away. Probably didn't. But just in case, needed to mark his territory, so to speak. Felt good. And honestly, she seemed to enjoy it too. Didn't fight him one bit.

FIVE

On the road. Gemma quiet. Think Denver messed her head up. It's like she's surrounded in gray fog. All the sunshine gone from her face.

Hazen doesn't know what to do. Trying to make plans, but it's damn near impossible. Wants to show her a good time, but his Visa's not working anymore. Guy at the Chevron station cut it up. Pompous little prick. "I'm sorry, sir. . . ." So smug. "I'm afraid I'm going to have to insist on cash." Like Hazen has a whole hell of a lot of that floating around.

Used up all the cash in his bank account, debit card is just for decoration now. So it's down to American Express, which he'd rather not use because they charge an enormous interest rate, and want him to pay the damned thing off every month.

Has to stop moving. Get a job. Used Gemma's finger, she didn't want to play, no matter, he shut his eyes. Pointed it at the map. Finger landed on Chicago. So Chicago it is. Day or two drive. Not much farther. Get a job. Settle.

Rented an apartment. A brownstone. By the tracks. Noisy as hell, like a goddamned earthquake when the trains whiz by. Can't be helped. Best he could get, given his limited financial situation. Pay by the week.

Purchases a lock to put on the outside of the door. A double-bolt lock to keep her safe. Has her stay in the trunk while he buys it, installs it. Has to keep her safe. Chicago is a dangerous place. A person could disappear in this city and never be seen again. He tells her that, over and over. Instills it into her brain. The Mafia runs Chicago. The sex trade. They have little girls like you for lunch. It's a city of whacked-out perverts. Can't be too careful.

Tells her over and over, but installs the lock too. Just to make sure. Just to be safe, in case she flips, isn't herself one day. He installs it as a safeguard, a safety precaution.

•　　•　　•

She was crying again. Not because he was doing her or anything. Just crying for no reason. When he asked her what was the matter, she just rocked back and forth, clutching her knees, face streaked, eyes swollen. Back and forth, like those scenes in the movies of crazy people.

He tried to get her to stop. Tried holding her, comforting her, tried yelling. Nothing worked. Nothing. He didn't know what else to do, so he left. Door double locked from the outside. Always double locked from the outside. Didn't want a repeat of Denver.

Denver, that's when he realized they needed to settle, couldn't keep traveling, trying to keep ahead of the lost-child posters that seemed to be popping up everywhere.

Needed to put down roots. Find a safe place for her. Impossible to keep track of her twenty-four/seven. Besides, he needed a job, spent too much trying to show her a good time. And what did she do? How did she show her gratitude? Ran away. Gave him grief. Messed his head up royally.

And now she was crying.

It's not his fault. He did what he had to do. That's what a man does. Takes care of things. Killed him to cut her beautiful long hair, but he had to. Cut it, dye it. Dyed it brown, so people wouldn't look twice.

Didn't mean to cut it so short. But she wasn't cooperating. Wouldn't hold still. It was virtually impossible to unwrap her scrawny little arms from around her head, all the while she's crying. "Don't do it. Please don't do it. I'll be good. I won't be bad anymore." Sobbing, wrenching her head from side to side, so he couldn't get the scissors near her. Scared he'd poke out her eye. Finally he sat on her. Had no choice, but to pin her down.

Legs gripped around her body, his knees tucked tight. And even then, she was kept wrestling her arms out from under him, grabbing what was left of her hair, in tight little fists, trying to clutch it to her head, even though half of it was already gone.

And now she's crying again. It's not about her hair, Christ, that was two days ago. She just started crying, and he hadn't done anything at all. It's like ever since Denver, something in her snapped, and it's freaking him out, because she's not acting normal.

Walking the block, round and round. No coat, thirty below with the wind-chill factor, blowing off the lake. Thirty below in the beautiful metropolis of Chicago, and he's trying to cool off. But his face is on fire, and the contrast of the hot and cold makes his eyes tear up, icy air searing his lungs.

Five times around the same stupid block, and then it comes to him. He knows what to do, and that's when the cold slams into him, into his bones, because his head's stopped spinning. He has a plan.

The store doesn't have fresh ground beef, only frozen. Corner store. Small, dark, cramped. Aisles piled high with tired, dusty cans. Boxes, labels faded, like they've given up hope of ever going home.

He finds the tomato sauce. Two cans. Onion, spaghetti noodles, salt, pepper. Finds what he needs. Pays. The cold is in deep now, and has him on the balls of his toes, bouncing slightly. Not much heat in the store. The Chinese man, his wife behind the counter, have coats on.

"Cold day," says the Chinese man. And Hazen doesn't know if this Chink is laughing at him or not. Laughing at him because he forgot his coat. His face doesn't seem to be, but Hazen never knows with these sly bastards.

The wife doesn't bother to look up from her newspaper, just sits on her wooden box in her parka.

Back outside. Cold. So cold. Runs up the apartment stairs, four flights. Hard to get the keys out, turn them in the locks. Hands, fingers numb. Can't hear her crying from out here.

Opens the door. Cautiously, slowly, like it's not really his to open. Doesn't hear anything. Opens it farther and he sees her. Gemma, lying on the floor, curled up on her side in a fetal position. Face pale, eyes shut, swollen. Her breath rapid, a shallow pant, like a cat in labor. Her body, shuddering, convulsing maybe every sixth or seventh breath. Hand curled up by her face like she wants to suck it. Did she suck her thumb when she was little, he wonders. Her teeth stick out ever so slightly when she smiles. He wants to ask her, but he doesn't. This probably isn't the best time. He'll ask later. After, when he's made her some homemade spaghetti with real meat sauce, not from a jar. He'll ask her then, when they are eating and happy.

.   .   .

The spaghetti doesn't do it. She just keeps pushing it around on her plate.

"You have to eat," he says. "You have to eat. . . . It's good. Home-made."

She pretends, but he can tell she's not eating.

"You're getting skinny," he says. "You're getting too skinny. You've got to eat proper so you can grow up and get big and strong and healthy."

She gives him a look out the side of her eyes that she's screwed up slightly, like she's trying to look mean. "I'm not a five-year-old," she says, real dismissive, like she can't even be bothered.

"You're acting like it," he replies. He doesn't say it harsh. It's more of a thought really. Christ, he could barely hear it himself, and he's the one who was talking. But she hears it, with those bat-radar ears of hers. And the next thing he knows, she's slamming her hand down into her plate of spaghetti. Her chair falling backwards, crashing to the floor.

"I'm not a five-year-old!" she yells. "I'm not a sissy, goddamned five-year-old!" Her face mean, so mean, all distorted and venomous. But she's crying too. Trying to punch the tears away with her fists.

He's never seen her behave this way. First the crying jag, and now this. Doesn't know what the hell to do.

He pretends she didn't say anything, keeps trying to eat his spaghetti. But she flies at him, right over the table. Sends his plate of spaghetti crashing into the wall. Flies at him, claws outstretched, like an electrocuted cat. Slashing at him, taking chunks of flesh out of his face, arms, neck, before he wrestles her to the ground. Has to smack her a few times across the face to calm her down. Fucking little ungrateful bitch. Smacks her a few times, kicks her in the stomach for good measure, and then leaves her lying on the floor. Lying there in the spaghetti and her own vomit. Stupid bitch. Goes to take a shower. Leaves her there, looking like shit. Hates that ugly brown hair on her. Short nasty hair has made her spiteful, like a mean alley cat.

·   ·   ·

He dreamt about the old Gemma. Smiling, running towards him, arms outstretched. She had her long, blond hair back and she was so beautiful, wearing a little white halter top, jean shorts, bare feet. Her colt legs kissed by the sun. "I love you, Hazen. I love you," she says. And he swings her around and around. And then she's kneeling before him and taking him in his mouth, and it feels good.

When he wakes up, it's like the dream was real. He reaches for her, but she's not there. And yesterday rushes back, her acting so crazy. "Poor little kid," he says. He gets up and goes into the other room. She's still lying there on the floor where he left her, curled up in a little ball on her side. She is shivering in her sleep, arms wrapped around tight. "Oh Gemma," he says. And he feels kind of like her father, her so young and all. "Oh Gemma."

He picks her up, and she nestles in, snuggles into him in her sleep. He carries her to the bathroom. She wakes up in the hallway. He can tell, because her body stiffens. But she doesn't fight him, and that is good.

He runs the bath, takes off her clothes, smooths the hair out of her face. "Poor baby," he says. She doesn't say anything. He washes her clean. All pink and shiny. Washes his little girl. She doesn't look at him, just looks down at her limp Raggedy-Ann hands, because she knows she was bad. "It's okay," he says soothingly. "Daddy forgives you," he says. She doesn't say anything. And he feels a surge of excitement. "Daddy forgives you," he says, heat racing to his groin. "Daddy forgives you. Give Daddy a kiss." She hesitates, but she does it. A shy, closed-mouth kiss. But he's the boss. He grabs the back of her head with his hand, takes her mouth in a deep, satisfying kiss. "Oh, you're good. You're good to your daddy." He takes her out of the tub and dries her off. He powders her, takes his baby to bed and fucks her. Gives it to his baby, again and again. Can't get enough. Makes her call him "Daddy." She doesn't want to, but she does, because she knows he is the king. And it is good. He goes at it until it starts to get light and she is asleep and exhausted. And even then he can't sleep. So excited by this new thing. So damned excited. Making new plans as he strokes her limp and passive body, licking, lapping up the traces of salt, the tired tears of her acquiescence from her face.

·   ·   ·

He wakes up to the sound of her vomiting in the bathroom. "Gemma?" he says. But she doesn't answer, stays crouched over the toilet. "Gemma? You okay?" She doesn't reply, she's too busy barfing.

She's in there for a long time, until there is nothing left to barf but dry, rasping heaves of air and snot.

When she finally returns to bed, she is shaky and pale and sweaty and smells of vomit.

"Are you okay?" he says. But she turns her back to him. Lies curled up on her side, eyes shut.

"Are you okay?" But he is talking to nothing, because she's shut him out.

•   •   •

She's better in the afternoon. Subdued. Stopped throwing up, which is good. Hazen takes care of her. Makes her Lipton's tea. She drinks it, all shaky and pale. And because she's been sick, he does her gentle, no games, or role play. He makes sweet, gentle love, soft and slow, so as not to disturb her stomach. He does her nice, because he's not an animal. He knows how to take care of his woman.

They have a nice, peaceful afternoon. Spend it in bed. She's not fighting, or crying, or trying to run away. She lies with him like she's supposed to, and lets him touch her any way, anywhere he wants. Doesn't fight him, slap his hand away, there is no biting. They have a wonderful day. She's finally growing up. Coming around, is realizing how much she loves him.

•   •   •

This flu of hers is not going away. Won't eat. Can't eat. Just keeps throwing up, over and over again.

"Tomorrow," he prays, praying all the time. "Tomorrow, she'll be better."

But she's not.

•   •   •

He gets a job. A temp job at a dog-grooming salon. Shampooing dogs. Clipping their toenails. The things he does for her. And he has to laugh here, because she has no idea. How could she? She's just a kid, for Chrissake.

Hasn't eaten properly for two weeks. Getting so skinny, throwing up all the time. Barely talks. Just lies on the bed, facing the wall.

He tries not to think about it. Gets too sweaty, plunges his whole body into hot-and-cold shakes. All the "what if's?" "What if the doctors can't fix her?" "What if he doesn't get her to one in time?" Got to work hard. Can't fuck up. Have to get some money. Doctors cost money. Lots of it.

He's hoping she'll get better before he gets his first check, because they could really use the money. Food and shit like that. Could really use the money.

•   •   •

He says he's going to take me to a doctor. I can tell that he's scared. I'm not. Dying doesn't seem like it would be so bad, just a letting go, like the rope swing at the community pool. Swinging out, far over the blue, sparkling water, hanging on with all my might, and then, when I can't hang on any longer because the rope is riding too rough on my hands, and I feel like it's going to yank my arms right out of their sockets, I release the rope. I'm scared, but once I let go, it's kind of beautiful. I tumble, in slow motion, to the cool, refreshing embrace of the water. I think that's what death is like, a stopping of the struggle. Might not be so bad.

I'm so tired. Everything is such an effort.

He's worried. "Don't die on me," he says. "Don't die on me."

But I have to say, if this is what dying is like, it's not so bad. Other than the constant throwing up, which I could do without, but besides that, it's not so bad. Getting tireder and tireder until one day, I fall asleep for good.

I wouldn't mind. It's not like life is such great hot shit.

•   •   •

"I told the doctor's office," Hazen says, "that your name was Angel Drummond. That was my grandmother's maiden name. Drummond. You would have liked her. Mabel Drummond. Used to make me baked Alaska for dessert. That's how much she loved me. Took her all day, making the angel food cake, hollowing it out. Letting me eat the left-over insides. My grandmother was a saint. That's how I came up with your name." His palms are sweating, skidding on the steering wheel. "Are you listening to me, baby?"

She's sitting, the side of her forehead resting on the window, like her head weighs too much. Legs tucked up on the seat, arms wrapped around her knees like loose, tired wrapping paper. And Hazen gets this bad feeling in his gut. He wants to turn the car around. Take her back to their apartment. But she's been so sick.

"What's your name?" he says, watching the road, watching her. "What's your name?"

"Gemma," she says. "Gemma Sullivan." Voice dull, face expression-less.

And Hazen gets that feeling again. That bad feeling, the taste of copper in his mouth.

"No! Your name, dammit! Your Angel-goddamned-Drummond name! Am I talking to a wall? Your new name! The name you got to use or they won't see you."

"It's a stupid name." Her gaze slides over him, slow, like it's an ef-fort. Slides over all slitty-eyed and sullen, lower lip plumping out.

"Still has a little fire in her," he thinks. "Talking back, even though she's sick." He loves it when she pouts like this, so cute, lower lip jut-ting slightly out.

Her lips are dry, cracked, from being so dehydrated, but it doesn't matter, still gets him good. That pout, even when he's mad at her. Can't help it. Has to pull the car over, into a parking lot. It's early so the lot isn't full. Pulls the car to a far corner where they won't be disturbed. And she's looking all nervous, skittish. Taking it back about his grandmother's name, but he makes her do it anyway. Broad daylight. Windows steam-ing up, rain beating down. Ten a.m. in the morning and Hazen Wood is getting himself sucked off in the Simpson Sears parking lot.

•   •   •

"What's your name?" he asks as he zips up.

"Angel," she says, but she pauses, is reluctant, isn't believable. So he smacks her a little. Not hard, just enough to wake her up.

"What's your name?"

"Angel." Eyes drooping, half shut, but she's forcing herself to talk faster now, so that's good.

"Angel what?"

"What?" A little panic in her voice.

"Angel what?" Smacking her around a bit. Got to be tough. This is too important. Got to beat some sense in her. "What's your last name? What's your last name, you dumb bitch?"

She's crying, making a halfhearted attempt to try to get away, but he's got a good grip on her arm, and she's weak, she's pretty weak now.

"What's your last name?"

"I don't know. I . . . don't know. I . . . I can't . . . remember."

"Drummond," he says, shaking the name in. Then he says it slow, into her face. So close he can feel the words ricocheting off her face and back to his. "An . . . gel . . . Drum . . . mond. Say it."

"Angel Drummond." Head drooping, like a broken buttercup stem.

"Again."

"Angel Drummond."

"Faster."

"Angel Drummond."

"Good. Ten times in a row, fast."

"Angel Drummond . . . Angel Drummond . . . Angel Drummond . . . Angel Drummond . . . Angel Drummond . . . Angel Drummond . . . Angel Drummond . . . Angel Drummond . . ." She's tired, but she'll say it. By god, she'll say it, over and over until he says it's enough. "Angel Drummond . . . Angel Drumm—"

"Okay. That's good. You can stop now. That's very good, honey." He strokes her hair to show her how pleased he is. "Strap in." And she listens. She listens good. She pulls the seat belt around herself and straps in.

"What's your name?" he says, as they pull out of the parking lot.

"Angel Drummond," she says, no hesitation. And his gut feels better. Just needed a blow job. Needed to let off steam.

•   •   •

He watches her walk into the building. Office number, instructions, written down carefully. Watches her walk into the three-story brick building, her shoulders scrunched, head tucked down against the rain. Looks cold. Wishes he had more money, would buy her a winter coat. Wrap her up snug. That's what he'll do with his next check. Buy her a coat. He tries to focus on that, but his stomach's racing. Wants to run into the building, drag her out. Doesn't want her talking to strangers.

"I got you a woman doctor," he told her. "Thought you'd be more comfortable. Wouldn't want some pervert touching you up, checking you out."

His stomach is goddamned racing. Breathe. Take a breath. Think about the nice, warm winter coat he's going to buy her. Maybe a sheepskin coat. A genuine sheepskin. Those are supposed to be warm as shit. Yeah, that's what he'll do. Buy her one of those. Will look good with her hair, when it grows back in.

But that's all he can squeeze out of the coat distraction. Mind keeps going back to Gemma inside. She'll remember her name. He made sure of that. She'll be careful, knows what she's allowed to say. The doctor will check her out, give her some medicine, and that will be that.

"I mean, what the hell was I supposed to do?"

It's getting cold in the car. Body is shaking. Shivering like a sissy, but he doesn't turn the heat on, doesn't want to attract attention, doesn't have the money to waste on gas. Keep moving. Keep talking. "It's not like she can run away, Hazen ol' boy. She can't leave the building without you seeing her. She knows you're in the parking lot. She knows you'll just find her again. So calm down. Calm down, ol' man. Besides, she's too sick to run."

Hazen stays in the car, in that parking lot, for what seems like forever.

Gets out twice. Is going to go to the phone booth on the corner. Call. See what's the holdup. But every time he gets halfway there, he gets worried. Won't be able to see the door from the phone booth. Might miss her. So he sprints back to the car.

And now, staring so hard at the doorway, his eyes are hurting. Staring, willing her to come out. Sweaty, so sweaty.

And sweet Jesus, she comes out. His heart leaps, and he's able to breathe again. Didn't realize he'd been holding his breath, didn't realize how much he'd been missing her until he saw her skinny hunched-up body. Worrying that something had gone wrong. Worrying that maybe she'd found a way to run again.

He jumps out of the car. Happy, so happy. Helps her into the car. Giving her little kisses all over her head. Strapping her in.

"What did the doctor say?" he asks, slopping the fog off the window with his hand. "What'd the doctor say?" And he starts backing out, but he stops, because she's acting weird. Puts on the brakes, stomach dropping like an out-of-control elevator. "What did she say?" Gemma is looking so small. Scared. Tiny. "Gemma?" he says, voice tamped down, so as not to scare her. "Gemma honey, are you all right? Did she give you medicine? What did . . ." He's looking for clues on her face. "What did the doctor say? Gemma?" She's crying now, so he prepares for the worst.

"I'm sorry . . ." she's saying. "I'm sorry Hazen . . . I'm sorry . . ."

"It's okay, sweetie." He's holding her, comforting her in his arms. "Tell me, baby. What's wrong? What did the doctor say?"

"I . . . I have to come back . . . this afternoon. . . ." She's crying so hard.

"It's okay, I'll bring you back. It's okay."

"Two o'clock . . ."

"We can do that. Don't worry. No problem. Two o'clock. We'll get you some lunch, and then we'll come back. How's that sound? Sound good?" She nods, her head buried in his chest, and he comforts her, soothes his frightened sparrow. Soothes her, because he's her man. A good man. "Did the doctor tell you what you had?" Inhaling her scent. Lips in her hair. "What was wrong, baby? You can tell me."

"She . . ."

"Uh huh. I'm listening."

"She says I'm . . . She says . . . The doctor . . ." Her voice box doesn't seem to be cooperating with her mouth. But he's patient, waits for her to find the words.

"She says, the doctor . . . She says I'm pr . . . pregnant."

"What? What did you say?"

"That I'm . . . I'm pregnant. . . ."

He needs to see her face. See what this is about. Takes her chin in his hand and tilts her head up, out from his chest, forces her to look at him, because this is serious. Serious, important stuff. He needs to know.

"Are you joking?" Searching her face. "Is this a joke?"

"No. . . ." Her voice small, looking sideways. She's shaking, trembling all over.

"You mean to tell me you're pregnant? That's . . . that's impossible. You don't have your period yet. Are you bullshitting me? Don't bullshit me!"

"No, I'm not, honest. That's . . . that's what she says." She's crying, panicky. And he's not trying to be harsh or anything, but he's got to know.

"But you're twelve. You're only twelve. You don't even have any boobs, for Chrissake!" And it's not like he's saying this as a criticism or anything, it's just that the whole thing is almost too weird to comprehend.

"She says that I am, that I'm pregnant. That it can happen sometimes, even at my age. And she says . . . that I have to come back for an ultra . . . an ultrasound to make sure that . . ." Crying, choking on her words. "To . . . to . . . make sure that . . . that everything's okay." Crying hard, so hard. "I'm sorry . . . I'm sorry. . . ."

"You're pregnant." Her head, bobbing up and down like one of those wooden dolls with the round, wobbling heads. The kind where a flick of the finger makes the head nods forever.

"You're actually pregnant."

He can't believe it. Feels like his chest is going to explode. He is going to be a father. Gemma is going to have his baby. And he was so worried. Worried for nothing. What a day!

And he's laughing. Of course, she was pregnant. That's why she was so sick. Laughing out loud. Body, still shaking with laughter when they pull up to Denny's.

"You can have anything you want. Eat the whole damned menu—it's on me.

"We're celebrating," he tells the waitress. Orders Gemma the full fried-chicken dinner and a glass of milk, because she's going to be a mother. But she's not hungry, pushes the food around on her plate. "I'm sorry," she whispers, because she doesn't get it.

"Don't be sorry. I'm happy, Gemma. I wanted to have babies with you. Granted, I thought it would be a few years down the road. But God works in mysterious ways, Gemma. And who am I to question God? God led me to you. He told me to take you. And now, God, in his infinite wisdom, has decided we are ready to take that next step. To have a family, to have a baby." And Hazen finds himself kneeling down. Right there in Denny's restaurant, he finds himself kneeling down on that grease-smeared floor, "Gemma . . . will you marry me? Will you do me the honor of being my wife?"

"Get up," she says. "Get up." She starts crying all over again. And Hazen, he realizes he did it all wrong. Should have done it romantic. Flowers and violins and shit like that. Girls like that kind of stuff. So he gets up and eats his eggs and bacon.

•   •   •

On the way back to the doctor's, she's trembling. "Don't worry, Gemma," he says. "It's okay, baby, it's the way of things." Soothing her, stroking her wrist. "Don't be scared. It's going to be wonderful." He smiles at her. "You'll see, Gemma. I'm going to be the best daddy in the whole wide world," he says, covering her hand with his. So romantic, him and Gemma, starting a family, his baby growing inside her.

He drives, eyes on the road, watching the traffic. Driving careful. Going slow. Got to keep Gemma and his baby safe. "Don't worry. We're going to have a beautiful life, you'll see."

His reassurances don't seem to be helping. Gemma, so tense. All knotted up. Face small, like a little, scared fox. A cornered fox. Ankles crossed, held. Hands, white knuckled, gripping. Like she's terrified, and trying to be good.

"What's your name?" he says when they get there. Says it in a jokey sort of voice, just to remind her. Jokey, so she'll know he's a nice guy. Know he's not going to hit her or anything. Just to remind her, so she won't forget and mess up when everything is going so good.

"Angel Drummond," she answers, eyes big, dark. Face so white, like she's going to faint or something.

"That's my girl." He ruffles her hair. Winks at her, trying to cheer her up. "Go knock 'em dead." Poor kid. So scared. She starts out the door, when he remembers the money. That he forgot to give her some money for the doctor. So he tries to catch hold of her arm, not hard, gentle, wasn't going to hurt her or anything. But it startles her or something, because she levitates a good foot of the ground and cries out like someone has stabbed her.

And he's trying to calm her down, trying to explain, but the weird thing is, instead of getting closer, it's like he's being propelled backwards. Something has slammed, lodged itself into his chest. His windshield, struck by something, pieces falling about him like candy flung from a parade. His car door bursts open and his body is slamming into the pavement. Body pulsating, jerking. It's discombobulating, and then he hears the noise, the loud explosion. Hears the noise, feels the heat. Like someone has slit his stomach open with a red-hot poker. Gemma's voice faint, far off in the distance. She's screaming, tearing her hair out, trying to get to him, but there's a woman. Some stupid, busybody woman has grabbed ahold of her, is gripping her tight. Where the hell did she come from? And Gemma, screaming, wanting to be with him, but this bitch is holding her.

And there is all this yelling, bodies jostling.

"Gemma . . ." he says. He tries to get up, go to her. Wants to help her, to save her from this bitch that's holding her back. "Gemma . . ." he says. And there is that noise again, more pain, unbearable. And it's like Gemma, she's a rag doll on a spin cycle, all her colors, her features blurring, running together. "Gemma . . ." he says. He can't see her now, he can still hear her, faint, so faint, like a carousel in the far-off distance. They rode a carousel once. And he bought her a lilac-colored cotton candy. It was sunny, windy, storm clouds on the horizon. Such a beautiful day. Wind kicking up swirls of dust. Little miniature dust tornadoes that got grit in the eyes and the mouth. "Don't cry," he says. And it's funny, his voice sounds far away. "Don't cry."

SIX

It's over. The police caught him. It's over.

They let me talk to my mama on the phone.

I was fine when the police officer dialed. All calmed down, except for the shaking, because that part won't seem to go away. I was fine until I heard Mama's voice.

"Gemma?" she said, her voice full of worry. "Gemma, honey, are you all right?"

"Yeah, Mama," I said, but then I started bawling like a baby. Big noisy sobs. I couldn't stop. Wanted to talk to my mama, so much I needed to say, but the words couldn't make it past all the crying that was flooding out.

"Are you okay?" Mama's saying. "Honey, speak to me." But I can't.

I'm nodding, but she can't see that. I'm nodding my head up and down like crazy, but that does her no good. She's crying too now. And the police officer, Mrs. Cindy, she takes the phone. She's smiling, but her eyes are filling up too. I didn't know police officers cried. Luckily, once she starts talking, she isn't crying anymore, so she's able to answer all my mama's questions.

I listen from where I'm sitting, to the tinny buzz that's my mama's voice responding to what Mrs. Cindy's saying. Listen to Mrs. Cindy answering, the blanket wrapped around my shoulders, my body, like an Indian child. I listen, bundled up warm, snatchy, hiccup breath still rattling through me. I can't stop shaking. Even my teeth are clattering away, like I'm sitting in a bathtub full of ice cubes. But I'm not. I'm warm. Got a blanket and everything, I even have an Oh Henry bar. I got away, have nothing to shake about. But here I am, shaking like my body's a maraca.

"Uh huh," Mrs. Cindy says, "That's right." She bends down to hold the phone to my ear.

"Your mother wants to tell you something," she says.

I try to calm my trembling down so I can hear good. I try to hold my hiccuppy breath. I hear my mama say, "I love you, pumpkin." She hasn't called me pumpkin since I was three and a half, so of course I start crying all over again. But I manage to get out "I love you too." And that's good. I was real happy to hear my mama's voice. She's flying out tonight, so I'll get to see her tomorrow.

.   .   .

Floating in and out of consciousness. Tubes attached, electrodes, monitors attached, spitting out data. Beeping noises, the "blip" of the heart, still beating. White walls, ugly curtains, metal rungs, sliding open, shut. Irritating noise. Pain, too much pain. So he sinks back, back into dreams of Gemma.

.   .   .

They are asking me all kinds of questions. Tons of them. Police officers, social workers, and now another kind of doctor, a police one, is asking questions. Collecting DNA, which basically means I have to get naked again and let them poke and prod me, scrape my tongue, the inside of my mouth, with a long, single-ended Q-tip. She collects samples from other areas too. Embarrassing areas, that I prefer not to talk about. I feel like I'm in science class, but instead of doing the learning, I'm the amoeba under the microscope. Being looked at. They run a little rake, a comb-like thing, through any area that had hair . . . and I mean any. Taking pictures . . . not pictures of my privates, she doesn't do that. Thank God. I don't think I could take that. Luckily, she just needs pictures of my bruises and whatnot.

Then they took me to a lady who talked in this stupid fairyland voice. Sort of like the voice that actress who played Glinda the Good Witch of the North used in *The Wizard of Oz*. I hated the way she talked in that movie, all phony and sugar and spice. All la-dee-dah, with her insipid, sappy voice, careening around like she's been tippling at the booze, wafting her arms about, like she's conducting an invisible orchestra. She ruined Glinda for me. Seriously.

That's the thing I hate about books being made into movies. They take the best books, the most wonderful magical books, and ruin them.

And this woman, this Ms. Lind-something, dressed in her earth tones, is driving me nuts, and to make matters worse, I have to see her tomorrow and the next day too. I don't know if I can take it. I really don't. I don't know what planet she was born on. I mean, I know she's trying to be compassionate and all. But please. I am twelve years old. I do not want to play make-believe with a doll. I do not want to paint stupid pictures.

"Oh. You've drawn a tree. And why is it, do you suppose, that your tree has no roots? Do you feel the lack of family roots, of support, perhaps?"

"No." I'm trying to be patient. "I didn't have time to draw roots. You said 'time's up.' Otherwise I would have drawn roots. Leaves too. I ran out of time." A perfectly good answer, but that's not good enough. Oh no. There's some deep, dark reason I didn't draw roots. I don't know why she's bothering asking me any questions, because, please, she's already decided what she wants me to say, and what she will and won't write down on her pad of paper.

I can tell. When I say something she doesn't like, doesn't agree with, her eyes narrow, and she sniffs. Sniffs, pauses, and then asks me the same dumb question phrased a different way. I mean, how stupid does she think I am? I know what she's doing.

Why doesn't she just ask me the things she wants to know? Not that I'd answer, but why doesn't she just come out and say it? Why does she have to tiptoe and be sneaky, try to pretend to be all sweetie-sweetie? She's not a nice person. I can tell, she's all wrapped in how "good" she is, how "wonderful." She doesn't care about me. Her *concern* has nothing to do with me, has everything to do with winning. This woman wants to win come hell or high water, and death to anyone who gets in her way.

There's nothing wrong with that. I can respect that. Just be up front about it. She shouldn't pretend she's something she's not.

I don't know. Maybe I get so mad at her, because if I'd been meaner to Hazen right off the bat, if I'd told him I thought he stunk, that he was a jerk, if I'd told him I couldn't stand his guts, maybe he never would have stolen me. He thought he was in love with me. If I'd been honest about who I was, what I did and didn't want, maybe he wouldn't be in the hospital right now, fighting for his life.

I just got a wave of grief. I don't know why. It's not like I liked him. It's so confusing. Everything's all mixed up. I feel sorry for him. I didn't know he was going to get shot. Shot twice. Didn't know they were going to do that. I hadn't thought it through. I was just thinking about me, saving my skin. Hadn't thought about his.

Feel bad. He took me to Disneyland, wanted to marry me. Let me wear his coat sometimes when I was cold. He tried to show me a good time. I feel kind of bad. He couldn't help it that he fell in love and needed to steal me.

Feelings.

Feel like a bad person. Like I led him on. I should have told him right from the start how I felt, even though I was scared.

And I definitely shouldn't have brought him back to the doctor's office. I knew they were going to be waiting.

"Act normal," the police said on the phone. "Don't let on. Don't tell him anything. You're just coming back here for an ultrasound. That's all you got to think about. That's all you have to keep in your head. You're coming back for an ultrasound."

So that's what I did. That's all I told him. I didn't tell him about the rest. That the doctor had figured out something was wrong, got it out of me. I didn't tell him that she'd talked to police for a long time on the phone. Didn't tell him they needed me to bring him back, so that they could set up the net to catch him. That they needed time to secure the area. I didn't tell him that they needed to catch him with me. "It's the best way," they said to me. "Need to do it clean and safe."

I didn't know they were going to shoot him. They hadn't told me that. I might not have gone through with it. Him, being so happy about the baby, wanting to marry me and all.

I just thought they were going to catch him, is all. Let me go home. Didn't know they were going to shoot him.

•   •   •

My mama wasn't able to get a flight last night. It was all booked up, but she's going to be here today. Today or tomorrow.

She said a strange thing, though, right before she hung up. Her voice, all quiet and muffled. It sounded like her hand was cupped around the mouthpiece, like someone was in the room and she didn't want them to hear. She said something like "Don't tell them about Buddy. . . ." all fast and breathy. Said something like that, I think. . . .

I'm not really sure if that's what she said. Not to tell them about Buddy. But if she did, what did she mean by that? Does she know about Buddy and me? Does she know what he did? Shopping me out? Fiddling with me? Doing me at night? Does she know all of that?

What did she mean? "Don't tell them about Buddy. . . ." What did she mean by that?

I already told them something. I thought it was all right to tell them. They got me away from Hazen. And they were asking me questions and one thing led to another, and they wanted to know how I met Hazen. . . . And, well, I'd told them. I mean, it's the truth. Buddy set it up. That's the truth. I didn't tell them about Buddy doing me too. I didn't tell them that. They asked me. They guessed at it. But I wouldn't tell them nothing about that. Just shook my head. Didn't let no words come out. I know I'm not supposed to tell about that.

But the thing is . . . what did Mama mean? "Don't tell them about Buddy. . . ." Does she know what Buddy was doing to me? Is she all right with that?

My belly is in an uproar ever since my mama's call. My head's hurting, heart too. I'm watching my words. Not sure what I can say and what I can't. Insides twisted. Careful, so careful. Who are the bad guys? Whose side am I on? Who's on mine?

So scared. I don't know when my mama's coming, what she's going to say. Don't know, but I've been thinking on it, and I'm figuring I heard her wrong. That happens sometimes. I think I'm hearing one thing, and really that's not what the person's saying at all.

I'll be careful with my words, just in case. I'll wait till my mama comes and make sure. Make sure I heard her wrong.

•   •   •

My mama came, smelling of Jack Daniels, face powder, and lipstick.

She was wearing a short skirt and high heels, and she looked fine. Her hair swept up, caught in a clasp at the nape of her neck. My mama signed me out of the foster home. Temporary care. I was glad to leave, too many messed-up kids in there. And some of them, their mamas are never going to come. They're in that depressing place for good.

I felt proud, walking down the hallway with my mama, holding her hand. Walked past Eunice, this big black girl. Big, stuck-up, fat girl. Bossy as all get up. Stupid too. Bet she can't even read. Walked past her, and it felt good, because last night, when we were supposed to be sleeping, supposed to be quiet, no talking, last night, she said I was making my mama up. I couldn't believe her nerve.

"Probably has no mama," she said. "Little Miss Priss is probably jus' makin' her up." And all her suck-up buddies were laughing. She reminded me of a female version of Billy Robinson. I would have fought her, but I'm no fool. If it was only her, I would have fought, but there were too many of them. So I did nothing. Ignored them. I pretended they were nothing more than pesky little mosquitoes, and rolled over and went to sleep.

But I had the last laugh. Yes, I did. My mama picked me up this morning, at 11:45 a.m. My mama signed me out. I didn't see no mom for Eunice. Didn't see no mom signing *her* out.

It felt good seeing the jealousy and longing on her face when we walked past. Like she wished she had a mama who flew halfway across the United States of America to get her girl out of foster care. I saw that look on her face, and I was glad. I felt like a mean person, being so glad, but that's the way it is. I liked it.

·   ·   ·

We're staying at a Howard Johnson, in a smoking room. Funny, I was missing my mom, but I forgot how much she smoked. That's one thing I forgot about. Hazen didn't. That was one good thing. He didn't smoke.

I don't like cigarette smoke. It clogs up my throat, stings my eyes.

But my mama, she's sucking away on those cigarettes like there's no tomorrow, huge, billowing clouds of smoke. The whole room is full of gray haze, and I have to squint in order to see through it.

My mama's pacing. She's not being so cozy now that we're out of the foster home. Away from curious eyes.

I don't know what I was thinking. I'm kind of wishing we'd stayed at McLaren Hall a bit longer, because it seems like the hugging that was going on there is all the hugging I'm going to get.

She's looking at me sly, out the side of her eyes, drawing in a huge drag off her cigarette. "Did you think on what I said?" she says, blowing out, head tilted to the ceiling, eyes still on me.

And I know what she's talking about. My belly can feel it. But I'm hanging on to the hope that I was wrong. "What?" I say. "What was that?" But I know. I know.

"Buddy." She's not even pretending to look at the ceiling anymore. She's looking directly at me.

And it's like I knew before, but I didn't really. But now, there's no getting away from it. My belly wrenches sideways, my mouth dries up, and my brain, my brain is scrambling around on the floor on all fours. Saying "Oh my God. She's known. She's known what Buddy was up to all this time."

Everything suddenly flips on its back. It's like I'm in one of those scary sci-fi movies where people shape shift, and I think this person is my mother, but she's really a werewolf, or an alien, instead.

It's like that. Somebody else morphed into her body. And my whole past, the last five years, ever since I was seven and Buddy moved in and started touching me, it's all zooming past, like a train in a tunnel. And I want to ask, I want to say, "You knew? When? What? How long? For how long did you know?"

But I don't say anything. I just sit there on the bed, in Howard Johnson, looking at my hands. Scared to look up. Scared of what I'll see. I sit there, feeling like I've swallowed a truck full of cement.

．　　　．　　　．

I'm still throwing up all the time. And everybody's wants to know, the doctor, the social worker, Mrs. Cindy, even my mom's asking me what I'm going to do about the baby. I have to make a decision, but I don't know. Christ, I'm only a kid myself. I don't know what to do.

Some people are talking to me about abortion, saying that's the answer, that it might be dangerous to have a baby at my age. That I have my whole life ahead of me to have babies. That I should get an education, go to college, build a future. I'd like to do that. Go to college, build a future. . . .

But I don't know. I saw President Bush on TV once with his friend Jerry Falderal, or something like that, and I can't remember clearly, but they said something about rape not being a good reason to have an abortion.

Something like, Murder is murder, and abortion is murder.

I can't get their words out of my head. I don't want to be no murderer, so I don't know, I think I have to keep Hazen's baby in my belly, whether I want to or not. Got to keep it, even though it's making me barf all day long.

The doctors actually did an ultrasound, so that made me feel better, like I wasn't lying to Hazen about that. They did do one, and there is a baby in there, so that part of it was true. I really am pregnant.

I'm kind of scared, about being a mother and all. Don't know how I'm going to afford to take care of it. Kind of scared, I mean, I did the best that I could with Boxcar Julie, and look what happened to her. She got flushed down the toilet. I couldn't take care of a damned turtle, how the hell am I going to take care of a baby? And that's another thing. I wanted Boxcar. Paid good money for her. I wanted Boxcar. And it's not that I'm trying to be mean or anything, I'm not trying to hurt the baby's feelings, but the truth of the matter is, no matter which way I turn it, around and around in my brain, I don't want to have a baby. Not now, and especially not his baby.

But the thing I keep coming back to is our president's words. He feels that abortion is murder. Doesn't matter what the circumstances are. He feels so strongly about it that he's trying to make it outlawed. That if someone had an abortion, they'd be a criminal and have to go to jail. That's what he wants. And he's the president of this country. And nobody gets to be president by being a dummy. They got to know something. They got to be smart. Otherwise, nobody would have elected him. He's got to know something.

Our president says murder is murder, and if I had an abortion, I'd be committing murder. So, that's the way it is, I guess. I'm probably going to have to keep this baby. I'm scared out of my skull, but I don't want to be no murderer.

.   .   .

Mrs. Cindy, the police officer, actually, she's a detective. That's her official title. I didn't know there were different ranks of police officers. A detective is better than a police officer, and a sergeant is better than a detective. Well, not better, just higher up, like the boss, or something. Anyway, she's a detective. She detects things, solves mysteries, murders, things like that. That's why she doesn't get a uniform. Detectives don't wear them. She used to have one when she was a police officer, but not anymore. I think I'd rather be a police officer, the uniforms look fancy, and I'd get to have all that stuff hanging around on my belt. Looks much cooler than a suit.

I have to say, I feel bad, lying to her. I have a soft spot for her, on account of her saving me from Hazen, and the bullets and all. Not only that, but she knew about the Hazen situation, that I had sex with him, broke the law with him being a grown-up and all. She knows about that, and she hasn't thrown me in jail.

Now, I don't know if she hasn't because she's being nice, feels sorry for me. Or maybe the law about that kind of thing is different here in Chicago. Hazen did say that in Chicago, men like to have little girls like me for lunch, so maybe it is different here, the sex with grown-ups thing. I don't know. But I have to say, I'm grateful not to be in no jail. Just wish I didn't have to lie to her about Buddy and all. I don't like being a liar. My belly hurts every time the subject comes up. I feel bad about it, but my mama was quite clear. She talked about Buddy well into the night.

Mama wouldn't touch on any specifics about Buddy and me, so I still haven't figured out if she knows or not. She won't talk about details, brushes past, glosses over it. Like we're whitewashing the fence. Arms making huge sweeping movements as if she's got a paintbrush in them, wiping, painting him white.

She doesn't want to talk about, go into, ask any questions about me and him.

It's kind of weird, everyone asking me questions about Buddy all day long, and my mama asking none. When I got up the courage, figured, what the hell, felt like I had to know, I tried to bring it up, but she got this closed look. All shuttered, like the storm windows I've seen looking at pictures of houses in Massachusetts and Maine. All slammed shut, bolted, and locked. So I let it go. Didn't talk.

Later, lying in bed, staring at the ceiling. All the lights off, the room dark, curtains drawn to block out the flash of Ed's Diner. I can still see a bit of the glow from the pink and green neon tubes that write the name in cursive, where Mama didn't draw the curtains tightly enough together. Can see Mama's silhouette, the shape of her face, her nose.

Neither one of us is sleeping. Minds spinning.

I feel so lonely, like I've lost my mother. And I want to crawl into her arms, like I did when I was a baby, and have her rock me, and sing to me, and smooth back my hair. Tears start to slide down my face, but she doesn't know. I can cry silent now. That's one skill I learned while I was away. I can cry so nobody can tell unless they are looking right directly at me.

Lonely, so lonely.

And she doesn't know that I'm crying. She's thinking about her life, running through her life. She starts talking up into the darkness, filling the room with words. Talking about what a good man Buddy is. How he helps with the finances. How she doesn't know what she'd do without him. How he's kind to her and buys her pretty things. How he doesn't beat her like my daddy did. Apparently my dad used to beat the crap out of her. I didn't know this, but he broke bones and everything. That's why they got divorced. He used to beat her on a nightly basis. "And you don't want that for me, do you, honey?" she asks, a pleading quality to her voice.

And I say, "No. . . ." because I don't know how else to answer. "No, Mama. . . ." I say, because I want her to be happy. Really I do.

She rolls over and wraps her arms around me, like I want her to. "Thanks, baby," she whispers. I breathe her in deep. She kisses me on the forehead. And I want to cling like a man drowning, but I can tell that she doesn't want me to, so I let go.

"Night. . . ." she says, and rolls to her other side, facing away from me, and falls off to sleep.

I listen to her breathe, a steady rhythm, in and out. I listen to my mother breathe and I know what I got to do.

In the morning, I lie to Mrs. Cindy about Buddy, and all the things he's done to me. I play stupid to her questions, my belly all messed up, like it's been sucking on lemons.

I lie to Mrs. Cindy, with my mother waiting outside the room, her ear to the wall.

I see the disappointment rise in Mrs. Cindy's eyes, because she knows I'm lying, right to her face.

It feels bad, like I'm disrespecting her. And I don't know if what I'm doing is right or wrong. I don't know anything, except it's what I have to do, need to do, because I don't want my mama going back to getting beaten up every night. I've had enough of that myself. Don't want it for her.

I'll do what I need to do to keep my mama safe. Out of harm's way.

•   •   •

They're back. The bull-dyke detective and her pussy-whipped partner. He remembers her. She was the one who was holding Gemma back while they were blasting the hell out of him. Detective Salyn, that's her name. Got to remember it for when he gets out, because that bitch is dead meat.

Her partner? Hazen doesn't remember him from the parking lot. Doesn't know if he was there. But one thing for sure, the dipshit sure loves to strut in here and fill up the hospital room with his so-called maleness. Blond, muscle-bound prick. Hazen Wood knows the type. Knows never to trust them. That's what he knows. Chisel-jawed, weight-lifting, steroid-popping perverts. There's a reason why this sort feels the need to spend so much time on his body. Only one reason, and Hazen is wise to this dickhead's ways. Not going to turn his back on this one, not going to bend over when he's in the vicinity. Incompetent, self-righteous faggot.

They're quizzing him, advising him, reading him his Miranda rights, like he's the criminal.

He tells them about Buddy. They got the wrong man. Arrested the wrong man. But do they acknowledge that they have screwed up royally?

No. The shits. Stuck him in some kind of hospital prison. Guards all over the place. What's the point of sticking him in with a bunch of psychotic criminals and guards? First of all, he hasn't done anything wrong. Hasn't done anything that any red-blooded male wouldn't do if he had been in Hazen's shoes.

Secondly, guards? Like he's going to be able to run anytime soon. He was blasted full of holes last time he checked, courtesy of the inept, incompetent Chicago police. He should have gone to Canada. Those Mounties, they would have treated him with respect.

Incompetent assholes. They don't listen to him, don't pay attention. He and Gemma were just friends. Buddy was the bad guy here. Buddy was the asshole. Told them they bloody well better let him out of this hospital prison or there's no telling what he'll do.

Going to sue them for all they're worth, filling him with damn bullet holes. Think they're the judge, jury, and executioner all rolled in one.

Told them about the situation with Gemma, that Buddy was raping her and she'd asked him to save her, take her away. "What's a man to do? She was in a bad situation. A very bad situation, and to be brutally honest, that mother of hers . . ."

He told them they were questioning the wrong man. He's the hero in this scenario. Hazen Wood is the goddamned hero.

But the bull dyke doesn't hear him. It's like his words are bouncing off her force field. Looks at him like she thinks he's dog shit under her shoe.

The faggot seems to listen better. Might be a faggot, but seems to understand the way of men. That Hazen was trying to protect the kid.

Wore him out with all their questions. The nurse had to ask them to leave. Tight-lipped automaton, but at least she could see that he was being overworked, overstressed, needed to rest. Needed to sleep.

·   ·   ·

"But what I don't understand is why didn't you run away?" Ms. Lindstrom keeps on saying. "There you were, in public places, why didn't you walk up to someone and ask for help?"

And I've tried to explain, really I have. I've tried to be patient, but my God she is stupid. I mean, Jesus Christ. I've told her how he locked me in the trunk, me trying and trying to get away, making noise, banging my feet on the trunk door, crying out until my voice was raw and ragged. I told her how, when he finally let me sit in the car, how *every* time the car would slow down, I'd jump out, run. *Told* her and *told* her. And people *saw* me, *grown-ups* saw me, *heard* me, and *nobody*, not one person, helped.

And I *did* run away. I got away in Denver. He just found me again. I mean Jesus Christ. There was only so much I could do, he was *holding a fucking knife* on me! What was I supposed to do? There is, I'm *sorry* to say, only so much I could do. Only so many times I could try to run away. He was just going to catch me again. And when he caught me, things were worse, way worse, the beatings. And nobody, *nobody* would help me. Because the simple fact of it is, people don't care. People just don't care. Turn away. "Not my problem," they say. It was as if I'd turned invisible. Like at Disneyland. How many people helped me? Not one *single* person.

I told her all this, how I tried, how it just didn't work, but she played stupid, acted like she hasn't *even* heard what I *just* said. Asked me, real patient, if maybe I *liked* Hazen, *liked* being with him, *liked* the excitement of being on the road. Being a runaway.

I mean, come *on*, am I crazy? No. I did not *like* being with Hazen. I did not *like* being on the road. I tried to get away. But after a while . . . what's the point? Nobody cared whether I lived or died, so what's the point of fighting? What's it going to get me? It'll get me a broken jaw, or worse, that's what it'll get me. I fight back, and I get slammed in the face, slammed in the trunk, get a damn knife in my ribs. That's what it got me. Stupid, judging, ignorant bitch!

She didn't seem to want to talk much after that. Got offended, quiet, sniffed a lot and wrote notes.

After having that pleasant chat with Ms. Lindstrom, Mrs. Cindy wants to talk to me again. I don't know why. Maybe I'm in trouble. Maybe the laws are the same in Chicago as California after all.

"What?" I say, as we exit the front door. "Did I do something wrong?'

"No, sweetie." Mrs. Cindy smiles at me. She doesn't look mad. "I wanted to talk to you a bit, outside of the police station. I thought it would be nice if we swung by McDonald's, picked up some lunch and took it to the park for a picnic. Would you like that?" She's stopped by her car and is holding open the front door of the passenger side.

I get into what looks, from the outside, like an everyday normal-looking car. But things aren't always what they seem. The minute I get in, I know that this is a police car pretending to be a regular one. I can tell the difference. For one thing, there's a lot of noise coming out of her glove compartment. It sounds like some kind of fancy calling radio walkie-talkie that crackles and snaps like super-loud chewing gum, like my granddaddy chewing on his Wrigley's, watching boxing on the TV. He could snap that gum good, but he wouldn't teach me. "It's a bad habit," he said. "Impossible to break, and once you started, God help you, you can't chew gum silently ever again. No," he said, sitting back in his Barcalounger. "I'd rather go to hell and back than teach a granddaughter of mine to snap her gum. Make you look cheap," he said. And that was the end of that. Wouldn't teach me. No way, no how.

Mrs. Cindy shut the door solid behind me and walked around the front of the car. Someone's talking out of the glove compartment now, a gravelly voice, forcing its way through all that static. Snapping out messages in some kind of code. Another voice is responding. I should enjoy being up front in a secret police car, but my mouth, my heart, are too nervous.

"Why's your glove compartment making all that noise?" I ask, when she gets in. I see this thing that looks like a police light, but it isn't attached to the roof, it sitting on the floor.

"Oh, sorry." Mrs. Cindy reaches over me and shuts off the noise. "I forget it's on. So used to it. It's a radio. Helps me communicate with the other officers, with the dispatcher at the police station, things like that."

"Oh," I say.

I'm sitting in an undercover police car. She's letting me ride up front with her, and I know what that means. I've seen enough police shows on TV to know that the police make the bad guys sit in the back. So that means she doesn't think I'm all bad. Isn't going to throw me into jail. I don't think so, anyway, because I'm riding up front, like a pal.

Must mean she trusts me, because she's got all kinds of fancy, secret police equipment in here—the police radio, the police light, and probably other stuff too, stuff I can't even imagine. This car is probably crammed to the gills with super-fancy, special, police-type things, and if she thought I was dangerous, she wouldn't let me near it.

She trusts me. She's telling me about her secret police radio, she's letting me ride up front. I guess she hasn't figured out that I lied about Buddy, didn't tell the truth.

"Strap in," she says. I put my seat belt on, careful not to touch or bump anything. I try to let her know with my actions, that even though I lied about Buddy, I lied because I had to, and in all other things I'll tell her the truth. I keep my hands on my thighs with the palms down, no sudden moves, as her car pulls out of the parking lot.

At McDonald's I order a Big Mac, some french fries, and a chocolate shake.

"Ummm," she says. "That sounds good." She gets the same thing and pays.

I'm kind of embarrassed because I have no money, but she waves me off, and we take our food and cross the street to the park.

It's a nice, crisp, sunny day. Cold out. I can see our breath. Our burgers steaming, sending trails of good, juicy smells up to my nose, getting my taste buds ready for that first bite.

And it tastes good out here, all warm-and-toasty good. There's something about fresh, hot hamburgers warming my hands and belly. Warming me from the inside and the outside. Something about sitting in a park, free, eating those hamburgers, that just seems to fill me up. Like God is eating hamburgers with us. Feels sort of like that. Not talking, just eating, side by side.

·   ·   ·

Driving back in the car, Mrs. Cindy starts talking. "I know about Buddy," she says, looking forward at the road. She doesn't say it mean or angry. Says it like a fact.

My stomach drops like I'm on a roller coaster at Disneyland. On a roller coaster blindfolded, so I didn't know, couldn't anticipate what was going to happen, and we'd just swooped, hurtled down. Don't know how far or how long we're going to drop. Don't know where we're going to end up. I'm blindfolded, see. Falling, blindfolded.

I keep my sweaty palms on my thighs, don't say anything, keep my head forwards, except for a quick glance to read her face. I want to look longer to find out what she's feeling, if she's pissed off at me, doesn't like me anymore, but I can't look long enough to figure it out. I'm too ashamed. Too embarrassed. Caught in a lie.

Maybe she's taking me to the police station, to book me and arrest me. I'm scared of jail. Maybe I should jump out at the next stoplight and run. Run fast. Get away. I don't want to go to the jail.

But, if she was going to throw me in jail, why did she take me to McDonald's? Why is she letting me ride up front like a pal, like a friend, if she already knew that I lied about Buddy?

The streets are passing, a psychedelic blur. Colors and sounds, whooshing by, nothing clear, distinct.

"I'm sorry," I say, voice, like a goose-down feather tumbling across the dashboard. "I'm sorry. . . ."

But she doesn't yell, get mad, doesn't even seem to be angry. Still looking forward, she covers my hand with hers. "It's okay, Gemma," she says. "I understand. Really I do."

.   .   .

"Do you want to talk about it?" she asks, her car stopped now. We are parked in the Howard Johnson parking lot, engine still running, exhaust blowing a cloud of steam past my window.

And I do want to talk about it, pour it all out, but I shake my head no. I promised my mom. Gave her my word. It's warm in here, the heat's on, but I'm shivering.

"Well, you think on it." She gives me her card. "Here is my phone number, day or night. If you need to talk, give me a call."

I take the card. It has her name, Detective Salyn, twenty-second precinct, typed out in dark letters, a tiny gold insignia or something in the right-hand corner. There are two phone numbers in the bottom left-hand corner. I hold her card in my hand, look down at it hard, because I can't look at her, my face and ears hot.

"Thanks," I say.

There is a pause. Nobody fills it.

114

"And thanks for the hamburger, and the milkshake, and fries," I say.

Then, there isn't anything else left to do, so I get out of the disguised police car. I feel a little funny, like maybe people who see me, people who know about unmarked cars and can recognize them, maybe they'll see me getting out and think I'm in trouble with the law. Maybe I am.

"Thanks," I say. I give my card a little wave at her, so she'll see that I have it, that I didn't leave it on her seat. See that I'm taking her offer seriously. I paste a smile on my face, a polite one. Not a jaunty one, or a "pulled something over on you" one. Not a happy, happy one, because to tell the truth, I'm not feeling particularly happy. It's just a "thank you for your time, see you again" sort of smile. Then I shut the door careful. I want it to be secure, don't want it flying open while she's driving along. Want it shut safe and sound, but at the same time, I've got to be careful because I don't want her to think I'm mad she brought up Buddy. I don't want her to think I'm slamming the car door and stomping off in a huff.

I close the car door carefully, firmly. Give her a wave over my shoulder, a half-turn wave as I head toward the door. A half-turn "nothing happened here" wave, an everyday, ordinary wave. An "I'll see you soon" wave, and head for the lobby.

· · ·

My mama's mad. Real mad. She's been raging ever since I got back. Circling me like a lion tamer with a whip, lashing me with her tongue. Eyes like fire, legs chewing up and spitting out every inch, every ounce of space in the room.

I stand here and try to make myself small, try to make myself invisible.

Feel like I'm inside a big beach ball and someone is sucking all the air out, and it's closing in around me, and doesn't matter what I do, it's not going to make no difference. They're going to keep sucking, closing the trap, nothing I can do, nothing I can say.

My mama raging and raging.

I don't move. She's like a cobra. Don't want to move, attract her venom. Don't want to move. Movement angers them, cobras. That's when they strike, cobras, mothers. Don't move, hold still.

I try to disappear into my shoes. Try to climb my staircase, but it doesn't work, trapped in this no-air room.

My mama raging at me. My mama not believing me. My mama thinks I told them about Buddy.

"I didn't," I say. "I didn't." But nothing I can say, nothing I can do, will convince her. And my protestations, they sound so weak, so wishy-washy, so fake, that I almost don't believe them myself.

"Did I?" I find myself wondering. Because how else would they have found out, known, if not from me? But, I don't think I did. I don't remember telling them. Mama told me not to. I'm almost positive I didn't. Did I?

But facts are facts. My mama knows, Mrs. Cindy says she knows, the police in Oakland know. Know enough anyway, because they dragged Buddy out of work in the middle of the day and took him down to the Oakland Police Station for questioning.

"How could you?" she screams, her lipstick a scarlet slash against the livid white of her face. "You selfish bitch! You little whore!" Her saliva spraying on me.

"The first decent man . . . the first decent man I've had in my whole life and you've got to ruin it." Pacing, pacing back and forth. "Inconsiderate little bitch. Stuck-up little whore. Nothing's good enough for you, is it?" Turning on me now. "Nothing's good enough for Little Miss Priss!"

"That's odd," I think, which is a really weird thing to pop in my brain, because I'm really scared, but here I am thinking, "That's the same thing Eunice called me at the home. Little Miss Priss." But I don't tell my mama. She'll think I'm talking back. I don't tell her about that coincidence. I keep it to myself, because I'm pretty damned sure she wouldn't be interested.

116

"Slut!" my mama calls me. "Whore!" Words shooting out like bullets.

Says I just had to go and try to scare him away. Drive him away, with my lies and deceit.

"Just can't stand it, can you? Can't stand to see your mama happy."

And I'm shaking my head back and forth. Can't stop crying. But it does no good, whatever I say, it does no good, she doesn't want to hear me.

·   ·   ·

Feel like a damned invalid. Eating lukewarm pudding with a plastic spoon. Slopping it all over the place, hands shaking. Has a tremor, like his Uncle Mike. Sad-assed Uncle Mike, shaking all over the place like he's hooked up to an electric socket. Parkinson's. Better not be getting Parkinson's. Wouldn't that just take the cake? Like he doesn't have enough shit going wrong. Gemma, setting him up like this. And after all he did for her. The little bitch. Just wait till he gets out of here. Just wait. He'll clear up this whole misunderstanding. He'll clear it up, and then she'd better run. Run fast, because he's going to get her and get her good. Little, two-faced, double-crossing slut.

And these nurses, what's up with that? Tight-assed nurses in their little uniforms, walking around with goddamned broomsticks up their butts. So smug. So superior. Like, who bought the world and made them God? That's what he'd like to know.

Think he's a goddamned pincushion. Jabbing their needles into him left, center, and right. Sadistic bitches. Bet they enjoy it. Bet they get off on it. Hurting innocent victims. Made helpless, forced to lie back and be accosted because they can't move. Can't move because of the ineptitude of Chicago's finest.

Can't move, can't even crap without assistance. "Excuse me, Miss, can I please have my bedpan?" Can't fucking move. Can't escape. Them, coming at him twenty-four/seven with their foot-long needles. Can't get away, attached to the bed by tubes, wires, and data-spitting monitoring machines.

Just wait till he gets her. Just wait till he gets that little two-faced slut.

.   .   .

It's kind of hard to cover my eye that's swelling up.

I was worried they'd find out my mom did it and get mad at her, and then she'd get madder at me. But I didn't have to worry about that. My mom getting madder at me, that is. Apparently, getting madder wasn't on her mind.

She took me to the police station for my appointment, all distant and removed, her face like ice.

Dropped me off outside of Mrs. Cindy's office.

"Good-bye, Gemma," she said. Kissed me on the forehead.

I remember thinking it was weird at the time. Not "Good-bye." People say good-bye all the time, means nothing. "Good-bye." "See you later." "Adios." Means nothing.

But there was something about the way she said it, her tone of voice was all cold and weary and sad.

"Good-bye, Gemma," she said. And that was it. Apparently, after I went into Mrs. Cindy's office and the door had shut behind me, she walked out of the building, down the steps, got in her car, and drove away.

When I got out, she wasn't sitting in the chair, like yesterday.

I waited for her for a long time. It got dark. I was scared to go to the bathroom, in case I accidentally missed her, if she decided to come back.

It was the end of the workday. People were gathering up their stuff and leaving, rattling their keys, the night shift bringing the night air in with them, shrugging off their coats. Mrs. Cindy came out of her office. She looked surprised to see me still sitting there. "Gemma?" she said. "Is everything okay? Did you need to see me?"

"Oh . . . nah . . ." I said, trying to be casual, my feet shifting around on the floor. "I'm just waiting for my mom is all."

"Your mom?" I saw her shoot a glance at her watch, eyebrows up around her hairline. "You've been waiting all this time?"

"Yeah . . . well . . ." I kept my voice light, no problem here. "Sometimes she's a little late. I don't mind waiting. It's warm here, people are nice." I smiled to show her I wasn't tired at all. Didn't let on my bladder was about ready to burst. "You go on home," I said, all reassuring. "I'll be fine."

Well, that didn't fly with her. She marched me back into her office and sat me down, made me call the Howard Johnson motel. I was praying my mom had calmed down and wasn't mad at me anymore. I dialed the number Mrs. Cindy got out of the phone book, fingers nervous.

"Hello," I said. "Could I please speak to Pamela Sullivan?"

"Who?" It was a smoker's voice, rough and scratchy.

"Pamela Sullivan, room two-eighteen?" I spoke carefully, didn't want to make a mistake and get the wrong room.

"Don't got no Pamela Sullivan here," said the voice.

"What?" I said, even though I could hear. My ears heard, but the rest of me was racing to catch up.

"Checked out. Checked out this morning. Around ten-thirty, according to my books."

"Okay. Thank you." I hung up the phone. Had to shut my eyes. Didn't want to take in the room, Mrs. Cindy, and the fact that my mama had gone and left me. I didn't want to take it in just yet.

"What was that?" I heard Mrs. Cindy say. I kept my eyes shut. Needed to, for a little bit longer.

"Is everything okay?" she asked.

"Yeah, fine," I said. "My mom went out for a bit. I guess she forgot to pick me up. No problem. I'll just walk back. She'll be back soon, I'm sure."

But my mom not picking me up, on top of my new black eye, which I explained to Mrs. Cindy was on account of me not turning on the light when I got up to go to the bathroom and accidently walking into a lamp. I guess all that made her suspicious, because she called the Howard

Johnson motel back and got the real story. And bam—I'm back at the stupid McLaren Hall. The dumb old foster home for messed-up kids that nobody wants.

I'm back in stupid Eunice's dorm. And when Eunice saw me, she got a bitchy smirk on her fat, ugly face, "Whassa matter?" she said. "Yo' mama didn't want ya?"

And maybe it was a little too close for comfort, or maybe I was just screaming mad and needed to hit somebody. I don't know what it was really, but I lost it. Didn't care how many buddies she had. Didn't care how hard she could hit. I launched at her like a nuclear missile, intent on damage. Intent on making somebody hurt as much as I did.

We got in trouble. Both of us. Not just me, which was surprising. Because honestly, after I cooled down and thought about it, it was pretty clear it was all my fault. I mean, she shouldn't have said that and all, but really, I overreacted.

Anyway, about my mama, apparently, she just upped and left. Walked out of the police building, got in her car, and drove away. Just drove away. Didn't look back. Drove to the airport, pedal to the metal, bought the first plane ticket back to Oakland. And that was that. Went back to Buddy.

"Good-bye, Gemma," she'd said. "Good-bye."

I called her collect from Ms. Finnegan's office, to ask her why. Trying to keep the hurt out of my voice, I asked my mama, Why? Why she upped and left me all alone here in Chicago?

When I asked her she said, "Buddy needs me more than you."

That's what she said. That's what my mama told me, and then she hung up. "Buddy needs me more than you." My own mother. Wouldn't take no more collect calls. Nothing.

"Buddy needs me more than you."

That night, I had a bad dream, a real bad dream. I woke up screaming, calling out, fighting. Sweating all over. My sheets soaked with sweat.

I was back in the trunk again. Couldn't breathe. Woke up crying, fist-in-the-gut sobbing.

And the weird thing is, when I woke up, Eunice was the one comforting me, shaking me out of sleep, drying my tears. It was Eunice, my claw marks fresh on her face, telling the other girls to mind their own beeswax. It was Eunice who held me. "Hush now . . . hush now. . . ." It was Eunice who made them all stop staring, shut their eyes, and go back to sleep.

SEVEN

I don't have it so bad. I mean, really, when I heard some of the stories flying about here, I realized, I've been pretty lucky. Pretty blessed. I mean, at least I've got a mama. I was really surprised to find out how many kids here don't.

Eunice, for example, her mama was a junkie, got shot dead. Don't know who did it. No daddy to speak of. She must have had one at some point or another. I mean, her mama couldn't have got pregnant by herself. So somebody's got to be Eunice's daddy, he's just never come forth to claim her, is all. Never let her know who he was. Could be one of several people, but she doesn't know who. She knows he loves her. He just doesn't know she's his, is all. That's what she's waiting for. She's waiting for him to find out, realize he's got a daughter. Hear about her mama being gone. Because she knows when he hears about that, he's going to come down to McLaren Hall right quick and sign her out. That's what she's waiting for.

Now, Kendra, she doesn't have a mama or a daddy. Nothing. And nobody wants to adopt her. She's just passing through, bouncing from one foster home to the next. Nobody wants her. She's not cute anymore. "Past the age." That's what they say, like she's a loaf of bread that's gone bad. Gone past its "sell by" date.

That's the way it is. Kids get past the cute stage, and that's it. Their chances of getting out, getting adopted, are about zilch.

And then there's Jasmine. She's pretty, cute as a button. Lots of people want to adopt her. She has blond hair and big, blue eyes, like one of those fancy china dolls in the toy stores, and not only that, she's smart too. She's only four, but she can read. I'm telling the truth. Read books like *Go Dog Go*, *Ten Apples Up on Top*, things like that. And that's good for a little kid who's only four. Real good! I tell her, "You're smart as a whip. You're going to do things with your life, girl. You're going to go to college and win scholarships and be rich and famous. You just keep on reading. Keep your nose to the books. You forget about boys. Pay them no mind. You study. You make something of yourself. You make me proud." That's what I tell her, because it's too late for me. Being pregnant and all. It's too late for me, but not for her. Lots of people would adopt her if they could. But they can't, because her mama won't sign the papers. Her mama's in prison for shooting her boyfriend, and she's hoping to get out someday for "good time." So that's why she won't sign the release papers. She doesn't want Jasmine going to anybody else.

There's a lot of stories here. Real hard, tough stories, sad stories.

It makes me feel humble, lucky that I don't have it so bad. I've got a mama who loves me. She's just mad is all, and is leaving me here to teach me a lesson. She loves me. I know she does. Just wants to teach me a lesson. She'll come around soon. Real soon, I hope, because Christmas is coming. Don't want to still be here at Christmas. I'm keeping my fingers crossed. Wishing on stars. Not just for me. Trying not to be greedy. I'm alternating my wishes, one for me, one for Eunice, one for me, one for Kendra, one for me, one for Jasmine. That's what I'm doing, spreading the wishes out.

· · ·

His grandmother came to him in the night while he was sleeping. There in the hospital. Sat by his bed. Her voice, face, eyes, full of sorrow.

"What have you done, Hazen, my boy?" she said, over and over. "What have you done?" And there was something about it, the sight of her, memories of cookies baking and childhood, that just messed him up.

"I . . . I thought you had died, Grandma," he said, but she didn't answer. Just looked at him with those dark, sad eyes.

"What have you done?" Tears catching, running down the creases in her wrinkled old face. "What have you done?"

And he woke up weeping. Weeping like he'd never wept before. Couldn't stop. Wept until his toes, his fingers, even the roots of his hair, every particle, every molecule of his body, was emptied into nothingness. The memory of his grandmother and her sad eyes, too much to bear.

Couldn't stop, until finally, exhaustion took over and dropped him back into sleep.

· · ·

I'm sitting with Eunice and the girls when Jasmine comes running up to me. "Gemma! Gemma!" she squeals, tugging on my arm, jumping up and down. "Gemma! Come quick! Ms. Finnegan wants to see you in her office! Ms. Finnegan wants to see you!" Her eyes are all lit up, sparkling like a Christmas tree.

Now normally, it's a little nervous making to get called down to Ms. Finnegan's office, but I knew it couldn't be bad. Not with Jasmine jumping up and down like she's got boingy springs on her feet.

"What is it?" I say, scrambling out from behind the table. "What is it?" There's an excited, hopeful feeling starting to dance just underneath my skin.

Jasmine pauses, proud to have all the big girls hanging on to her every word, her little chest puffed out like a baby penguin. "Well . . . ," she says, looking around slowly, eyes enormous in her elfin face. "Somebody is . . ." She gives an excited squeal and hop. "Somebody . . . is here. . . ." And then it's like she's been as patient as she could, but it's too much excitement to keep welled up in her little body and it all comes out, in an excited rush. Bubbles and tumbles out, words bouncing, leaping over one another, ending on a such a high pitch, it's a miracle the windows don't shatter. "SOMEBODY'S HERE TO SIGN YOU OUT!"

Everyone is excited now. We're jumping up and down. People are patting me on the back, crying, talking at once. "Oh! Lucky!" "You deserve it!" "I'm so jealous!" "Write! Don't forget to write!" "Bet it's your mama!" "Bet it's your mama, come to get you for Christmas!"

Jasmine and I run out, my heart in my throat. Someone's come to get me out! "My mama!" I think. My mama's forgiven me, and loves me, and wants me back!

I hurry. I get a plastic bag from the kitchen staff. "I'm going home," I say. "I need a bag for my stuff."

"She's going home!" squeals Jasmine, her arms flapping like a bird trying to take off.

Martha, the cook, a big black lady with cornrows and a hairnet, gives me a bag, a floury hug. Tucks me in to her big, soft, squishy breasts that smell like cooking and tired-out caring.

"That's good, sweetheart," she says, patting my back. "You go on home." Calls all of us girls sweetheart, because there are too many of us to keep straight.

"Have a Merry Christmas!" I say, sprinting out the big, gray, swinging doors, the plastic bag billowing out behind me like a flag.

I gather all my belonging from my room. I don't have much. It takes all of two minutes to jam my stuff in the bag. And then we're back on the move, Jasmine and me, out the door and down the hall towards the office. I don't want to keep my mama waiting. Don't want her to change her mind about taking me back.

We come around the corner, my heart all full of hope and forgiveness and anxious love. Come around the corner, but my mama's not there. My mama's not signing the forms.

It's someone else.

At first I don't recognize Mrs. Cindy. I wasn't used to seeing her out of her work clothes. She's wearing blue jeans and a cranberry-colored sweater. It feels odd seeing her like this, with her hair down, all soft, deep brown, shiny, like a coffee table that's been polished a lot.

"Where's my mama?" I say. A jumble of emotions, confusion, sorrow.

"You're coming home with me, Gemma." Mrs. Cindy smiles kind of shy. Hesitant, like she's not sure of my reaction. "That is, if you want to. . . ."

Jasmine has gone quiet beside me. She slips her hand in mine, looking up at me, worried, like maybe she screwed up.

"I'd have to remove myself from your case," Mrs. Cindy's saying, "but I've talked to Bonnie, Detective Bonnie Sheffman, and she's agreed to take over for me."

"Oh," says Ms. Finnegan, nodding her head at Mrs. Cindy. "She's good. Real good."

Then Ms. Finnegan turns to look at me, head still nodding, only slightly now, like a toy that hasn't quite wound down. "You'll be in good hands with her, Gemma," she says, like I should know what she's talking about.

Jasmine gives my hand a little tug. "Wha . . . who?" her voice, a tiny, barely there whisper. "Is . . . not your . . . mom?"

"It's okay, Jasmine," I say. "It's Mrs. Cindy."

And I don't know what this all means, if I like it or not. It's hard to compute, sort out. But I nod my head, like everything's fine, put a smile on my face, even though my belly's in a mishmash of feelings. "Great!" I say, looking down at Jasmine's worried face. I act all happy and excited. "This is GREAT!" And Jasmine looks relieved, like she can breathe again.

"Oh, good," Mrs. Cindy says. "Then it's all settled." She pulls me in

126

for a quick hug, which feels weird, because she's a policeman and all. It's a brief hug, and then she releases me, and turns to finish the forms.

"Are you sure you want to do this, Cindy?" Ms. Finnegan flips a paper over, points her finger at a line on the bottom. Mrs. Cindy signs it. Ms. Finnegan is talking low, quiet, thinking I won't be able to hear, but I can hear her all right.

"Twelve's a difficult age under any circumstance," she says, turning another page. "And Gemma here," her voice drops even lower, so I have to strain my ears, "she's had more than her share of troubles."

"I know," Mrs. Cindy says. "I'm her—" She corrects herself. "I *was* the investigating officer on her case. I am aware of—" but Mrs. Cindy doesn't get to finish. Ms. Finnegan is talking again in a hushed, hurried whisper.

"It's just these kids, I mean, I know, my heart breaks for her too." She takes a breath. "But Cindy, honey, you're only asking for trouble."

I want to argue back, tell her that if Mrs. Cindy wants to take me home for the holidays, that's fine with me. It's better than staying in this stupid, stinking place.

But I can't, I'm not supposed to be listening. So I keep a smile on my face and pretend I'm playing with Jasmine.

"If you want company, adopt yourself a baby, or better yet, a dog. Less trouble, and you'll get more back. I'm telling you as a friend, don't do it. The repercussions for this type of abuse . . . Well, you of all people should know."

A look crosses Mrs. Cindy's face. Irritation? Impatience maybe? Not sure, it passes so fast.

"I know what I'm doing, Linda," she says, like it's the end of the conversation.

And I'm not sure what exactly they're talking about, but I know that it's about me. That Mrs. Cindy wants to take me home for the holidays, and Ms. Finnegan doesn't think it's a good idea. I don't know why she is wanting to stand in my way. I thought she liked me.

And Mrs. Cindy removed from my case. What does that mean?

I'm not sure what this is about. How I feel. It's mixed. My mom didn't come. Apparently, she hasn't forgiven me yet. Mrs. Cindy is signing me out, and in an odd way, I'm okay with it. I'll be going to someone's home for Christmas, even though I'm "past the age," and on top of that, pregnant. Somebody is willing to take me in for the holidays. Wants me. And that makes me feel kind of okay, kind of good.

It's embarrassing, though, that all the kids think my mom has come to get me, but when I look at the overall picture, think about it, compared to being in the trunk of a car, or spending Christmas in this place . . . Or actually, to be perfectly honest, staying at Mrs. Cindy's is probably better than me going to my mom's house too. Because over the holidays, my mama drinks like a fish, and with Buddy being there and everything . . . Especially with them thinking I ratted them out, when I take into consideration all of these things . . . Mrs. Cindy's house . . . even though I don't know her very well . . . Mrs. Cindy's house is looking pretty damned good.

.   .   .

Able to walk. Get out of bed. Doubled over like an old man. Thirty-seven years old, hobbling around like he's ninety. Feet dragging, sucking breath in through clenched teeth. Doubled over, one hand, trying to hold his stomach together, the other clutching at the back of his ridiculous hospital gown, which is always trying to gape open, show his ass to all and sundry. Who designed these things, anyway? That's what he'd like to know. Go out personally and gun the asshole down. Do the world a favor.

Impossible for anyone to get better wandering around in garb like this. Fucking inhumane. And these slippers. These ludicrous regulation hospital slippers, dangerous is what they are, could break his neck in these things. Can't walk normally. Not that he can, but if he could. If he didn't have these damn bullet holes blasted through him. If he was healthy, he'd still be walking like an idiot. Asinine, poorly made, piss-stupid hospital slippers. Has to slide his feet, one foot in front of the other, carefully, inch by inch, shuffle along so they won't fall off.

They say they're going to be transferring him soon, transferring him to the regular population as soon as he's on his feet. Well, screw them. He's on his feet. He's on his goddamned feet. Let's go! Pompous incompetents. Think he's so scared? Think he's so fucking scared of jail? Hell no! Take him there! He's ready! Anything would be better than this idiotic place.

•   •   •

"Are you sure you're okay with this?" Mrs. Cindy glances over at me, sitting beside her in the car.

"Oh yeah." I nod my head. "I'm really glad, Mrs. Cindy." It feels a little awkward. Shy. I turn and watch the city pass by. As we whiz by an alley, I notice a teenage boy digging through a Dumpster and I'm glad it's not me.

It is quiet, both of us lost in our thoughts. Then Mrs. Cindy clears her throat. "Gemma," she says, "you can call me Cindy. There's no need to be formal, plain old Cindy is fine by me."

"Okay." I take a breath. "Cindy," I say, and it feels kind of strange to be calling her by her first name, but it feels good too, closer to a friend.

"That's better." She smiles at me and I smile back, a warm feeling in my belly. It feels good to be driving along with her, in her regular car, not her camouflaged police one. Driving along, like we're family. Like if someone looks in through the window, they might think we were a mother and a daughter out on a drive. Maybe coming home from the grocery store, or from doing some last-minute Christmas shopping.

And when I think about the last-minute Christmas shopping, for the first time, I get an excitement in my belly. Not because we're shopping, we're not. And it's not because I expect any Christmas presents, because I don't. I get this excitement in my belly because in thinking it, like with Gemma travel, in thinking it, I almost believe it! That I really am her daughter! That we were Christmas shopping! That I really do come from one of those happy, happy families that I see on TV, where the worst thing that happens is they lose their favorite family dog and then find it again.

And it's weird, it's like I get lost in the story of it. I don't even realize that I'm bouncing on the seat, grinning out the window, until Cindy says, "What are you thinking?"

"What?" I say, because I heard her, but, what I was thinking is a little weird.

"You looked so happy."

I don't know what to do. Feel kind of embarrassed, don't know why, but I feel sort of like I forgot to get dressed and went out in public in my pj's or something.

I don't know what to do. She's smiling at me, and I don't want her to think I'm rude, not answering her question. She might decide to turn around and take me back to McLaren Hall.

"Um . . . ," I say.

"You don't have to tell me if you don't want. It won't hurt my feelings."

And all of a sudden, I want to tell her. Feel stupid for not telling her right off the bat. I mean, come on. I was thinking about teaching Gemma travel, maybe making it a profession, and here, the first person who asks me about it, and I clam all up.

So I tell her. I don't tell her I was pretending to be her daughter and we were coming home from Christmas shopping. I don't tell her that, because number one, I don't want her to think I was hinting about Christmas presents, because I'm not. Hell, I know I'm lucky to be going home with her. Number two, if I told her I was pretending to be her daughter, she'd think I was pathetic.

I do, however, tell her about Gemma Travel and creating places and making food and eating it. I tell her all about how I learned it in the trunk. And as I'm talking, I find myself getting excited about my invention. My mouth says, "I'll teach it to you if you want."

And then my ears hear her say, "Okay," which makes my body feel all jangly. Not that I don't want to teach her, I'm happy to. A little nervous is all. My face feels like I just ate a red chili pepper by accident.

"Um . . . Okay, it's like this." I'm trying to be like a professional teacher, but the minute I start, I realize Gemma travel is a hard thing to explain. I don't want to come off as some kind of goofy weirdo.

"Um . . . Let's see. What you got to do . . . is, like, you pretend something. You start off with something easy . . . um . . . and then . . . you . . . um . . . you build it. See?"

"Hmm," Cindy says. "Not quite." She nods, encouraging. "But keep going. I'll get it."

"Oh . . ." And as I'm thinking back on what I just said, I can see how she didn't understand it. I didn't explain it well, didn't approach it in the right way. "Okay," I say. "Just a minute." I think about it for a minute. "Okay, what you got to do is first, you have to shut your eyes."

I shut my eyes, and it's better already. I can't see her, so, I don't feel as nervous. "Now, you *might* be able to do it with your eyes open. I mean, you might, if you got good enough at it. Got to be an expert. I'm not at that stage yet. Well, maybe I am. I haven't tried it actually. . . . But for now, just shut your eyes. . . . Wait!"

I open my eyes.

"You're driving, so um . . . I don't think you should shut your eyes." I feel real dumb, because I'm supposed to be the teacher, and with my stupid instructions, I could have gotten us in a car crash. "Shut your eyes." How stupid is that?

I look at her. She doesn't seem mad, like she thinks I'm the dumbest thing that ever set foot in her car. She's smiling.

My face gets hot. "I mean, unless you want to shut your eyes. Then you're welcome to. It is easier with your eyes shut. But maybe, because you're driving and all, maybe you should pull over to the side of the road."

And then I worry that she might think I'm bossing her, ordering her around. So I say, "Unless it's not convenient to pull over right now,

131

and then probably the best thing to do is, I'll tell you how to do it, and then you can practice when you get home, it would probably be kind of hard for you to do it properly, get the knack of it with me watching you."

"Okay," she says. "That sounds like a good plan."

When she says that, I feel so much better, because she thinks I made a good plan. It gives me courage, like maybe I'm going to be a good teacher after all.

"Okay," I say. "I'll shut my eyes, so I can describe it better. There. Now, what you do is you imagine something, it can be anything, and you build on it. You start off something small and specific. You got to be specific or it won't work. If you're doing a place, doesn't matter if you've ever been there before, you have to be specific about the details. Like say you're choosing a field . . . I'll do that, it's one of my favorites. So . . . Imagine you're lying down."

"You have to be lying down?"

"No, I guess I always did, on account of being in the trunk. The more things you can use that are actually real, the better. It's like you steal little truths from your situation and you hang the place you're creating on it, sort of like the truth is a coat hanger, and the image you're creating is the dress. So, see, if I'm lying in a trunk, then I imagine I'm lying in a field. One less thing to create. Does that make sense?" I look at her to make sure.

"Um hmm," she nods and she seems to mean it.

"Okay, good." I shut my eyes again. "So, you're imagining you're lying in a field. Now you have to choose, are you lying on your back, or on your side? Are you face down? Decide your position and then create the earth under you. Is it damp? Does it soak through your shorts, your T-shirt? Or is it dry and dusty, with the hum of summer insects? Does the grit fly up so you can taste it in your mouth? Is the ground soft? Lumpy? Is there one irritating little rock that is digging into your hip and you got to pry it out with your fingers and toss it away? What kind of field is it? Mine was always grass, tall grass, swaying slightly, a gentle breeze, just rustling the tops of them. . . . Tall grass . . . No one can see me. . . . And I lie stretched flat out, arms and legs wide. . . . I take up space, because it's okay. The grass is tall, nobody would be able to see me, even if they were walking right close by. I can hear the birds singing, calling to each other. The sun is warm on my face, and the breeze . . . it kisses me. And it is beautiful, so beautiful. I could lie here all day. . . . Nowhere to go. . . . No need. Just lie here soaking up the sun, the smell of the grass. Wide open field . . . Boxcar on my belly and . . ." Suddenly my voice stops, because I get this swell of sadness in my chest, thinking about Boxcar and how her little feet used to tickle across my belly. . . .

I open my eyes, and I'm back in Mrs. Cindy's car, the rumble of it under my butt.

"And that's how you do it," I say. "That's how you Gemma travel." I don't look at her though, just look at the gray glove compartment, hair tipped in my face.

"Wow," she says. "That's amazing. I'll have to try it when I get home."

I sneak a look at her, and she seems genuine, smiles at me like she means it. So that's good. Made it worth it, even though Boxcar snuck up on me.

•   •   •

I got my own room and it has a bathroom attached right to it! I don't have to go out into the hall. Just get off the bed, or up from the desk, open the door, and there's the bathroom. I have my very own bathtub, toilet, everything!

At first I thought the bathroom was for the whole house and that everybody would have to walk through my bedroom to use the bathroom and brush their teeth. And that was fine. I felt lucky that I got to be the closest to it, in case I had to go in a hurry. But no. This house has *three bathrooms*! One in my bedroom . . . I'm calling it my bedroom even though it's not really. It belongs to Cindy and Joseph. I'm just saying it's mine while I'm here, because it's more fun, makes me feel special, and doesn't hurt anyone. I'm just pretending. I know it's their guest room.

Anyway, back to the subject, there's one bathroom in "my bedroom," one in Cindy and Joseph's bedroom, *and* one downstairs off the hallway.

The one downstairs is a sweet little bathroom, tucked under the stairs. It doesn't have a tub or a shower, just a toilet and a sink and a real pretty mirror with gold all around the edges. And there's a tiny table near the toilet with magazines, a couple of books, and a vase of flowers on it.

The flowers aren't real. They look real, but they aren't. Crazy, huh? I'd never know just looking at them. I found out by accident. See, I was sitting on the toilet, and I saw them, thought they were real pretty, so I leaned over to take a deep whiff, buried my face in them, and that's how I found out. The feel. They feel different than real flowers, and they don't have a smell. I just got a nose full of dust. . . . Not a lot of dust, just a little, no disrespect to Cindy's housecleaning. Actually, I probably didn't get any dust, just sneezed because I've got a sensitive nose is all. No dust. This house is clean as a pin.

They both clean up, and me too. I'm trying to be real helpful. Chase them out of the kitchen. Say, "I'll do the clean up. Don't you worry, go relax, watch TV, talk about your day."

I want them to be glad they asked me to stay. To know that Ms. Finnegan was wrong and I'm not going to be any trouble. I want them to know that I'm a good worker.

They look kind of reluctant to leave. "It's okay, Gemma, you don't have to work so hard." But I chase them out, wave a dish towel at them, "Shoo . . . shoo!" I say, and it makes them laugh. "I like it," I say to them. "It's peaceful doing dishes."

And it is. I said that so they wouldn't feel guilty, but honestly, it is peaceful. Hot soapy water, making dirty dishes clean. It's a good feeling. And another thing, it makes me feel happy in my heart to do something for them.

I like the way they joke and goof around and look at each other with such tenderness in their eyes. It makes me feel good to see them loving each other so much. Makes me want to be around them all the time. Like they are the sun, and I'm a lonely bit of outer-space debris, something no one has any use for, a broken window from a satellite or something. And I'm bumping up against them, trying to soak up, collect, store for safekeeping, a few rays, a few bright moments, a few memories to sustain me for later. When I have to go back to McLaren Hall. Because I've realized it's time to stop kidding myself, my mama's not coming back. No way. No how. Not a chance in hell. If she's was willing to drive away, not come back, not take my phone calls, leave me in that foster home, especially at Christmas. If she's willing to do all that, then who am I kidding? She's not coming to get me. She's given up on me. I'm more trouble than I'm worth. Especially, with the baby coming. . . . Well, hell's bells, why would she want me?

I've got to say, when it first hit me, that my mama didn't want me. That she was never coming back, it was like a fist to the face. Hit me hard. Unexpected. I was eating dinner with Cindy and Joseph, and we're talking and the food was good, and then all of a sudden, *bam*!

I don't know what kicked it off. Maybe it was the skinny black-and-white stray yowling outside. Skinny cat, mean-eyed, all claws and sharp teeth, who doesn't want to be anybody's friend. I tried sneaking it some scraps, but it wouldn't come close enough to get them. It's been yowling and yowling all the time. Joseph says it makes that noise because it's in heat. I don't know how, it's pretty damned cold outside. But if Joseph says it's feeling hot, then it must be, because I haven't been here that long, but I don't have to be Einstein to figure out pretty damn quick that with Cindy and Joseph, anything that's not the truth is just not going to fly. It's like they got truth radar or something.

Like yesterday. See, they got this bowl on the kitchen counter.

Actually, they've got several. One has fruit in it, bananas, couple apples, some oranges, and that's for everyone to eat. I don't have to ask. If I feel like a snack, I'm supposed to help myself. They got another bowl that has onions, garlic, and a couple of not very happy looking potatoes. The last bowl has odds and ends—bobby pins, paper clips, rubber bands, and spare change—quarters, nickels—and things.

So anyway, to make a short story shorter, I took some money, not much, some quarters, a few dimes. I was going to say, I thought it was like the fruit, "help yourself," but my belly knew when I was taking it that I was doing wrong. I don't know why I did it. I didn't need the money. Nowhere to spend it. Didn't need it, just took it. I don't know why. It was scaring the hell out of me that I was taking the money, but once I started, it was kind of like a dare, once I started, I couldn't back down. Maybe I wanted to see if they'd notice. If they were paying attention, if they knew how bad I was.

The first day nothing happened, so I took a little more. Next day, still nothing, so I took some more. I'd taken all the quarters now, so I started on the dimes. Had six dollars and eighty cents weighing me down, burning a hole in my pocket, making it impossible for me to meet their faces and talk in a comfortable way.

I had six dollars and eighty cents before they sat me down in the living room, their faces sad, serious. They asked me about the missing change. And me, embarrassed, running hot and cold, like I got diarrhea. Sweating, cursing my stupid self out. Expecting to get hit, kicked, screamed at, didn't know what. Definitely expecting to get sent back to McLaren's.

But they didn't. Just looked sad. Like their hearts were hurting. Talked to me about truth and honor and trust. And I have to say, I felt way worse than if I'd gotten a beating. Way worse! I'd rather get a million beatings than risk disappointing them again.

So this is what I've decided: I'm not going to steal.

I'd done it with Hazen, but he deserved it, so I stole a little bit here and there. I'd steal money, a sock, his toothpick, just little things, and throw them in the garbage. Watch him go crazy trying to remember where he put the stuff. It drove him nuts. He would go ballistic! Yeah, I'd steal things from him, wouldn't keep them, although that would have been fun. I couldn't risk him finding the things on me. I'm not dumb. It made me feel good, powerful, like I was stealing something back. And he never knew. Never found out it was me disappearing those things.

I stole change from Buddy too, took it out of his slacks when I was doing the laundry. Didn't give it back either. Kept it and bought candy and stuff.

But taking from Joseph and Cindy was wrong. I'm not going to steal from them ever again. I'd rather put out my eyes with burning-hot pokers. Seriously. They've been so good to me, and what do I do? How do I repay them? I steal their money. It makes me feel kind of nauseous, disappointed in myself, thinking about it. And I know one thing for certain: I will *never* steal from them *ever* again!

That's how I found out that truth and honor and trust are so important to them. And if Joseph says the cat's yowling because it's warm, so be it.

Anyway, maybe it was the cat, and the cries it was making, that triggered it.

Or maybe, it was remembering how I stole and then lied.

Or maybe it was just the sound of the neighbors' back door. Maybe it was that. The sound of that door slamming real hard, like someone's mad. Don't want me coming in. Someone slamming the door in my face. It sounded like that kind of slam. Maybe it was the noise of that?

I'm not sure what it was, but all at once, for no reason, I got this overwhelming rush of homesickness and it made Cindy's baked cheese-and-tomato ziti clog up in my throat. Didn't make any sense. I'm in the nicest home I've ever been in, and Cindy and Joseph are so kind. And yet there I was, enjoying myself, tasty food on my tongue one moment, all stopped up and emotional the next.

I had to leave the table because the tears were coming fast and furious. Had to leave before they made their way to my face. Got to my bedroom before they fell. Stuffed the pillow over the top of my head so they couldn't hear me. Didn't want to disturb their dinner. Held the pillow down hard, because noises are trying to come out. Body doubled up in two, like I've swallowed a fistful of double-sided razor blades. Because I'm thinking about my mom. Her face, her smell, how she looks when she's happy. Images of my mom, ripping through me. Loving her so much, and knowing she doesn't want me, couldn't care less. Left me here in Chicago. Hurts. Hurts so bad. Pillow wrapped around, gripped tight with both fists, face, gaping mouth, like a beached fish trying to suck up air, everything that can express anything, slammed into the bed. Into the lilac-colored, spring-scented sheets. Slobber, mucus, snot. Can't help the sheets. It's like those documentaries on TV, where the floods are just too big, and they destroy everything in their path. Homes, bridges, factories, schools. Everything, wiped out, destroyed, totaled.

And I know, in this moment, that my mama's never coming to get me. And it hurts so damn bad. And no matter which way I turn it, I can't make it into something happy-ever-after. I can't. She's not coming back. She doesn't want me.

I hear the door, and I'm embarrassed to be caught in this out-of-control, crying-so-hard position. But even embarrassment won't stop the flood. It's just tearing through me, ripping me apart, destroying things. And I think I'm going to die, going to be demolished by the force of it.

But just when I give up hope, and this is how I know there is a God, just when I feel the absolute bleakest, I feel a gentle hand come to rest on my back, and I'm breaking into a million pieces, but I feel this hand, Cindy's hand, and it's like it is filled with light, all calm and serene, like a cool breeze when I got a fever.

And it guides the hurricane out of my body.

And I'm okay. I survived, and I am in my borrowed room again.

Cindy gathers me into her lap, scoops me up, like I am her baby. She holds me and rocks me gently, back and forth. And I cry for everything that has happened, and everything that won't. My face buried in the comfort of her bosom.

• • •

I felt kind of shy this morning about last night, crying and all, disturbing their dinner. That on top of stealing and lying about it the day before. I don't mean to cause trouble, but somehow, I seem to be.

Cindy's trying to act the same, being friendly and all, but I don't know if it's true or not.

Joseph is a little quiet. Maybe it's my imagination, but he seems . . . I don't know, careful, not relaxed, like he expects that at any moment I'm going to knock something over, spill my breakfast in his lap.

Maybe Joseph is being so quiet because they've decided I'm more trouble than I'm worth. I'm still here though, so maybe not. Hope they don't take me back to McLaren Hall.

EIGHT

The priest left. Thank God! Been driving him fucking nuts. At first Hazen was happy to see him, thought it would be nice to have someone to talk to. A man of the cloth. A man of God. Someone who would understand why Hazen had to do what he did. Understand the ways of God. The demands of Him.

But this nebbish? No idea! None whatsoever! Don't know what God he thinks he's talking to, but it sure as hell isn't Hazen's!

Was starting to really get on his nerves. Yammering, yammering, yammering. On and on and on with his drivel. An endless droning on, talking about some wimpy, wipe-ass version of God, simpering on about "redemption" and "forgiveness."

Fuck that! This man doesn't know God! Doesn't know what he's talking about! Fucking forgiveness? Please! God doesn't believe in *forgiveness*. He believes in brimstone, fire, vengeance, and absolute, total destruction! Jesus Christ, hasn't the dipshit even read the fucking Bible? It's full of mayhem and murder, floods and plagues. He even has a few messed-up dudes killing their own families, children. He asks them to do this, to show their faith! And they do.

And what about hell? What about that? The little pansy couldn't explain that away, no matter how many flowery words he used! No way to misconstrue that one. Forgiveness? Come on! God has you descending to the fiery pits of hell for all eternity, for some minor mistake or another!

Fuck forgiveness! That's not God's way! Screw forgiveness! He's going to kill the little slut. Kill the little two-faced bitch that got him into this mess in the first place. Kill her nice and slow.

Her first, and then Buddy. Wipe Buddy out too. Then deal with the mother. Wipe them all out. Clean slate. Do the world a favor.

Little ass-wipe doesn't know what he's talking about. Fucking forgiveness!

They're moving him this afternoon. The doctor's given the okay. So they're moving him from the hospital ward to the jail ward, and then to make it even more cozy, they're slapping him on the bus tomorrow, early, to take him to the courthouse to be arraigned. Six forty-five in the morning! It's inhumane. Bad enough that they're incarcerating him, slamming him in a county jail for nothing. Absolutely nothing. Following his dick, that's probably the worst "crime" he committed. Well hell, if they're going to start locking people up for that, for falling in love with the wrong person, for trying to do good and save some kid. If they're going to lock people up for that, well, just forget about it!

They're moving him to jail, and he's trying to be cool, but his damned hands got the shakes.

At least in the hospital, he could pretend things were status quo. Nothing out of the ordinary here, all hospitals feel like jail. What's the diff? But now, they're moving him. Messing him up just to think about it. Got the runs again. Got them bad.

It's not that he's scared. It's not that Hazen Wood is fucking scared, he's not. It's just that this is county jail, and if things don't go well in court, we're talking about jail, not some nursery school. Those guys aren't going to want to be sitting around doing watercolors and knitting. There's going to be some seriously messed-up dudes in there, and they aren't exactly going to want to sit around doing the hokey pokey.

Not just that, the prison part, who cares? That's not what bugs him. It's the unfairness of it. What ever happened to justice? What ever happened to "innocent until proven guilty"? Innocent! So how can they just lock him up like that? Where was his trial? Why wasn't he invited?

"You have to be arraigned," his lawyer said. "Then you can have your trial." Arraigned! What the hell is that? And what does that have to do with anything? No jury, no trial, no proof of anything, and yet, they're moving him to jail on the hearsay of some messed-up, demented twelve-year-old. A maximum-security, lockdown prison. And the inept, dweeby, ass-wipe of an attorney that the courts have assigned him is a joke. The imbecile couldn't find his way out of a paper bag, let alone figure out a plausible defense.

Always fiddling with his papers, avoiding Hazen's eye. It's like he's scared of him or something.

"And you're going to help me?" Hazen had said. "You're like a bad joke." The guy didn't even have the balls to get offended.

"You're entitled to your opinion," he sniffed, acting like Hazen is slug scum. Like sitting in the same room with him is like sitting in a room full of vomit. Superior little shit!

"You're entitled to your opinion. . . ."

That was it. That was his mighty comeback.

The asshole has no balls. No pizzazz. And this is what's supposed to win him his freedom? This is what's supposed to win Hazen Wood his God-given right to freedom?

He's going to kill that slut. Just wait. She's dead.

·　　·　　·

I've been having bad stomach cramps and it's making it hard to work at full capacity.

I'm trying to make up for the trouble I've caused. I heard them arguing last night. Not loud and angry, like Mama and Buddy. Just quiet, low voices, but it was an argument all the same. I think it was about me. Maybe that's why my stomach is hurting so bad.

I'm worried that maybe Ms. Finnegan was right. Maybe having me here is too much of a strain on them. Too big a burden.

Wish I hadn't stole that money. Maybe that's what they were arguing about. Maybe they were wishing they never took me. Were regretting it and are trying to figure out a way to send me back. Maybe they're tired of getting no sleep at night, because I keep having these stupid nightmares. I'm trying not to. Trying so hard to be quiet, to clean and do chores to show them how good I can be, that I'm not all bad news.

The trouble is, I'm trying to clean but the cramps keep doubling me over. It hurts bad, like a side ache from running too fast. But the side ache isn't in one spot, below my rib cage on the right-hand side or anything like that. This is a big side ache, but not on my side. It's in my belly, low in my belly. Doubling me over, snatching my breath. Hitting me every few minutes. Hurts real bad, like I accidentally swallowed several fistfuls of broken, dirty glass.

I cover it up, try to breathe through it, act all natural. Don't want them to think I'm one trouble after another.

Sure hope I don't have cancer like my granddaddy. He was always doubled over too. The cancer grabbing his breath away. Hope that's not what's going on here, but I'm sweating too. And my granddaddy, he was always sweating. Hope it's not cancer inside of me, gobbling me up. I'm kind of scared.

·　　·　　·

It got real bad. The cramps. I ran to the bathroom, right in the middle of mopping the kitchen floor. I wanted to get it done before Cindy got home from work. Wanted to surprise her.

I couldn't get through it though. The cramps were getting worse and worse. I ran to the bathroom. Thought maybe I had food poisoning or something. That maybe I could poop it out. But instead of poop, blood came out. First a little, then lots. A sploosh of it. Blood and gunk out of where I pee, filling up the toilet with blood.

It was like somebody had exploded a bomb inside me. And at that point, I was pretty sure I had cancer and it was just gobbling up my flesh, devouring me whole, ripping out my guts, and spitting up blood.

I remember calling out. I remember that. Calling out for Cindy, even though she wasn't home, blood everywhere. I remember that, I don't remember anything else. Guess I fainted. I don't know. All the blood freaked me out. Don't know what happened next. Don't remember.

On the toilet one minute, in the hospital the next.

.   .   .

I had a miscarriage. That's what they call it. I lost the baby, because God decided that it wasn't the right time, the right circumstances, for that baby to be born. That God had made a mistake, giving it to me. He'd made a mistake, even though he's God. And when he realized that, he fixed it. He decided that it would be best for me and the baby to give that baby to another family to raise. A family who wanted and needed it. A family that wouldn't be complete without it. That's what Cindy and I talked about in the car on the way home from the hospital.

So that's good, it's better for the baby. I'm glad about that. No question, real glad. Just the same, I felt funny too, didn't want the baby to feel like . . . I don't know, hard to put into words.

I guess, what I'm trying to say is, I didn't want the baby, to feel bad, like I'm so *happy* it's dead. Like I hated it or anything. Like I didn't want it to have a chance at life. Didn't want it to think that. I was worried, is all. That's why I'm glad it's gone. I was real worried about being a mother.

When we got home from the hospital, I went into my bathroom to see the miscarriage. Cindy said I should go to bed, that she'd clean it up, but, I don't know, I had to see for myself. Make sure it happened. I was looking in the toilet, the water was red from all my blood. And that's when I saw it, this little bloody lump of something, around the size of half of my thumb, the top half. A little smaller, but around that size, and I scooped it out and held it in my hand. It didn't look like a baby, was just a little splodge of bloody, mushy stuff. Might not have been my baby, but just in case, I didn't want it to get flushed down the toilet like it was a piece of pooh.

It was different with Boxcar. She was a turtle. It was a good thing, because if she was alive, she got to live in a lake. And if she was dead, which she probably was, then at least the other turtles would have found her body when it arrived at the lake and given her a nice burial. But it wouldn't be a good thing for a baby to get flushed down the toilet. It didn't feel right. Not for a baby.

I didn't know what to do with it, didn't want to drop it back in the toilet, just in case. So I just stand there looking at it, resting in my hand.

Cindy comes in. "What's going on?" she says, cleaning supplies clunking around in a bucket in her hand.

I show her. "Do you think it's my baby?" I say.

"I don't know, sweetie, it could be." She puts her arm around me. "Are you okay?"

I nod, but I'm feeling kind of funny. Kind of mixed, holding a little splodge that could have been my baby. Not that I wanted a baby, but I feel weird anyway. "What should I do with it?" I ask.

"I don't know. What do you want to do?"

"Maybe," I feel kind of foolish, hope she doesn't laugh, think I'm ridiculous. "Maybe I should bury it. . . . Just in case."

Cindy doesn't laugh at me, or make fun of me. She gives me a little squeeze. "That sounds like a wonderful idea, Gemma," she says.

She finds a pretty scrap of fabric from her sewing basket, all pink and soft and cozy, and we wrap it in that, like the scrap is a little blanket. I want to make a cross, so God will know where to come and pick up the baby's spirit to bring to the new family, so I get two little branches from the tree outside and we cut them to the right shape with scissors, and I fasten them tight with red yarn. I glue glitter and silver confetti stars to it, and it looks so pretty. And while I make the preparations, I feel sad for the baby, but glad too. My heart feels so full and heavy and light, all at the same time.

When I've got everything ready, Cindy says she'll come with me, but I don't know, I feel like it's something I need to do alone.

I go out by myself. It's dusk, shadowy, almost night, but not quite. I can still see.

I decide to plant her at the base of the oak tree in the back yard. The one I got the branches for her cross. Bury her among the roots.

The ground is real hard. It's frozen, and difficult to dig up with Cindy's tablespoon. I have to chip away. It takes a long time, but I manage to make a big enough hole. I put the baby, or at least, what I think might have been the baby in the hole. I place it in tenderly and stroke it with my finger. Real gently, because it's so small, even with the blanket wrapped around it. Then I put a cherry lifesaver that I'd been saving in my pocket in the grave as well. I give it to her so she'll have a treat to nibble on while she waits for God.

Wish I had some flowers, but when I give it some thought, I realize that wouldn't have been good, because I never would have been able to chip away a hole big enough to accommodate flowers. I would have been chipping away at that frozen ground until May, for sure.

I wonder how they bury whole grown-up people when they die in the winter. It wouldn't be so bad in Oakland, but if someone was planning on dying in Chicago, they'd be smart to wait until spring, when the ground had thawed. They'd get better flowers then too, which would make for a way prettier funeral.

However, I have no flowers, which is a blessing and a curse, so I put the crumples of frozen dirt back into the hole, my fingers, clumsy, numb with cold. I pat it down and stick the cross in. But it keeps tipping over, so finally, I prop it up with three little rocks and that holds pretty good.

I say a prayer. Thank God for my second chance, and for giving my baby a second chance too. I ask him to find her a good family this time. A loving family like the Salyns. And then I say, "Amen." Even though I'm not Catholic, I cross myself, because it seems like the right thing to do.

Then, even though the wind is blowing chills through my body, making it rattle and shake, whipping my hair, snake like, across my face and into my mouth, me making little *plah* noises spitting it back out. Even though it's cold, with the wind whirling in off the lake, freezing me to the bone, the moon disappearing in and out from behind clouds, which are flying fast, like a witch on a broom, thick-veined clouds, so that at times, even with the moon behind them, I can still see the glow shimmering through parts of it, and blackness through the rest, even though it's this kind of night, I lie down on my back on the hard, frozen ground, beside my baby's grave, and we look up at the beautiful sky. The old oak tree making black-lace patterns in the sky.

We look up at the clouds, the moon, gliding across the night sky, the occasional star, winking in and out, playing hide-and-seek. We look up at the beautiful sky and breathe in long. Cold air, searing my lungs. Breathe in long and deep, full of thanksgiving.

Later, when I go inside, hunched over and shivering from the cold, Cindy makes a pot of Constant Comment tea. I add some milk and sugar in mine and we drink out of Christmas mugs. Mine has a smiling snowman with a carrot nose that bumps into my chin if I'm not careful. The hot tea feels good, comforting, cupped in my hands, warm, wet steam enveloping my face when I tip my head to take a sip. It feels good to sit there and talk with Cindy, like I'm a grown-up.

We talk about God and his wisdom and goodness, and that maybe he gave the baby to another family, but maybe he decided to save it for me, for a later date, when I'm big and grown.

That's one of the many things we talk about, sitting at the kitchen table, sipping tea, nibbling on Scotch shortbread.

And now, lying here, snug and warm in my bed, the chill gone from my bones, I'm thinking over everything we talked about and I have to say, I feel so much better. I was worried that maybe I'd killed the baby with all of my bad feelings.

But Cindy says I didn't.

I'm so relieved that I didn't have to have a baby. Didn't have to get an abortion. It's such a relief! I was worried about that baby, if I was going to be a good parent. I didn't know how I was going to take care of it. Feed it. It was doubtful that I was going to be able to get an education. Especially with my mama kicking me out. I didn't know how I was going to manage, because I couldn't work, couldn't legally get a job until I turned fifteen, almost three years away. How was I going to support it?

I have to say, I had a lot of sleepless nights, worrying about that baby.

But now? It's like God has given me a second chance at life. Like God still loves me, hasn't given up on me! It's like God has said, "Here, Gemma, another chance. Don't screw up."

And I won't! I'm going to go to school. I'm going to work so hard! I'm going to get straight A's. I'm going to try to be a good person, and help other people, like Cindy does. I want to be a person that does good in the world.

God has given me a second chance and I'm not going to mess up. I swear it on all that is holy! I am determined to do big things with my life.

·　　·　　·

That was a total fucking waste of a day. Started off bad and didn't get better. Waiting around to get his day in court, locked in a cramped holding cell like he's a rabid animal. And then, when they finally got before the judge, Hazen's "attorney," *Mister* Partap, didn't do anything. Just rustled through the disorganized reams of paper he carries around in that beat-up briefcase of his—and that's another thing, he should get a new briefcase, because that one frankly, is an embarrassment. It's beat up, tired out, and inspires no confidence whatsoever. Got his lunch in there, for Chrissake! No kidding. Hazen saw it with his own two eyes. Fucking squashed egg-salad sandwich wrapped in Saran Wrap rolling around with the paperwork. And Hazen's sitting there thinking, "This is my attorney? This is what's going to make the difference between prison or walking free?" And he wanted to reach over and pop the guy. Would have if they weren't in court.

Partap wanted him to plead guilty! Said he might be able to get him a shorter sentence.

Needless to say, Hazen told him where to shove it.

"Not guilty, your honor," Hazen said. Threw the "your honor" in, Partap hadn't told him to say that. But Hazen, he's smart. He knows how the game's played. Figured it was a good touch, soften the judge up, show him a little respect, no criminal here. Gave him a little smile, like they were at a Sunday barbeque, a baseball game, passing on the street in front of the pharmacy. That kind of smile. But the guy was not very sociable, didn't smile back, looked down at his papers, tapped his right forefinger on his desk a few times and then set the trial for February first, provided there's a courtroom available. February first. Fifty days away!

"Do you mean to tell me that I have to stay in that county jail for fifty goddamned days?"

"That's about it," Partap said, packing up his briefcase. "Unless you or your family can come up with the five-hundred grand." Superior snot-faced shit. Five-hundred-thousand-dollars bail! Who the hell's got money like that?

.   .   .

Guess what? Another good thing happened. I made a mistake! Cindy hadn't just signed me out for the holidays. She'd signed me out for good. I get to stay for as long as I want! Forever, until I'm all grown! That's what she said. And the funny thing is, I'm happy right, I'm so happy, and yet when I found out, I started bawling. There I was, jump-ing up and down, smiling so big and bawling like a baby. Cindy started crying too, and we're hugging each other. It was great! I get to stay for-ever. They want me to stay forever. And not just Cindy, Joseph too.

I know that, because I asked Joseph. I did it when Cindy was gone, so he wouldn't feel like he had to be nice or polite or anything. I told him I understood that taking on an almost teen, someone who's had some challenges and is past the sell-by date, isn't what most people would want to do. That I understood if he didn't want me to stay, no worries, not to feel bad. I wouldn't tell Cindy, I'd just go away, make a life on my own, would be fine. I've lived on the streets before, it's not like I'm a baby and can't take care of myself, so no obligation. That's what I told him. All of it coming out faster than I'd practiced in my room. It came out in a rush of words, like a water balloon hitting the hot pavement.

He seemed startled at first, looked around, like he was hoping Cindy was still here and I was talking to her, because he's kind of quiet and lets her do most of the talking. But I wasn't talking to her. I was talking to him. She was long gone.

"Oh . . . um . . ." He cleared his throat, tipped his head down so he was looking at me over the top of his reading glasses. "It's . . . it's fine by me," he said. "I'm . . . I'm happy for you to stay."

That's what he said. "I'm *happy* for you to *stay*." Those were his very words!

And the weird thing is, I had *no* idea they were going to be my fos-ter parents. None! I thought it was for the holidays, because they were charitable. I had no idea that they *wanted* me! That they chose me out of all the boys and girls in the whole world that needed, wanted a home. They *chose* me! And not only that, I was *past the age*! I was *preg-nant*! And *still* they wanted me!

Makes me feel all humble and good, like I got a belly full of warm cocoa.

I didn't really realize it, but after he said that, the "I'm *happy* for you to *stay*," I was just standing there beaming at him. Wearing the biggest damned smile.

"Well . . . ah . . ." Joseph cleared his throat again, looked embarrassed. "So . . . ah . . . anything else?"

"No," I said. "Nothing else." I went to my room, so he wouldn't think I wanted more flattery. I've got to say, though, it sure made me glad that I screwed up my courage and asked him.

I lay on my bed with its ruffled, girly bedspread, looking up at the ceiling, thinking about what he said. Playing his words over and over in my mind. I say them out loud, softly so he won't hear me, but loud enough so I can hear them again, dance around and fill the room.

And the coolest thing of all is, I've been here for almost two weeks, and he hasn't tried to touch me once. Not my top, or my butt, or nothing! Hasn't tried to stick anything in me either.

He's funny too, in a fuddy-duddy way. He says these made-up swear words, because he's trying to be a good role model and not to swear around me. Which is really hilarious, that him and Cindy are trying so hard not to swear, because they have no idea! Really, they have *no* idea, the kind of words I know.

All this effort to protect my delicate ears from words I've heard, said myself, a million times. But it's funny, it kind of rubs off, because now I'm trying not to swear too. I figure if they can do it, so can I. It's a good habit to get into. Because walking down the street, it's rare to hear a fancy person cursing up a blue storm.

. . .

He's in isolation. They put him, an innocent man, not only in jail, but in fucking isolation! Like he's some kind of freak. Wearing some pansy orange jumpsuit. An orange jumpsuit, so everyone in the whole county jail thinks he's a freak. A faggot, some sort of sexual deviant.

It's an outrage! He pays his taxes! He pays his dues! And for them to throw him in here, on circumstantial evidence, on the hearsay of a demented twelve-year-old. It's an outrage!

He's going to find out who the senator is. Who the damned senator of the state of Illinois is. Give him a piece of Hazen Wood's mind! How dare they? Locking up innocent men. Incarcerating peace-loving, law-abiding, men! Find out who the senator is. Give him a piece of his mind. Tell him he'd better change his policy or he'll be losing Hazen Wood's vote. Better look into this outrage they call the penal system!

It's inhumane! Locking him up like an animal. Fucking eight-by-ten cell. Minuscule TV. No cable. Hard mattress. Food sucks. Tastes like somebody crapped it out and dished it up. Damned well sucks! Going to be a skeleton by the time he clears this mess up. Gets out of this freak house.

And to top it all off, the straw that's breaking the camel's back, they've stuck him in an orange jumpsuit! Why the fuck did they have to do that? Should be in blue, like the rest of the population! Should be able to go out in the yard, with the rest of them. But no. He's stuck in his cell all day. No one to talk to. Can drive a man mad. Stuck in the silence of his own brain. Too much time to think.

"For your own safety," they said.

His own safety? He's stuck in here with a bunch of perverts! A bunch of faggots and freaks! Makes him sick just to look at them.

Told his lawyer that they'd made a mistake. Put him in the wrong jumpsuit, have him segregated, isolated. Told his lawyer that, and the asshole laughed. First time Hazen had ever seen him so much as smile.

"What's so funny?" Hazen demanded.

But it didn't deter him. Mr. Partap, Mr. Richard-tight-ass-Partap just kept laughing, swiped at his eyes behind his Coke-bottle glasses.

"That would be good," he said. "That would be good. I'd like to see that. Throw you in there with the general population."

"Yeah," said Hazen. "I want a blue jumpsuit, like everyone else."

But the Partap putz wasn't listening. He was back rustling through his papers. Ignoring him. The asshole was ignoring him.

So, Hazen slammed his fist on the table, slammed it down hard. Made Partap jump.

"Did you hear me? I *want* a blue jumpsuit. If I going to be stuck in here, due to *your* incompetence, at least I should be dressed in the appropriate color."

But Partap just looked at him, over the top of his papers. "Don't be an idiot," he said, face tired, bored. "They'd eat you for lunch."

•   •   •

We put up the Christmas tree. A real one. We bought it at a Christmas-tree lot. They had tons of trees. Millions of them. And we stomped around in our boots and winter coats. Did I mention I have a winter coat? Yeah, I got one. Cindy's sister gave us a whole bunch of clothes. She has a daughter who's eleven, one year younger, but she's taller, on account of my being so small for my age. Anyway, Cindy's sister Camille had a bunch of extra clothes lying around. Her daughter had gone through a growth spurt and couldn't wear them anymore because they didn't fit. And some of these clothes are almost brand-spanking new. Beautiful too. Fashionable.

It's a weird feeling actually, because I love these clothes, and want to show them off, but I'm kind of nervous about going to school here. I don't know what I'm going to be walking into. Kids might not like me. I sound different, have a different accent from the people around here. They might think I'm weird, odd. Might gang up on me, like the kids at my old school did on José.

But I'm hoping that maybe, wearing these fashionable clothes, maybe they'll give me a chance. Think I'm normal, one of them.

I've been trying on outfits the last few days. Trying to decide what to wear the first day of school. Looking in the mirror. Looking hard. Studying myself real close, right up in bright, harsh light. Looking so my nose is almost up against the mirror, fogging it up, and even looking that close, that careful, looking for any trace . . . I got to say, other than my dumb hair, and a few little belt-buckle scars I can barely see, which could be chicken-pox scars for all anybody would know. Looking up close . . . I don't think, and I could be wrong, but I don't think there's any way anybody could tell, by just looking at me, all my troubles.

Unless, of course, they saw one of those stupid missing-child posters. Unless they saw one of those. Paid attention.

I hope not. I really, really hope not.

Maybe Cindy would let me change my name. If I changed my name, they wouldn't know it was me. Maybe that would help.

I hope nobody at my new school saw the posters. That would suck. That would not be good.

Too bad I like learning so much. Otherwise, it would be no problem. If someone recognized me, figured it out, no problem, I'd just walk out the front door and never go back. Walk out, hit the road, sayonara, baby.

But I can't. Even if someone figures it out and things get tough. I have to stick it out because I've got my plan. I promised God, promised myself. I've been given a second chance and I'm going to make something of my life. I'm determined to get a higher education. To go to college. And if I'm going to do that, I have to work hard and get a scholarship. I've got to get straight A's. I can't expect Cindy and Joseph to pay for everything. I'm already a financial strain, not that they'd admit it, but I know about these things.

So, it's a mix of feelings. I'm scared to start school, but I also can't wait. Good or bad, I want to get started. This not knowing how it's going to be is getting to me, big time.

I'm trying not to be negative, to think positive. "Yay!" I say to myself, "I get to go to school here. Wear my new clothes. Make lots of friends. Get to work on my plan!"

That's what I tell myself. I do such a good job that sometimes I actually convince myself that I can't wait to get started. Feel a bit like one of those race horses on TV, all stompy and snorty, kicking at the stall door. Trying to get that little latch door lifted so I can bolt out, run like the wind.

Yeah, sometimes I get excited, like school, life, everything's going to be good now. And then other days, I want the clock to slow down, stop, so I don't have to deal with the future. Don't want to go to school. Just want to stay here with Joseph and Cindy, happy and safe. Want it to remain Christmas forever.

Anyway, enough about that, I want to talk about the tree. We got a beautiful Christmas tree. Must have looked at about a hundred trees. Pulling them up, turning them this way and that. Noses red, fingers and toes going numb. Feet stomping. "Feels like snow." Everyone's saying it. "Feels like snow."

And I stomped my feet too. Slapped my hands together. Said, "Feels like snow," too. Just like an old pro. "Feels like snow. Uh huh." "Yep," I said. "Feels just like snow"

I said it to everyone I met, so they'd know I live here, and think I'm an old pro with this snow stuff and Chicago weather. "Feels like snow," my face matter-of-fact, knowledgeable, like snow's just a matter of time. Everyone is saying it now! Everyone! So snow must be coming! And even though I act all casual, the fact is, I can barely sleep with the excitement of it.

We looked at lots and lots of trees. Tested them out, buried our faces in them, breathing in their scent. We looked at hundreds of trees and then we found it. Actually, I was the one who first discovered it, but I'm saying "we" because I don't want to brag.

And it was the most beautiful Christmas tree that any of us had ever seen. It was just the right size and shape. Had the right feel and smell. But, most important of all, it had that Christmas magical feeling that only special Christmas trees have. That feeling that called out and swirled around my heart and head, promising miracles and happy-ever-afters. And that tree we found . . . *it had it all!*

So naturally, we bought it right there on the spot. Bought it, and tied it to the top of our car. We had to leave the car windows open a crack for the rope to go through, which made the inside of the car pretty chilly. We tied it down good, and Joseph drove home, nice and slow, so the tree wouldn't fall off. Then, when we got home, we carried the tree inside the house, got it set up in the stand, and decorated it to kingdom come!

•   •   •

Partap is gone. Mr. Richard Pompous-Ass Partap is officially gone. "A family emergency," Hazen was told. "A death in the family."

Bullshit. He's gone because Hazen got rid of him, plain and simple. He told that "Mr. Richard Partap." Hazen Wood told that idiot. Showed him who was boss. Made him sit up and take notice. Partap may have thought he was just dealing with another schmoe, but he had another think coming. Thought he'd get Hazen to agree to waive his right to a "speedy" trial. Like, who the hell are they kidding? Fifty days in jail? Not to mention all the time he spent in that hospital bed, recuperating from the goddamned bullet holes Chicago's finest blasted into him, with no just cause.

"You . . . want me . . . to sign this?" said Hazen, being oh-so civil. "And why, might I ask?"

"We want to wait, put the trial off as long as possible. . . ." Partap would have kept talking, blathering on. Pontificating fool. Would have kept talking, but Hazen, he wasn't feeling in a listening mood. He had listened and listened. And for what? To what end? To end up rotting his life away in jail?

"Wait. Back up a minute." And the guy, the poor putz, he actually flinched at Hazen's tone. Must have known something was coming.

Hazen spoke slow, distinct. "Let me get this straight. You want to *wait*? Put it off as *long as possible*? You want to play casual with my life?"

"Listen. It's in your best interest—"

"Fuck you!"

"Look, you go to trial now, you've haven't got a shot in hell. The kid's holed up with Detective Salyn, and she's not going anywhere. They've got DNA. Granted, it's not conclusive, but they've got it. They've got witnesses. And they've got the kid. And what do I have? What do I have to work with? I've got you. An asshole who not only *did* everything he's accused of, but he actually doesn't have a problem with it. That's what I've got. And I'm supposed to try and get you off? I hate my job!"

At first Hazen was stunned by the ferocity of Partap's outburst. Didn't think he had it in him. Just sat there, looking at him.

"Wow," Hazen said, because what the hell could he say? The guy was flipping on him.

They sat there for a bit more, nobody talking, and just when Hazen was starting to feel a modicum of respect for the guy, Partap apologized.

"Look, I'm sorry, I was out of line. The baby was up all night. Colic." Partap was massaging his temples like he had a headache coming on. And that's all well and fine, but they need to get to work, figure out a strategy.

"That's okay," Hazen said, being generous, getting the ball moving. "That's okay, man. Look, that's something we have in common, I'm going to be a father too. That's why it's real important I get out. Got family to attend to."

But the personal touch wasn't working. Partap looked like he just took a slug of sour milk.

"Whatever," he said. "The way it stacks up is, the best thing to do is stall. Hope Salyn gets tired of the kid and sends her back to Oakland. We have to try to draw it out, maybe their witnesses will die or forget. If we really get lucky, they'll lose the DNA. Don't count on it though. What we're waiting for is a shot in the dark."

"Uh huh," said Hazen, and he was trying to be calm, keep on track, but it wasn't working. He could feel his neck going red. Felt the rage building up. Partap. Playing God with his life. "I see. You want to wait. You want to wait for a 'shot in the dark.' That's what you want to hinge your defense on?"

And when Partap's Adam's apple bobbed in his scrawny little neck, and he started nodding his stupid gargantuan turnip head, like that was a reasonable plan, something in Hazen just snapped. "A *shot* in the dark? *Are* you out of your *fucking* skull? *Jesus Christ!* You don't give a *crap* about me! My *life.* You just want me to *sit here,* twiddling my thumbs, *rotting* my life away, sit here, waiting for a *'shot in the dark'*? I don't think so!"

Partap wanted to speak, Hazen could see that. Opened his mouth, but Hazen came down on him like a fist of fire. A fucking fist of fire. Grabbed him by his little, pansy, button-down shirt, his Brooks Brothers cheap-imitation pinstripe shirt.

"Now you *listen* to me. I've been reading up. Yeah, that's right. I *can* read. And I know my rights. I know my rights, *asshole.* Now I've tried to be patient with you. I've been a saint. But no more. I want my trial. I demand, as an American citizen, my right to a speedy trial. Do you know what that means? Huh? Do you? That means no, I will not, I will *never* waive my rights to a speedy trial! You got that? You *got* that, *asshole?*" By that time Hazen was shaking him like a scarecrow. The guard had to come in, drag him off. "You got that! You *got* that, asshole! No way in *hell* I'm *waiving* my rights!" And then Hazen couldn't see Partap anymore, because the door had swung shut, two more guards arrived and wrestled Hazen to the ground.

So that's the true story. That's the real one. Not some "family emergency." Partap's "mother" didn't have a "heart attack." The wuss was scared of him, plain and simple. Even better, the new guy, Partap's replacement, he's sharp. He's real sharp. Not some sad-sack, court-appointed attorney. No way, not for Hazen Wood, he's the man. And apparently, according to the guys on his cell block, he got one of the best, one of the finest lawyers in the country. Mr. Samuel Levy, that's his name. A Jew, not that it bothers Hazen one bit. He's not prejudiced, hell no. He'll take a Jew any day of the week, not to dinner mind you, but as a lawyer, they're the best. Smart, sneaky, wily little bastards.

What happened is, this Levy guy apparently had been following Hazen's case on the news and decided, on a whim, to take him as a client.

"What about payment?" Hazen asked him. "I'm broke, you know."

"Don't worry," Levy said, his hand waving away the question like it was no big deal. "We'll work something out." That's the kind of man Mr. Levy is. A class act, even though he's a Jew. A triple-A class act.

•   •   •

Cindy got a phone call from the station and it got her all worked up. She's slamming the pots and the cupboard doors in the kitchen. Joseph said it was best not to go in there when she was like that. "Give her ten minutes and she'll calm down," he said. So I stayed where I was, sitting in the living room. I sat there, pretending to read my book, watching the clock on the mantelpiece out of the corner of my eye. Ten minutes came and went, and she was still banging, so Joseph went in. She was mad, I could tell. She was trying to keep her voice down, but it was rising all the same. She was yelling about a Samuel Levy, and swearing, and saying things like "blood-sucking ambulance chaser," and "Why . . . why . . . why?" I could hear Joseph's voice, calmer, soothing, couldn't hear everything, just a few words here and there, floating to me, like "TV" and "publicity" and "It's not the end of the world." And when he said that, Cindy started yelling again about "You don't know!" And "This guy is good! Really, really good!" And going on about all the cases that he's won, and then all of a sudden she started crying, soft, like she was trying to hold it in. I wanted to go to the kitchen and comfort her, but I didn't want to intrude, because maybe she would have been embarrassed, me seeing her like that. So I stayed on the sofa, like I was a mummy, not moving, barely breathing. I could hear her saying, voice all choked up with tears, "It's not fair. . . . It's just not fair."

•   •   •

The nightmares keep coming. I can't seem to get rid of them. They visit me every night.

It's gotten so bad that I'm nervous about going to sleep. I like my bedroom during the day. It's all cozy and pretty and homey. But when it starts to get dark, I find all kinds of excuses not to be in there. Reading a book, comfy on the sofa, drinking tea in the kitchen, want to watch TV. It doesn't matter what is playing. Well, actually, that's not true. I don't want to watch anything scary. Can't. It makes me too nervous to sit through shows with killing, or shooting, or people being mean. Even corny shooting shows, like John Wayne, cowboys and Indians. I can't even watch that. I get too scared. Only seem to be able to watch happy-ever-after shows.

And movies like James Bond and things like that? Forget about it. Even if they didn't give me panic attacks, I wouldn't watch them, and that's the truth. I mean sheesh! Why would I do that? Pay good money to get scared? That's the stupidest thing I ever heard of! Life's scary enough.

I don't know what to do about the nightmares that keep visiting me, night after night. Waking up screaming, Cindy having to come in, comfort me, stroke my head until I go back to sleep. I'm glad she chases the night terrors away, but I feel bad too. She doesn't complain, but I know I'm tiring her out, because in the morning, Cindy's shoulders are slumped down, and her head is practically buried in her coffee cup. She didn't look like that in the morning when I first moved in. Now when she gets up and goes to the sideboard to refill her mug, her legs are moving slow, like she is having to push her body through invisible sludge. Moving around the kitchen. Dark shadows under her eyes.

I wish I could get on top of it. Stop keeping her awake with my tomfoolery. Wish I didn't have such bad nightmares coming to me in my sleep.

And when I'm not dreaming about him, about Hazen Wood, when I'm not having nightmares about him, then I'm dreaming about my mom. Dreaming about her shape shifting, coming back to get me. At first I'm happy, so happy to see her. And then she shape shifts, shape shifts into a monster, and she's trying to kill me. And I can't fight, and I can't move, and I have to kill her or I'll be killed myself, but I can't. It's like I'm petrified rock and everything in me is yelling, "RUN!

160

SAVE YOURSELF!" But I can't move. Can't run. Am trying to call out, but it's like my vocal cords are underwater, in slow motion. And I'm trying to move my mouth to make noises, to let her know that it's me. Her daughter! But it's not working, and she's laughing and laughing, head tossed so far back I can see all the metal fillings in her teeth. And she's got a big knife and is laughing like it's real funny, and stabbing this huge bloody knife down at me.

And then I wake up. At that moment, I always wake up, and my face is all wet from crying and my heart is making my body rock because it's beating so hard.

That's the moment that I wake up, right before the knife slashes through my forehead.

I hate those dreams.

And it's like, when those dreams start, it's like my brain remembers it from before. Starts out normal enough, my mom comes into my room to ask me something. Starts out normal enough, but my brain remembers, doesn't remember quite what, but it remembers, and my stomach drops, and my mouth has that metallic feeling like I've been sucking on a handful of change. My heart starts racing and I have that trapped feeling, like I'm in a runaway car that's heading straight for a brick wall and there is nothing I can do about it.

I hate those dreams. But at least I don't wake up screaming and calling out from my mom dreams. At least I don't wake up the whole house with those dreams, like I do with the Hazen dreams. The trunk dreams. At least I don't do that.

I just lie there, heart pounding, still crying. And then I start thinking about my real mom, not the shape-shifting one. Wondering if she misses me. Worrying that she's going to come get me. A part of me, wishing she would. Wanting her to want me again. Or at least call me once in a while, to make sure I'm okay. Act like she cares. Not that I'd go with her. At least, I don't think I would, but I want her to want me just a little. I want her to wish she hadn't been so mean, leaving me here, losing her rights. Want, wish, she'd have just a little bit of regret.

And sometimes, when I can't shake the dream, the memory of her trying to kill me, wanting me dead, I turn on all the lights and walk around the room. I walk quiet, so I won't wake anybody up. The comforter from the bed wrapped around me, because they turn the heat down at night to save electricity.

I try to outwalk the dream. Sometimes it works, and after an hour or two, I can crawl back in bed, go to sleep. But sometimes it doesn't work. I can't outwalk it, and then I have to keep all the lights on and do something else. So I write.

I write poetry now. I haven't told anyone. I'm keeping it secret. I started that night I had the miscarriage. Didn't know it was going to be a poem. Just started writing and it helped, felt good, and the words came out as a poem. I don't know if my poetry is any good. Just know that I need to write it. Write about things. That it releases suffocating feeling somehow, to write it down.

So sometimes, if the dreams won't go away, and walking doesn't work, I take out my pen and some paper, and I write. Keep scribbling until morning light starts to come up, just a hint, scaring away the blackness. And then, when I see the light start to change, the first tinges of gray creeping in, it's like all of a sudden, my body gets heavy and my eyes get tired, and I crawl back into bed and go to sleep.

NINE

When I first saw Detective Sheffman, driving up the drive, I figured she was here to see me, being the investigating officer on my case and everybody being so tense about this new Levy guy. I thought she was here to talk to me some more, but she wasn't.

"I need to talk to you, Cindy," she said, as she banged through the kitchen door. No "hello." No, "Oh, what are you eating? Can I have some?" She didn't even seem to notice the food. "I need to talk to you," she said to Cindy, Sheffman's face like a brick wall. "You too, Joe."

They got up, no questions. Me, sitting at the table, a chicken leg sticking out of my fist like a question mark.

They filed out of the room, like it was a dance or something, no need for words, everybody knowing the steps but me. Out they went. Their food left on their plates to get cold, mine too, appetite gone.

Now they're holed up in Joseph's study, talking real low, so even with my good ears, even though I'm sitting real quiet in the kitchen, which is right next door, even though I'm sitting real still, with my eardrums turned on high, I can't hear a word they're saying. A low murmur is all

I hear. I can make out different tones, Joseph's rumble, Cindy's voice, Detective Sheffman's, but no words. It's sort of like the writing on a chalkboard when someone's rubbed a forearm over them. I can see that they were words, I can see that, they're just too blurry to read. That's the way they sound in Joseph's study, a rumble of blurry words, impossible to make out.

I listen to the rise and the fall of them. Hoping the words aren't about me, knowing they probably are. Something bad I've done wrong. I don't know what, but I know it's something bad, and there's nothing I can do about it. No way to defend, explain, whatever it is. They're in there and I'm out here. All I can do is hope. Fingers crossed, toes crossed, legs and arms crossed. Hoping and talking to God. Praying they aren't sending me back, that they aren't tired of me, that I'm not too much trouble. Praying hard.

Then, in the middle of all that praying I hear the study door open. I uncross everything real fast and act like I'm still eating my dinner.

"Gemma." I look up. Cindy is in the kitchen doorway, her brow furrowed, face drawn. "Gemma honey, Bonnie . . ." She pauses, glances around, like she's trying to settle herself by looking at solid, tangible things, the refrigerator, the stove, the sink. Only for a moment and then she looks back at me, "Ah . . . we'd like to talk with you, honey."

I put the chicken leg on my plate, wipe my hand on the napkin, and get up from the table. I walk to where she is standing in the doorway. She holds out her arm and I slip into the crook of it, like she's mother bird and I am her baby robin, all safe and protected. I feel her body soften slightly as she pulls me close. We walk back to the study like that, her arm around me.

Joseph is at his desk, his hair rumpled, like he's been running a hurricane through it. "Hello, dear," he says. He looks like he's trying to smile but his mouth muscles aren't cooperating.

Detective Sheffman is standing in front of the empty fireplace. Her hands behind her back, like she's warming herself.

164

"Gemma," she says. I'm used to her voice. When I first met her, she scared me. She was so abrupt, brusque, so different from Cindy, but now I'm used to it. I don't take it personally. It's just her way. "We were having a discussion, and realized we weren't sure what the appropriate thing to do is. Sit down," she waves at the sofa. "No need to stand, this might take a while."

I sit on the sofa. Cindy perches on the arm of it. She doesn't look comfortable. Seems nervous, as if she might take flight at any moment. I want to tell her it's all right. But I don't know if it is, so I don't say anything. "Anyway," continues Detective Sheffman, "we decided, since it involved you, it is only fair we let you in on it. And ultimately, let you make the decision as to how you want to proceed."

The room is quiet, the clock's ticking. The house shifts, creaks.

"Okay," I say.

There's a pause. Like everybody is holding their breath. Then Cindy clears out the silence. Her voice calm, matter of fact. If I wasn't looking at her hands, giving her away, I would have thought she was talking about something unimportant, like whether Tide or Cheer cleans clothes better.

"Your mother called the police station, Gemma. She was trying to get ahold of you."

"She has no rights," Detective Sheffman cuts in. "It is totally up to you if you want to talk to her."

Cindy continues, as if Detective Sheffman hadn't spoken. "She wanted to know where you were."

"We didn't tell her." Detective Sheffman again.

"What . . . what does she want?" I say, playing for time. Because I know what she wants. My belly knows. Feel suddenly like I'm wrapped, trapped in cotton gauze. Layers and layers of it. The kind they use for operations and injuries to soak up the blood. So removed from myself, my mouth, my body. Like I'm sitting up in the corner of the ceiling, watching myself on the sofa be calm and rational and ask questions.

"What does she want?" my mouth says again.

"She wants you to come home," Cindy says, eyes, face, worried.

"You don't have to." Detective Sheffman's voice is brusque, almost angry. "It's totally up to you. Don't even have to talk to her if you don't want to. She has no rights whatsoever. The courts have taken away all rights she had over you when she walked out that door and left you stranded in Chicago."

And I'm hearing everything, from a faraway distance, like I'm listening through a keyhole.

"Is Buddy still there?" I hear myself ask.

I see Cindy nod. Eyes watching me, sad, dark.

Detective Sheffman snorts. "Yeah. He wants you home too." She looks at Cindy, jaw set, like she'd like to punch Buddy on the nose. Like she knows about Buddy too, even though I haven't spoken a word about him to anybody.

And the image of Detective Sheffman slugging Buddy with his big beer belly, slugging someone she's never even met. Walking up to him, "Hi, how do you do? I'm Detective Sheffman," and then *Pow!* Smacko right on the old nose! The image of that, because Detective Sheffman looks real powerful, even if she's a woman. She's all muscles and might. And Buddy . . . Well let me put it this way . . . Buddy is kind of soft. Squishy, like uncooked bread dough. Soft and clammy.

And the image of him going "Ooff!" Flying backwards, clutching his nose. Has me busting up laughing, even though I know I shouldn't. Know this is serious. Know this is absolutely no time for laughing, but I can't help it. It's bubbling, burbling, tumbling out of me. Won't stop. And they're looking at me, shocked, like they don't understand, can't figure out why I'm laughing. And I want to stop, but I can't.

"I'm . . . sorry . . . ," I'm saying, choking on spit, on words, on laughter. "I'm so sorry. . . ." But even though I'm sorry, the laughter won't stop. Laughing so hard that it hurts bad, like someone is pounding me hard in the gut, over and over, pounding into me like the butt of a machine gun. It's that kind of laughter. The out of control, hurting

kind, and tears are coming too. "I'm sorry . . . I'm sorry I'm . . . laughing . . . I'm sorry."

Cindy gets up and wraps her arms around me. "It's okay," she says,
to each of my "I'm sorry's."

"It's okay . . . It's okay . . . Gemma. I'm right here . . . I'm right
here. . . . Don't worry, you're safe. . . ."

She holds me until the laughter stops and it's just crying.

And after that, she holds me still. Takes me onto her lap, even
though I'm big. Wipes away my tears, her hand smooths the hair out of
my face, gives me some Kleenex to blow my nose while Detective Sheffman and Joseph clean up in the kitchen.

When I can finally get words out, I tell her about Buddy, my promise to my mom, how my mama knew about Buddy and the things that
he did. And when I tell her all this, I start crying again, and she holds
me. And by the end of my story, she's crying too.

•   •   •

All cried out. Tired of crying. Tired of all this sadness and tears. Said
good night and went to bed. Too tired for bad dreams. Off to bed.
Detective Sheffman gone. Left now.

I haven't called my mom. Don't know what to do, or if I even want
to call her. My stomach, twisted in knots, hurts whenever I think about
it. I wish she hadn't called. Wish they hadn't told me. Left it up to me
to decide.

"Sleep on it," said Joseph. "Take your time. No hurry. See how you
feel. Maybe you'll have more clarity in the morning." He says this kind
of thing, practical, pragmatic. "Maybe you'll have more clarity in the
morning." Very Joseph.

Cindy tucks me in. "You okay?" she asks.

I nod. I'm tired, but I don't want her to leave me just yet. "Cindy?"
"Uh huh?"

"Why'd you take me in?" I ask, because I want to know. Need to know. Not sure why. I guess I want to know if she likes me a little too, or if I'm just a charity case, a good deed.

"Do you regret it?" I say, looking down at my bedspread, smoothing out all the folds, all the wrinkles with my hands. "Signing me out of McLaren Hall, asking me to stay?"

It's kind of embarrassing to speak it out loud, but I need to know. It will help me decide what to do, about my mom and all.

I don't want to be a burden. I like Joseph and Cindy too much for that.

Not pregnant anymore. That's one good thing. That's one good blessing. But still, Ms. Finnegan is right, twelve's a difficult age. And given all of my troubles, how I stole from them, and lied, and how I'm always acting weird and crying, having stupid nightmares and everything, and then tonight, laughing inappropriately.

Cindy sits down on the side of my bed.

"I'm a lot of trouble," I say.

She takes my hand in hers. "Gemma," she says. I don't look up, I'm too nervous. "Gemma." She puts her hand under my chin and tilts my head, so my face, my eyes are looking directly at her.

"Not, for one moment." She pauses, eyes searching mine. "Not for one millisecond have I, or Joe, regretted taking you in," her face, her voice, serious. "Okay?" she says.

I nod my head. Feel like a big weight has been taken off of my shoulders. Feel like the elephant just got off of my chest and I can breathe again. Because part of me, back in Joseph's study, with Detective Sheffman and all, part of me was worried that they were letting me choose because they didn't want me anymore.

"Oh good," I say. "I don't regret it either." We smile at each other. It's cozy quiet. I can hear Joseph moving around in the kitchen, finishing up the dishes.

"Now," says Cindy. "The second question . . ."

She looks out the window. Even though there's nothing to see, not with the bedside light on. Can't see the moon or the trees, or the glow of other houses. Just looks like blackness, like a sheet of black glass. But I don't tell her it's pointless to look out the window at night when the light's on. I figure she probably knows that. I don't say anything. Just wait for her to speak.

"Why did we take you? Well . . ." She looks back at me, like maybe she can find the words she's searching for in my face. "It's a little more difficult to explain. Not so clear cut. I guess the easiest explanation is that you reminded me of myself."

"I did?" I want her to elaborate, but she just nods. "How?" I say. "When? When did you realize I was like you?" I like saying it, hearing it out loud, that I'm like her.

"Well," she says, and I can tell by the way she says it, that she's going to tell a story. So I snuggle down, settle in for a story about me and Cindy, and how alike we are.

"It was almost instantaneous actually. The first time I saw you, getting out of that gray Dodge Intrepid. I felt a connection. You were such a skinny little bundle of clothes, and you looked so scared and small and beaten down. He was grabbing for you, and it was like this enormous surge of protective power roared through me, and I'm not sure how it happened, how I got to you so fast. But I was damned if I was going to let him get away with you." She laughs, remembering. I laugh too.

"I was scared," I say.

"Me too," Cindy says. "I didn't even know you, but I was terrified that we'd lose you."

"I didn't notice you, didn't know where you came from. Thought I was suppose to go to the building."

"That was the plan. The plan was to get you safely into the building, and then apprehend the perpetrator. But when he reached for you, everything changed. We were scared he was on to us. Worried he was leaving with you as a hostage. Maybe we'd get him, maybe not. But the thing was, especially with the risk that he was on to us, you'd have been in more danger. And that was not a chance I was willing to take."

"Where were you?"

"Behind the navy blue sedan, two cars away. I was the shopper fumbling with my keys, the trunk, some packages. Bonnie loves teasing me about it, says it was like I was Superwoman or something, that I vaulted, literally flew over the trunk of the car and had you in my arms before he even blinked."

"I didn't see you."

"No."

"I felt you, but I didn't see you," I say.

And I don't talk about it, but I'm remembering Hazen too. The sweaty smell of his clothes, his hamburger breath, the smile on his face right before it happened. I remember being yanked backwards, away from the car. I remember the noise, the yelling, everybody yelling all at once. Hazen flying backwards, his car door bursting open from the impact of his body, arms outstretched like he's still reaching for me, still going to grab me. I remember peeing my pants. Blood, spurting out of his side. I remember him hitting the pavement, looking confused, not sure what was happening. Calling to me, trying, even though he's shot, to get me. I remember that.

"I remember what you said," I say. "You told me your name. Told me you were Cindy and that I was safe with you." I nestle in close, to remind myself, because Hazen's on my brain now. I try to keep my mind from him, turn it to other thoughts. But sometimes, Hazen sneaks up and grabs ahold of me and won't let go. And when I think about Hazen, it always makes me feel a little, I don't know really, a little creepy, I guess. Makes me feel dirty, like I'm a bad, yucky person. A bit like that, and a bit like I'm coming down with the flu or something, kind of like I get chills and nauseous all at the same time. Feel like that. Guilty too. I feel guilty, like it was all my fault.

I keep having dreams that he's coming back to get me. And he's mad, real mad. I keep worrying about that, that they're going to let him out of jail, because he's good at talking, he's good at convincing. I get scared they're going to listen to him and let him out, and he's going to come and get me again. And this time, because he's mad, this time, he's not going to be so nice.

I nestle in closer. "I'm glad you're a police officer," I say, because my heart started running fast again, from all this thinking about Hazen.

"Me too," Cindy says. "Otherwise, I never would have met you."

She smiles, and I try my best to return it. Hard, though, because Hazen's angry face is still stuck in the center of my forehead.

"And what else about me reminds me of you?" I say, partly because I want to know, and partly to change the subject, to get my mind off him.

"Well," she says, "you remind me of myself, a long time ago."

"Really? Why?"

I see thoughts, images, tumbling across her face. I wait. When she starts talking, she picks her words careful, like she's walking barefoot across a minefield.

"I . . . I also had challenging times . . . difficult times . . . like you," she says.

"When? What?"

"When I was little."

"Really?" I say, and I can't quite believe it. "You did?"

"Uh huh."

And then she tells me. But I'm not going to say. Not going to tell what happened to her. She told me because we're close, because she knows she can trust me. She told me, and that's as far as it goes. But I have to say, I had *no* idea. I never, *ever* would have thought that she'd had such a difficult time growing up too. Makes my heart ache. Her own flesh and blood. And she was younger than me. Way younger when it started. I'm not saying what, let me just say, he's lucky he's already dead.

But Cindy, she says that our challenges are the very things that have made us who we are, that give us our strength, our compassion, and our endurance.

She keeps saying "us," "we," "our," but I don't know, to be honest,

I don't know if I have those qualities. Cindy does, but I don't know about me. I'm pretty mad a lot of the time. Feel sometimes like a downed electrical wire, snapping and arcing and trying to destroy everything in my path. Like Cindy's father, when I think about what he did to her, I don't feel any compassion or forgiveness in my heart! I want to destroy the son of a bitch. And I'm sorry I'm swearing, but I got to let it out somehow, because I just don't think I can keep it inside.

"What are you thinking?" she says.

And I tell her what I'm thinking, how I'm feeling about her dad.

"I know," she says. "I feel the same way about Hazen. But we have to keep working on letting it go. We have to leave it in the hands of the law and hope that the courts are able to do what is just."

"But what if?" I ask her. "What if the courts fail? They do sometimes. What if Hazen gets out? And what about your father? He didn't go to jail. So what then? I mean, shouldn't we just go out and get them? Knock their blocks off?"

"No," she says. "Because then they'd win."

"But how? They'd be dead. That would be good."

"But you'd be in jail, and that wouldn't. No. The best thing that we can do is to try and live a good, fruitful, and honorable life. To walk right in the world. That's the only thing we have control over."

And I want to do that, be more like Cindy. Make the world a better place. Not to let them to win. I tell Cindy and she says, "Good."

Then because we've finished our talk, she hugs me good night and kisses the top of my head. Cindy, my new mom, tucks me in and pulls the blankets up around my shoulders so I'll be warm. I never had anybody do that before. But Cindy does it every night. Me, all cozy and clean in my new flannel pajamas.

Then she turns out the light, leaving the hall door open a crack, just the way I like it. Leaves it open, so the night terrors can't get me.

I lie on my bed, thinking about her, what we talked about.

Cindy says that the person I am, the person I'm going to become, is a choice. She says that good things and bad things happen to everyone, and it is how I meet these challenges, what I learn from these experiences, that makes me who I am today, shapes who I'll be tomorrow.

And I try to send my thoughts towards being all good and honorable. But I can't help it. My mind keeps going back to her father. How I wish he was alive, so I could kill him slow and horrible. Crack open his skull and pee on his brain. I'm a bad person, I guess, because when I think about doing that, it makes me feel good.

I think about Cindy too. About how she has a gun and knows all kinds of fancy self-defense stuff, and yet, she didn't do it. She didn't kill her dad. He died of old age. He went out to get the mail from the mailbox one day. Came back and told her mom that he felt a little funny, sat down in his favorite armchair, and died. Just like that. Nice and peaceful! And I wonder how God could have let him have such a peaceful death. Such a bad person! Shouldn't he have had some horrible disease, where he had to suffer long and slow, like he made others suffer? I don't understand it. I just don't understand God sometimes.

And I asked Cindy, "Aren't you mad? Aren't you mad that he didn't suffer? That God let him die so nice? Doesn't it make you mad?"

"What would that accomplish?" she said, head tipping slightly to the side. "How would that change things? He's dead, it wouldn't affect him, and I'd be walking around carrying it." And I guess I know what she means, but it's a lot to get my mind around.

I lie there in bed in the darkened room, the moon smiling at me, casting a pattern of the oak tree on my wall, so I won't be alone. I can hear the rumble of Joseph's voice, Cindy's voice, softer. The water is running. They're probably brushing their teeth. I listen to them talking, bumping around their bathroom, getting ready for bed. And it's comforting, these night getting-ready-for-bed noises. So different from the bedtime situation at my mom's house, with all the fighting, and the drinking, and Buddy coming in. So different.

But I'm here now. I'm here. I breathe in deep. Cindy and Joseph downstairs. I can see out of the window now that my bedside light is off. The air fresh and cold, and I can see everything, the night sky, the moon. Can see it all and as I watch, right before my eyes, the stars twinkle on, one by one, filling the sky with their brilliance.

I lie in my bed and think about Cindy and me, her life and mine. I think about the fact that if Hazen hadn't stolen me, I never would have met her. And if her dad hadn't been such a jerk, maybe she never would have seen her in me and me in her. And I realize that if these two bad things hadn't happened to us, then I wouldn't be lying right here, in this wonderful, cozy house, with sweet-smelling sheets, and comfy flannel pajamas with fluffy, big-eyed kittens on them, all tangled up in blue balls of yarn. And when I think of all these things, all my anger and madness, it just melts away like an ice cube on hot cement. Just melts away, and I am trembling, so full of thanksgiving. Because it's like my body, my whole room, the whole house, is near exploding with blessings. Everything humming and vibrating and my heart is filled right up, bursting wide open with a million hosannas.

TEN

He dreamt of her last night. Woke up hard. Thinking about how good she felt. About his baby growing in her stomach.

Woke up, thinking about forgiveness, compassion, and their future after all this is done.

She messed up, just a kid, for Chrissake. The busybody doctor probably put her up to it. Knew he'd made a mistake the minute Gemma disappeared into that building. It was a mistake to send her to a woman. Should have gotten a man, a male doctor. Then none of this would have happened.

What was that doctor's name? The bitch. What was her name?

He reaches into the back of his mind, rummages around.

Dr. Fries. Dr. Janet Fries. That's it. The cunt. One more person to take care of. One more person to clean up, once this mess is over.

But not Gemma. Not his Gemma. Changed his mind on that. Just a kid. Didn't realize what she was doing. Poor messed-up kid. What good would that do? Getting rid of her. Who would that help? And besides, and this makes Hazen laugh, his crazy cock would never for-give him.

Been awake for forty-five minutes at least, and the thing's still stiff as a board. Demanding, insisting he deal with it. So he does.

Would like to take his time, but there's no privacy here. Any asshole with a uniform can look in, barge in, whenever they damned well please. Can just sally on in, don't need a reason to pay a visit, rip up his room, destroy it. No reason. Just for the hell of it. Just to mess with his mind.

He used to fight them, but not anymore. Does no good. Just get the crap beaten out of him, because they like that kind of shit. They like trying to control him. Smug little pricks. They come marching in with their riot gear, bunch of sissies! Won't fight fair. One-on-one. Hell two-on-one, and it'd be worth it! But no way.

And if he tries to fight, tries to resist, even when he's only talking the talk, in they march, like marionettes. All geared up. Bring at least half-a-dozen assholes to knock him to the ground, beat the crap out of him, and then on top of that, he loses privileges.

Yeah, he used to fight. Hazen Wood. He used to fight. Not any-more. Nope. Just sits there, lets them do their inspections. Lets them rip the place apart. Just sits there planning. Because this jail thing? This isn't permanent. Not with Mr. Samuel Levy on the case. The guy's *bril-liant*. Fucking brilliant! Putting together one hell of a defense. Got a way of twisting things, saying things, that makes Hazen shout with laughter, at the sheer pleasure of being in the room with somebody who is so skillful. It's like Hazen's watching a magician at work, things Par-tap had said were insurmountable obstacles, and Levy keeps coming up with ways to make them disappear like smoke. Hazen Wood, he's as good as free. They got nothing on him. Not really. Nothing.

So he can afford to sit, let the guards strut around, tear up his cell. He just sits, calm as can be. Doesn't rise to the bait, because he's going to be out of here soon. This is just a pit stop. This is just a rest stop until he fixes his flat tire and gets on with his journey.

Got to think about the future. When he's out of jail. A free man. The baby's going to need a daddy, Gemma too. They're both going to need someone looking out for them. Someone to take care of them, feed them, bathe them. Going to need someone to make sure their hair is brushed. Got to get out of this place, take care of Gemma and his baby. Hope it's a girl. A little baby girl like Gemma.

That would be great. That would be fantastic! Then when Gemma starts getting too old and saggy, starts to lose her appeal . . . Voilà! Baby Gemma's right there to take her place. Perfect. Life's going to be perfect.

Going to have to wait for a while, lie low. Let the authorities forget about him, move on to someone else, and then he'll strike, claim what's his, get his family back together again. First order of the day is to clear up this mess, the smear on his name. Straighten out this little misunderstanding. Might even sue the Chicago police department for aggravated assault, use of a deadly weapon, bodily harm, because, as Sam pointed out, correct procedure was not followed. Yeah, maybe they'll slap a lawsuit on Chicago's finest, smug little bastards. Yeah, that would be good, that would be real good. It would pay for Levy's bills, and maybe there'd be a little left over for Hazen. A little nest egg to start a new life. With a new baby coming, he'll need it.

·   ·   ·

It snowed last night. And it was the most beautiful thing I ever saw.

Joseph was the first one to notice. We were eating dinner, Cindy was telling us a funny story about her and Eric "on the job." That's what they call it when they're at work. "On the job." I think it's a police thing.

Anyway, I was paying attention to Cindy, listening to her story. That's how come I didn't notice right away.

Now Joseph, he was listening too. But maybe he wasn't listening as hard, because all of a sudden, he got a smile on his face. "Gemma," he said, right in the middle of Cindy's story, because he knows how long I've been waiting for snow. "Gemma," he said. "Look outside."

Cindy stopped talking. I stopped listening. We both turned and looked, and lo and behold, there was snow!

Little snowflakes drifting down, floating down from the sky.

We probably wouldn't have noticed them if the porch light hadn't been on. But it was, and we did. I leapt to my feet, jumping up and down.

"Can I go outside? Please? Please? May I be excused?"

"Yes," they said, laughing at the expression on my face.

I ran outside, the snowflakes falling like dainty little fairy kisses on my face, and the feel of it made me delirious with joy. I started dancing a wild, mad, crazy-woman jig. My face turned up to the heavens, arms outstretched wide. I heard Cindy call, "Gemma! Your coat!" I didn't want to stop my celebration, but I didn't want to disrespect her either, so I ran back to the door, where she was standing with my coat in her hand. Joseph's arm around her shoulder and both of them, smiling. I put on the coat, my legs still dancing their joyful jig. My smile so big it felt like it might split my face in two, like an overripe melon.

Then, coat on, I was back in the yard, whooping and hollering, whirling with the snow. And next thing I knew, I heard Joseph say, "What the heck!" And he came out on the lawn with me, and he started hollering too. Waving his arms, dancing around, leaping up, clicking his heels together like he's Gene Kelly, and Cindy was doubled over, laughing so hard she has to clutch at her belly to hold it together. And we were yelling, "Come on! Come on!" And Joseph had a big goofy grin on his face. "Come on!" he called, with an extra-fancy twirl. "It's so much fun!" So Cindy came out, and the three of us danced a wild, wonderful, snow dance!

The neighbors' upstairs lights came on and we could see them, dark cut-out silhouettes, pressed against the window, elbows bent to shade their eyes.

"Come on!" Joseph yelled up to them. "It's fun!"

But they didn't. They stayed in their nice, warm house, shaking their heads, thinking we'd gone crazy for sure.

We danced a little more, but it didn't have quite the same "joie de vivre" with someone watching. So we gave one last whoop for good measure, and then rushed back inside, shivering, teeth chattering and snowflakes clinging to our hair like little icy stars.

Joseph made a big, roaring fire in the living room. We huddled around it, trying to warm our bones. It was wonderful. Family, a roaring fire, and *snow* falling outside, and best of all, Joseph said it looked like it was going to stick.

It was a perfect, beautiful night.

In the morning, when I woke up, at first, I didn't remember. I knew there was something, but my mind wasn't awake enough to know what it was. And *then* I remembered! I flew to the window and, oh my, there was a ton of snow.

I stand there with my nose pressed up to the cold windowpane, and then I realize, I don't have to stand here inside.

I run to my dresser, pull out my clothes, put on two of everything for warmth, two pairs of pants, two pairs of socks, and a sweater and a long-sleeved shirt. Two of everything, because last night was real fun, but I have to admit, I did get cold.

Then I run to the kitchen and get my coat that I left on the kitchen chair. Don't normally leave my things lying around, but last night, I was so excited, I plumb forgot.

"I see the snow hasn't lost its appeal," says Joseph, from behind his paper. He's wearing his pj's, robe and slippers, and his hair is sticking up every which way.

"Yep," I say, stuffing my feet into my black rubber boots. I have to push a bit, wrestle my feet in, on account of wearing two pairs of socks. "Want to come?" I ask, although I know it's unlikely, he looks pretty sleepy and he is still in his pajamas.

"No, thanks," he says, with a little half laugh. "Last night's frolic should do me for the next twenty years. I could barely get my old bones out of bed this morning." He tousles my hair, takes a slurp of his coffee, and goes back to his paper.

I run around outside. I make snowman, an angel, then after all that, I flop back and lie in the snow. Just lie still and watch the snowflakes drifting down. Everything, so beautiful, the trees, the branches, the fences, the roofs, even the old metal garbage cans, are covered in a thick, white blanket of snow that muffles everything, making it quieter, more still. Like magic has happened, and everything, the traffic, the trees, the birds, everything, is holding its breath. Just a quick little intake, like, "Ahhh . . . perfect . . ." It's that kind of feeling. "Ahhh . . . perfect . . . Snow. . . ."

. . .

In my bed, thinking about the day. Feeling, somehow, like the snow coming is another sign. Like God's talking to me again, saying, "I've given you this fresh start, this clean slate. What are you going to do with it? Which path are you going to go down, Gemma? Which path?"

I think about my mom, the one in Oakland. I think about her wanting to talk to me. And me putting it off, not calling, and I feel bad, because I know what I want. I know already. I know how I feel when I think about going back, and I know how I feel when I think of staying. It's two totally different feelings.

And it's hanging over my head, this whole calling thing. It's present even in the real fun times. It's sort of like wearing a sweatshirt that's mildewed. No matter what I do, try to ignore it, put perfume on, powder, wash it a million times, nothing will work. That sickly sweet mildew smell will just follow me around, smelling everything up. Nothing I can do except take the sweatshirt off and throw it away, because it's going to stink no matter what.

So I get off my bed and go to the living room. Joseph and Cindy are sitting on the sofa watching a show about the migration patterns of the polar bear. It looks sort of interesting, and if I wasn't all scrambled about my mom, I probably would sit down and watch it with them.

Instead, I just stand in the doorway and watch them watching the show.

Cindy looks up. "Hi, honey," she says. "Did you need something?" Because I'm just standing there, trying to pull the words out.

"I . . . um . . ."

Joseph looks at me too. "What's up, Gems?" He clicks the remote control at the TV and turns it on mute.

"I'm . . . ," I say, feeling embarrassed. "Uh . . . ready to call my mom and wanted to know if it was okay . . . to use the phone?"

"Oh sure. That's fine. She'll be real happy to hear from you," Cindy says.

"If you like, you can use the phone in my study," Joseph adds. "It'll give you a little privacy."

"Oh thanks," I say. "That would be great." My stomach is tied in a million knots. "I'll go do that." There's no more reason to keep standing there, so I make my legs walk me into the hall. I don't make it to his study, though, get too scared, return to the living room. The TV is still on mute. Joseph and Cindy are talking in hushed tones. I can't make out what they're saying. They stop when they see me.

"Wasn't she in?" Cindy asks. She looks tense, nervous. Way different than when I left a few seconds ago, like she's about ready to cry or something. Joseph's arm is around her, and I feel like I walked into a private conversation.

"Um . . . ," I say, and I'm uncomfortable to ask, especially now that they seem to be having a talk and everything. But I don't know what else to do, and I've already interrupted them, and this should only take a minute or two. "Um . . . I'm sorry. I didn't mean to interrupt, but the thing is, I haven't called yet. See, I'm . . . I'm kind of scared." I try to clear the lump out of my throat. "And I was wondering . . ." My dumb, stupid eyes start to cry. I can't help it. Hope they don't notice. "And

I . . . I was wondering if one of you would mind holding my . . . holding my hand when I call?"

And Cindy, it's like she's stuck for a moment, like a fly on sticky paper, like she wants to get up, but her body won't let her. And then she unglues herself, leaps up, Joseph too.

"Of course we will. Do you want one of us? Both of us?"

"Are you sure you don't mind? I know you're busy."

"Gemma," Joseph says. "We were watching a TV show. How important is that? If you need us, all you have to do is ask."

We walk to Joseph's study. They let me sit in his chair with the armrest and the swivel bottom, which I have longed to twirl around and around in, ever since the first time I saw it.

But I don't, because this is too important.

I take a deep breath. Cindy and Joseph are behind me, their hands resting on my shoulders, like they are anchors and are holding me safe to the earth, so I don't float up and disappear into the night sky.

I pick up the phone.

It feels odd, punching out my old phone number. I've known it for years. Called it six, seven, eight times a day that first week I was in McLaren Hall. Sometimes more. Listened to it ring. Listened to the operator asking her if she'd accept my call. Listened to my mama say, "No."

I dial the number, and the peculiar thing is, I have to hesitate. Am not quite sure, for a moment, what my phone number is. Have to think, to pull it up, out of my past. There is only a split second of a pause, and then it comes back to me. Nobody would have noticed. Nobody but me.

And I find it strange that something like my old phone number, that was such a part of my past, that was ingrained in my life for so many years, could just slip away like that. Disappear. Evaporate, like it never existed.

I dial the number. Listen to it ring. My palms slick, slippery wet, with nerves.

It rings once. Twice. Three times. She picks it up.

"Hello?" she says, her voice husky, low, like maybe she and Buddy were right in the middle of going at it. And it's like I'm paralyzed or something, because I don't say anything.

"Hello?" A little more impatient this time, like if I don't speak soon, she's going to hang up.

And I got to say, the chicken part of me would like that. She hangs up. There. I called her. Did it. Done.

But I don't discharge my responsibilities like that. Cindy wouldn't do that. She'd call, say why, explain things face-to-face. Or in my case, phone-to-phone.

"Hi, Mom," I say. My voice sounds weird to me, like someone sucked all the color out of it. Sounds like wind blowing through a crack in the window.

"It's me," I say. "Gemma . . ."

"Gemma!" My mama, she sounds like she's scrambling, either sitting up from lying, or grabbing a chair and sitting down from standing. I'm not sure what, but there is a movement of some kind or another.

"Jesus Christ! Thank God. Do you know how hard it's been trying to get ahold of you? It's like trying to deal with the fucking gestapo! I miss you, baby. When are you coming home?"

My hands are sweating, my back too. And my throat, my throat's all closed up.

"I'm . . ." My heart is hurting bad. Hurting just hearing her voice. Hurting with the hurt I'm going to have to do. "Mama . . ."

"Yes, baby?" she says.

"Mama . . . I'm . . . I think I'm . . ." I try to suck in some air. "I've decided I want to stay here." I've said it. I know I've said it. Can feel it ricocheting back and forth along the phone line, vibrating, buzzing, hanging in the air, gobbling all the oxygen.

I've said it. Told her. Got it out. Cindy, Joseph's hands calm on my shoulders.

"I see," my mom says after a pause. Voice cooler. Not so friendly now.

There's another long pause. I don't speak. Don't know what to say. Underarms clammy. Don't know how to fill the space now. Half expect her to hang up on me. She does that a lot. Hangs up on me. But she doesn't hang up, and I hadn't figured out the conversation beyond that point. Didn't expect there to be one.

"Look, Gemma . . ." Her voice tired now. Like she's all worn out. Like life is just too exhausting.

I feel bad.

"I know you're mad," she says. "I know I hurt your feelings. I know you're scared. But the thing is, the thing you got to understand, Gemma, is that I forgive you."

And I'm thinking, "You . . . what?" Trying to catch up. But Mama, she's still talking, not hearing my brain.

"I forgive you, Gemma," her words are saying, but the sound, the tone of her voice, that's telling me a whole other story.

"All that stuff you did with my Buddy. All that sneaky two-timing stuff you did? I forgive you. And that's a hell of a lot to forgive. But I forgive you for all of that, and I want you to come home where you belong. We'll let bygones be bygones, okay? How's that sound?"

And honest, I didn't expect her to want me, to try to talk me into coming home. Didn't expect her to talk about Buddy, because she's always avoided the subject. Don't know what I expected, but I didn't expect this. Got no answers for this.

"Why?" I say. That's it. Which is a real dumb response, but it's all I can come up with? "Why?"

"Why what?" she says, a tinge of impatience, like she's got somewhere to go, something to do, and I'm just being difficult by asking such a stupid question.

"I . . . I don't understand. . . . Why?" The words aren't coming out right. "Why do you want me?"

"Gemma," she sighs. I can hear the match, the inhale, long and deep. Can hear her as she blows a thin stream of smoke out through her lips.

Can see her in my mind, puffing on her cigarette, waving the smoke away. "Why do you have to make," she sucks in again, "things so complicated? All the time, everything . . . ," exhales, "so complicated. Why?"

"I . . . I just want to know."

There's another pause. Then she talks, all removed from her voice, like she's pissed off that I've asked her and she's trying to cover it up, but I've known her all my life. I can tell.

"Why do I want you? Well, let's see. The house doesn't feel the same. I miss you. Sometimes," she snort-laughs through her nose. "No, seriously, I'd like to have you back, and besides, you not being here . . . ," sucks on her cigarette again, "it's making things real hard down here. They're asking all kinds of questions, wanting to know why. Things like that, think it'd be easier all around if you came back."

Her voice has that slightly blurry, slurred quality it gets when she's been drinking too much. And I remember how she kissed me on the forehead and then left me at the police station. I think about her on the phone, choosing Buddy. In the Howard Johnson motel knowing about Buddy. Knowing and not saying, not caring.

I think about all of this and I say, "No." Just like that. "No. I love you, Mama, but, I'm not coming home." Just like that. Calm and firm.

She starts yelling and screaming. Calling me all kind of foul words, but I just listen for a while, and then I hang up. Her voice getting smaller and smaller until the phone receiver is resting back on its body and the connection is broken.

.　　.　　.

Had another bad dream about Hazen. A real bad one.

.　　.　　.

They had me hang a Christmas stocking. Which seems kind of funny, because I haven't had a stocking for years.

I tried to tell them, didn't want them to think I was trying to get free stuff by pulling the wool over their eyes and pretending I still believed in Santa Claus. Didn't think that would be right. Wouldn't be fair, honorable.

"You have to hang a stocking," Cindy insisted. "It's Christmas Eve." Her eyes, disappointed, forehead scrunched up, so I shut my trap, because the stocking thing seemed important to her.

I felt a little foolish pretending, but excited too. Like in pretending for her, it almost made it real. Made me feel like maybe Santa really does exist. Even though I know he doesn't.

We hung my stocking above the fireplace and put my name on it with a tag of paper that I decorated with three little snowmen, and a candy cane and a Christmas tree. Cindy made me write GEMMA right in the middle, so, "Santa will know whose stocking it is."

We put out milk and cookies and a carrot for the reindeer.

When all the Christmas Eve preparations were done, I gave them a hug good night and went to bed.

It was hard to fall asleep. I could hear rustling of packages and paper in their bedroom. Whispers and footsteps up and down the hall, little bumps and thumps and muffled laughter.

It really felt like Christmas! The old-fashioned kind that I'd read about in books, cocoa and gingerbread, that kind of Christmas. And just as I was drifting off to sleep, I thought I heard jingle bells and a faint "Ho . . . ho . . . ho . . ."

I'd swear I heard it, even though I know I didn't. Because honestly, even though I'm pretending for Cindy, I'm way too big to believe in Santa.

So I figure, it must have been my imagination playing tricks on me. It does that sometimes. Must have been my imagination playing tricks on me, making my Christmas even more magical.

· · ·

We had a most beautiful Christmas. Nobody got mad or drunk or yelled. It was great! Best of all, Cindy and Joseph loved what I made for them. They really did. Which was a happy something, because I was

186

worrying a bit, but when Cindy opened her present, she really seems to like it, and she said that homemade gifts were the very best kind.

As for me, I really raked it in. They gave me a sled and mittens! Good ones. Nice and warm. Waterproof too. It's going to be way better than wearing Joseph's old wool socks on my hands. I got candy and all kinds of cozy knickknacks in my stocking. A Santa Claus Pez, where the little square candy comes out of his mouth, and a little stuffed reindeer with a red nose, so soft I can't stop rubbing my cheek on it. Cindy likes to feel it too, all soft and cuddly against her cheek.

When I came downstairs, the reindeer was the first thing I saw. His head was sticking out of the top of my stocking. Like he was curious and wanted to see what was going on with the world, to check out the house and the Christmas tree. Poking out of my stocking, right next to a big candy cane. And there was an orange in there, and nuts in their shells too! Safeway always had them in the store around Christmas time, big bins of them. But Mama would never buy them. Said they were too expensive, too messy, and a pain in the ass to open.

So I was pretty stoked to get some real nuts, and Joseph said they had a nutcracker in the kitchen, so I'm going to crack them later.

And I got a new hairbrush. It works real good, and makes my hair all soft and fluffy and floaty around my face because of static cling. And I got some pretty hair clips, and a new toothbrush. And there was nail polish in my stocking. Pale pink, with a pearlish tinge to it, sort of that soft, foggy color, like my old abalone shell. I got all kinds of great stuff. Real girly-girl stuff, that made me feel all, I don't know, fancy, I guess. Special. And . . . last but not least . . . I got a new top. It was rolled up in the toe of my stocking and tied with a red ribbon. It's real pretty and I'm going to wear it on my first day of school.

•   •   •

Levy dropped by, unexpected. An earlier court date opened up, did they want it? Apparently, some poor sucker had been iced in the yard, so there was a vacancy. January third.

187

The odd thing was, Hazen had been wanting, waiting to go to trial, and here was an opportunity to get there sooner. Get it over and done with, and his first impulse was to say no. Found himself scared, hands shaking like a goddamned junkie.

"Ah, forget it," Hazen found himself saying, trying to sound nonchalant. "Why don't we just leave it where it is?"

"We could," Levy said. "But the thing is, the kid's in a good environment right now. The longer she's there, the more stable she might become. Less traumatized, everything not so fresh, close to the surface. This might make her harder to intimidate, not as malleable. On the other hand, it might backfire. She might be the kind of kid where time makes her less reliable, gives leeway for her story to shift. It's an either-or situation. So I thought I'd run it by you. You know the kid, what do you think? We've got to give them an answer by two. Now, we have several choices. We could take this new opening. We could stay with the original court date of February first. Or you could, and, yes, I know you've told me you don't want to, but I must mention it again, because it is a viable option, you could waive your right to a speedy trial. We could draw this thing out, take our time, and hope everything unravels for the prosecution. The kid gets cold feet, they lose witnesses, et cetera. The third option would give us more time to prepare, but it also gives them more time as well. There are no easy answers. What do you want to do?"

"If we draw it out, I waive my rights, do I have to stay here?"

"Yes."

And just then, it was like a curtain parted and everything seemed clear. This date opened up for a reason. God must think it's better to go sooner. Doesn't want Hazen wasting his life away in jail. He wants this thing resolved, wants Hazen to take his rightful place as father and husband and provider.

"Let's do it," Hazen said, his voice strong, impressive. "January third it is." Felt good about it. Righteous. Made the decision. Took the plunge.

But now it's night. He's lying on his bed and Manuel, a skinny Hispanic boy, is sobbing next door. And there's something about the sound that's messing with Hazen's head, and the kid won't shut up. And it's pissing him off, because it's making him feel small, the sound of all that weeping. And he's worrying, wondering if he made the right decision. Sleep is impossible, because Hazen's got all kinds of scenarios ricocheting around in his head and none of them are good.

•   •   •

Bonnie came over last night with her girlfriend, Lisa. It was a social call.

I'd never met Lisa before. Actually, I didn't know that Detective Sheffman was gay. But she is, and Lisa's her partner. They've been together for ten years, so that's something.

I liked seeing the two of them together. Gave me a whole different perspective on Bonnie. She laughs a lot when Lisa's around, doesn't look so stern, so much like an angry bulldog.

Lisa's real pretty. She's short and has sparkly eyes and curly dark hair. She wears red lipstick. Not the red, red my mama wears, more of a bright, cherry red. All spadang and shiny, like life's real exciting. I like it. I think maybe, when I grow up, I'll wear that color of lipstick.

I would have thought it would be weird, seeing two women, all in love and everything. At school, the kids act like it's the worst, most disgusting thing ever. But it isn't. Doesn't feel weird or nothing. Once I got my mind around it, it felt fine. Certainly didn't feel like anything "bad." Seemed natural. Like, of course Bonnie would be with Lisa, they're so cute together, make a great couple. That's the kind of thing that went through my head.

Anyway, they were over last night. A social call mostly, but then, at the very end, Lisa asked me to show her the snowman I made. It was mostly melted, but I took her outside anyway, and when we came back inside, Cindy and Bonnie were talking business.

Apparently Hazen's lawyer has changed the date for the trial. Guess he's allowed to. We'd thought it was going to be a while before I had to go to court. Not until the beginning of February. But apparently, it's going to be in eight days. On January third. I'm kind of nervous. I'm going to have to see him in eight days. I'm kind of scared. Hope I do okay.

Anyway, everything's changed. We were going to go to Navy Pier, have a family day, and see this beautiful indoor botanical park. Then we were going to take a ride on this enormous hundred-and-fifty-foot-high Ferris wheel. That's what we were going to do.

But instead, stupid stinky pants ruined everything, and Cindy and I are going to have to go over to the D.A.'s office instead, so he can go over some stuff with me. Everybody's a little nervous. Wondering what Hazen's side has, why they're rushing it.

Cindy says we'll go to Navy Pier another day, to celebrate after this is all over. That there's nothing to be get anxious about. Everything's going to be fine. But I don't know, she looks real worried to me, and everybody is acting skittery.

·   ·   ·

On the way back home from the DA's, we stop at the beauty parlor. Not only do we stop, but we stop for *me*! I'm telling the truth! It is an extra holiday treat that Cindy and Joseph planned so I could get rid of my stupid, dumb, stinky, two-toned hair! And believe me, when I say my hair looks bad . . . I am *not* exaggerating.

My old hair is growing back in, and the stupid, dyed-brown hair is growing out, so it's like my head is a badly striped sweater, all jaggity and crooked and yucky looking.

And another thing, whenever I look at it, at my hair, it reminds me of him. Of Hazen. Of what he did to me.

I avoid mirrors, store windows, fountains, anything with a possible reflection. Because I never know when the sun's going to burst out from behind the clouds and make what seems to be an innocent window into a reflection of what I don't want to see. Have to keep my eyes moving around pretty fast. Don't let them settle on anything that might morph into a mirror.

But after today, it's going to be gone. All gone. It'll be like it was before Hazen Wood ever came into my life and stole me and did all those things. I can't even put into words how good it's going to feel.

When I first come in, the beauty shop lady says, "Oh my . . . what happened to you?" Cindy and I don't tell her. We just smile and Cindy says, "She'd like to go back to her natural color."

"I should hope so. Whoever did your last hair color deserves to be shot. Hmmph!" Sharon the beautician says, her nose in the air, like she's smelling a bad smell, her fingertips running through my hair. "And I have to say, I'm not too impressed with the haircut either. Looks like it was done with a hacksaw."

"Just about," says Cindy, because she's heard the whole story. "Just about. Anyway, do you think you can fix it?"

"I'll try." Sharon gets me out of her chair fast and takes me in to the back room. Makes me hustle, because she doesn't want anybody to come into the shop and see me. Doesn't want them to think I got my last hair job there.

She washes my hair in a special hair-washing sink that has a fancy chair, which tips way back into a sink with a hole carved into it, for my neck to fit in. It doesn't sound good, sounds uncomfortable when I describe it, but actually, it really feels nice. She puts a folded towel under my neck to cushion it.

The water comes out of a special hair-washing sprayer hose. Kind of like the sink-cleaner hose Cindy and Joseph have on their kitchen sink. But this one has a bigger head, flatter, rounder. The water that comes out of it feels so good. It's like a warm waterfall, swishing all over my head.

The beauty shop lady talks and talks nonstop.

I can't tell if she's talking to me, or Cindy. Can't really hear what she's saying too good, on account of the water. But I say, "Uh huh . . .

Uh huh . . . ," every now and then, just in case, so I won't hurt her feelings if it's me she's talking to.

"Uh huh . . . Uh huh . . . ," I say, while she scrubs and massages my scalp. She uses lots and lots of shampoo. Can't see it, but I can feel it, all thick and luxurious.

She rubs and scrubs and I feel like a cat, feel like purring. I feel like a fine lady. A fancy lady, getting my hair done in a real, live beauty parlor, with Cindy sitting in the chair beside me, both of us, smiling.

ELEVEN

Today's the big day. He's going to see his Gemma. Set the record straight.

Feels good. In fighting form. Going to make those fuckers sorry they ever set eyes on him. Going to burn the Chicago police! Today's the day he gets vindicated. The day Hazen Wood walks out the door a free man, and it's going to feel good.

First thing he's going to do, is get himself down to Denny's. Get himself a big meal. Steak. Yeah! A New York steak, medium rare. That's what he'll have. A steak with the works. Mashed, no, baked potato, sour cream, bacon bits, butter. Lots of butter, maybe a little bit of those green things, what do they call them? Chives, yeah that's it. Get himself a sprinkling of chives. Cheesecake for dessert, strawberry sauce, whipped cream. Wait, maybe he should save the dessert for when he's back with Gemma. Eat it off her. He likes to do that. Where was the last place he did that? Somewhere in Oregon. Eugene maybe? That was the best cheesecake he ever had. It made a big mess of the bed, but sweet Jesus, it was worth it.

Going to see his girl today. Wonder if she's showing? Going to see his sweet baby doll Gemma.

.　　.　　.

His mother's here. His mother! Who asked her to come? Who the hell told her about this? Shit! The bitch! Sitting there so sanctimoniously, so piously, with her little Bible. Playing the long-suffering mother role, oh so well. Two-faced hypocrite! Fat cow! Who the fuck asked her to come?

Then, the answer to his question, dickhead Levy gets up and goes over to her, shakes her hand. "Thank you so much for coming. Your support means so much to Hazen."

"Like hell it does ... . stupid cow," Hazen mutters.

Levy was out of line on this one. *Out* of line. Should have talked to Hazen about this. Should have given him a choice. He doesn't want that old hag here. Shit. Not that he cares, of course. It's just looking at her face makes him want to puke. Stupid cow.

What pisses him off even more is the fact that he's a grown man. Full grown, and he's still scared of her. Scared she's going to cuff him along the side of his head and tell him he's a screw-up. Finds himself trembling at the sight of her.

And, at the same time, there's something about seeing her, sitting there, supporting him, that undoes him, and he finds himself having to fight hard not to cry.

In the courtroom, in this goddamned arena where he's supposed to conquer the world, and he's got tears in his eyes. Dumb bitch! Levy should have asked him if he wanted her to come.

.　　.　　.

We're driving to the courthouse. I'm wearing the new clothes Cindy bought for me.

It was fun going shopping in the mall, looking at all the clothes, picking out my new pale blue pants with a little, thin belt. Nice pants and a white top to match, with long sleeves, and a butterfly on the front. A pale-blue butterfly with spots of pink and yellow on her wings, and she's got her wings stretched out wide, like she's getting ready to fly.

I love my brand-new clothes. Love them. We had such a good time shopping. Everything was fine, laughing and joking. Buying the clothes. But then, when we were leaving the store, this really embarrassing thing happened. I don't know why, I mean I know he's in jail but all of a sudden, as we were going out of the store, a bunch of people pushed by, and . . . I thought I smelled him. I have a real sensitive nose and, well, I thought that I smelled Hazen, and I kind of freaked out. Thought he was coming to get me. Guess I started screaming and crying. I don't remember it so well. Don't want to. Kind of embarrassing. I remember grabbing onto Cindy, not being able to let go. Remember that. Remember her telling me over and over, "He's in jail . . . he's in jail, sweetheart. . . . It's okay. . . . You're safe. . . ." I remember her saying that, calming me down. Then the two of us picking up our bags off the floor, me keeping my eyes down. Trying not to look at anybody, hoping nobody from my new school saw me acting so weird.

Of course Hazen wasn't there. He was nowhere to be seen. I freaked out for no reason. Passed somebody who smelled like him is all. How embarrassing.

And now, driving to the courthouse, and the car seems to be traveling faster than usual. I want everything to slow down, need a little more time to calm, get ready. The clock is moving too fast. We are going to get there too soon. Not ready to see him yet.

I'm being brave though. Not carrying on. I'm pretending I'm all calm like Cindy. We're talking about the weather, my new school that I'm going to start the day after tomorrow. We're talking about things like that. Both of us. Me too. We're chatting all normal like, and I wipe my palms on the sides of my pants, not the front. Dry them off on the sides of my pants so the sweat stains won't show.

The car swings into the parking lot. We're here. The car turns off.

"Are you okay?" Cindy asks, because I'm shivering slightly, even though I got my coat on. I feel my lips, my teeth shaking. Can't stop them. They're shaking on their own accord. Not because I'm scared or anything. I'm strong, real strong. They're just clattering a bit.

"Are you all right? Do you need to wait a moment?"

"No, no, I'm ready," I say, and I smile my lips so she won't worry. Teeth still rattling together, hoping she won't notice. But I don't know, the smile doesn't seem to convince her, so I pull open the door handle, like "let's get this show on the road." I get out of the car. "I'm ready," I say, looking at the courthouse. There are lots of grown-ups milling around in front, TV cameras, and flashbulbs.

"Oh no," says Cindy, because she's looking at them too. I don't know what they're there for, but if I focus on the excitement over there, I won't have to look at her. Don't want to look at her. Don't want to cry.

See, this fear hit me back there, hit me like an old, greasy dishrag to the face. Just back there in the car. Slammed into me unexpected like, when she turned the car off and asked if I was all right, if I needed a moment. Something about the expression on her face that got me panicking. This slap of fear hit me like a slug to the gut, threatening to pull me under. Not that these panic attacks are so bad, I mean, no problem, I can deal with them, it's just I wasn't expecting it, is all.

"Wow. A lot of steps," I say, and I can hear my voice, it's higher than usual, more crackly. Cindy moves to hug me, but I move away. Don't want to hurt her feelings, but honestly, I don't think I can take it, kindness right now. Might break me, splinter me into a million pieces. Move away. "Better get going," I say. "Don't want to be late." Voice sounding like someone else's.

•   •   •

Waiting. I'm waiting now. Am in a little room. We got through the crowd in front. They were pushing, yelling, saying things. Got through them, and now I'm here, in this room. The walls have pale-green paint on them, not pale green like Easter, not delicate or anything, it's more like somebody took some vomit-green paint and thought maybe it'd look better if they mixed some white in it. Or maybe the paint's so ugly because the painter got a good deal on it. Was able to buy it cheap. Or maybe they paint the waiting rooms in back of courthouses these colors to depress people, make them feel like the world is coming to an end for sure.

The paint's been put on thick, globbed on, like my grandma's old lipstick that she'd accidentally left out in the sun. It melted. Wouldn't roll up or down. She had to scoop it out of its container with an old Popsicle stick that she'd use to smear it on her lips. She said it looked just fine. But it didn't. It went on a touch too chunky, not all smooth and silky, not all glossy like my mama's.

My mama's lipstick always looked pretty. Didn't matter if she was passed out drunk on the living room floor, her red lipstick was always in place.

Once when I was little, and she was passed out but good, I ran my finger over her lips. I did it real soft, gentle, so she wouldn't wake up, and she didn't, and a little bit of her lipstick came off on the tip of my finger. She didn't wake up, so I leaned in close and placed my mouth on her mouth, like I was her boyfriend. I laid my lips on hers, and tasted my mother. She tasted of gin, and vomit and cigarette butts. I did it gentle, soft, sneaky, and she didn't wake up. It didn't matter to me that she wasn't awake. Didn't matter. It was one of the first kisses I remember getting from my mama. But I'm sure she kissed me lots. Probably kissed me lots when I was a baby.

After our kiss, I dragged a kitchen chair into the bathroom. It was hard work because I was small then, but I managed. I stood on the chair and looked in the mirror on the wall in front of the sink. I looked at my reflection for a long time, tracing my mouth, gentle with my fingertip, so I wouldn't take any of it off. Looking, feeling different, feeling loved, my mama's crimson lipstick staining my lips.

But enough of that. I'm not going to think about my mama now. There's no point really. Things are what they are, and I should count my blessings. How lucky I am. And I do. I count my blessings every night, a million times a day. I know how lucky I am. I know how blessed.

I'm just a little scared now. That's all. Just a little scared. Worried somehow everything's going to come undone. Unravel, like a sweater with a slipped stitch. Everything's going to come undone, and the last four weeks are going to get pulled out from under me, going to vanish like fog coming out of my mouth. Worried that he, Hazen, is going to figure out a way to trick them, to fool them and get me back. Kind of worried about that.

It's hard to keep my mind off it, sitting here in this room by myself. Cindy's in front now, in the courthouse where the trial's going to be held. She's sitting with Joseph. He came here earlier, in case there was a delay in our case. He brought his cell phone to call Cindy if there was, because he didn't want me sitting in the courthouse any longer than necessary. I'm glad he thought to do that, because already I feel like I've been sitting here too long, like a cat wearing someone else's skin. All prickly inside, like I'm going to jump right out of it. Nervous. Heart banging away. Scared. I'm scared now. Can smell him. Feel like I can smell him all the way from here. Scared. Trying not to move. Trying to keep my legs from running me out of here. Am humming little songs to take my mind off it. Off him. Humming anything I can think of: radio songs, lullabies, Christmas carols, the "Happy Birthday" song. Just keep myself humming. Keep my mind busy. Keep it off of him.

"Are you going to be okay?" Cindy had asked when we got to the little room I was supposed to wait in, until the bailiff comes to get me and brings me to the judge. "Are you going to be all right here by yourself?"

I nodded, acted all nonchalant. "Oh yeah . . . sure, no problem. You go get a seat."

She hesitated, and I knew she was thinking of staying, and I really wanted her to. But that was short-term wanting, because the thing is, I also wanted her in the courtroom, needed her there, and I was scared they were going to run out of seats. Or that all the close-up seats would be taken and she'd have to sit behind a pole or something and I wouldn't be able to see her. I don't know why, but I feel safer with Cindy around, like Hazen won't be able to get me so easily.

She's got her gun. I made sure she brought her gun. Had her check a million times before we left the house. "You got your gun?" I'd said. "You didn't forget your gun? Didn't take it off when you went to the bathroom?"

And she said, "Yes, Gemma, I have my gun." She was patient with me. "But you don't have to worry." She said, "You're going to be safe in the courtroom. Even if I wasn't there, you'd still be safe. He'll be shackled. He'll have a guard. He won't be able to get you." Still, I had to check before we went out the door, make sure, see with my own eyes, that her gun was secure and in place. And I saw it, all metal and polished wood, hiding in the sling under her jacket. Her jacket which is Christmas red, so I'll be able to see her easy.

I'm grateful Cindy and Joseph are here. Glad I have somebody and am not going through this alone. My mama's not here, she's not coming.

I called and asked her, but she just sniffed. "Don't see why I should," she said.

We didn't seem to have much to say to each other, all my words stuck in my mouth, none coming out of hers. So I told her I loved her and hung up.

I really don't know what's going to happen there, if I'm ever going to get to see her again. My mom. I don't know if she's going to want to, now that I chose to live with Joseph and Cindy. Sometimes, lying in bed, I wonder about that. If my mama and me will hook up sometime. Maybe later, when I'm grown, no longer such a burden. I wonder if she'll want to see me then. I'm hoping she will. I'm hoping she'll learn to love me, forgive me, let go of that tight gripping in her heart. Maybe she has already, just doesn't know how to show it. Is too messed up by Buddy. Stupid, dumb, asinine creep. His fault this all happened. Stupid jerk.

Who knows, maybe my mama does love me, maybe she always has. She just doesn't know it, that's all.

Anyway, enough of my mama. The reason I told Cindy to go get her seat is because it was a question of which was worse. Keeping Cindy here, and risk her not getting a seat in time, or toughing it out, sitting here by myself for a few minutes, how hard could that be? Then, for sure, she would be in the courtroom for the worst part, the scary part, the part where I have to see him again.

So I smiled like I meant it, like I was calm, cool as a cucumber. "No, really, I'm fine," I said, nodding and smiling, not looking her in the eye. I hope it doesn't count as a lie, because I'm really trying hard not to do that. Don't think it was a real lie, more like a white lie, a "No, your haircut looks real pretty" kind of lie.

She wasn't going to, but I made her leave. And now I'm here by myself, trying to keep my mind busy. Trying not to think about him sitting two doors down.

Because really, there's nothing to be scared about, he can't get me now. Cindy pointed out the guard to me when we arrived. He was wearing a uniform and was sitting outside Hazen's door on a metal folding chair. I saw him. He had a gun. It wasn't hidden under his jacket, it was out on his hip for everyone to see. A gun and a badge too. He looks real strong. So Hazen can't get me. Can't get out of that room. There's a guard at the door with a gun, there's bars on the window, and the windows in these rooms are up real high, and small too. He wouldn't be able to fit his head out of that window, let alone his stupid, mean ass, even if the bars were gone he wouldn't be able to do it. No, he can't get me. I'm safe. Cindy told me. I'm safe here.

I have hummed all the songs I know, so I've got to start from the beginning again. I don't know what's keeping them. Cindy said it wasn't going to be long. Don't know what's keeping them. My hands are sweating, clock on the wall, ticking so slow.

The DA came in. Said hello. Made sure I was okay. Asked me if I wanted a soda from the Coca-Cola machine down the hall. I said no.

Was scared it would make me have to go to the bathroom. Didn't want to have to go into the bathroom. What if Hazen was going to the bathroom? What if he had a soda, and he had to go to the bathroom at the exact same time as I did? That wouldn't be good. I mean, maybe the guard wouldn't go to the bathroom with him. He might have found that too disgusting. Maybe Hazen would get to go to the bathroom by himself, and the women's bathroom and the men's bathroom are usually right by each other, side by side. And if I was going to the bathroom and he was going to the bathroom, he might see me and grab me, and that would be that.

So I told the DA no thank you. Couldn't remember his name. It's a long, complicated one that twists around itself. I didn't remember his name. Cindy would. Cindy remembers everybody's name. She's good at things like that.

"No, thank you," I said. I didn't take a soda, even though I like them. Even though they're a treat. Didn't want to have to go to the bathroom.

Maybe I should have said yes, though. I could have saved it for later, as a reward for when it's all over. I could have drunk it on the way home, in the car with Cindy. Could have shared it with her, I would have too. Maybe I should have taken the soda. It would have been nice to give Cindy a treat for a change. Darn. I should have said yes and gotten a root beer. Cindy likes root beer, me too. Root beer would have been good. A&W. That would have been tasty. I should have said yes.

Wonder how long it's going to be. How long I'm going to stay in here. Wonder if he'll be in the courtroom when I'm there, when they're asking me questions.

Cindy said that most likely he would, that I'd be able to see him, and not to let it throw me. "Just tell the truth," she said. "Answer the questions, truthfully and honestly, and you'll be fine. Judge Phillips is nice," she said. "He's an honorable, fair man. You're in good hands with him. I'll be there, Joseph too. We'll be right there in the courtroom. So if you get nervous, or scared, all you have to do is look at us.

We'll be there, loving and supporting you. I'm going to wear red so you can find me easily. Look at us if you get scared. We'll keep you safe. Don't worry. You will be able to see Hazen, but he can't hurt you. He can't hurt you now. You will be safe."

That's what she said, over and over, "You will be safe."

I'm glad she kept saying it. It made me feel better. Calmed my tummy a little. I say it to myself when I'm not humming. "You're safe. . . . You are safe, Gemma. . . ." I say it over and over. "He can't hurt you now. You are safe. . . ."

I heard a door down the hall open and shut a while back. Heard footsteps going down the hall. I don't know if it was Hazen or not. My heart is pounding so fast. Didn't know if it was him. Could have been, came from the right direction, the direction of his room. Another door opened and shut, further down the hallway. Could have been him going into the courtroom. I hope so. Hope it wasn't the guard taking a coffee break, going to the bathroom. Don't know.

Waiting, hands twisting. Waiting in this room.

More footsteps, coming closer, closer, and I'm holding my breath, because I don't know, maybe just a secretary, or someone who works here, walking by. But maybe not.

Maybe Hazen's guard did go to the bathroom, and Hazen's scouting, roaming the halls looking for me.

Someone knocks on the door, on my door. *Boom . . . boom . . .* Sounds like that, big and hollow. Makes me jump, jolts me up, like white-hot light shooting through me.

I don't answer, sit still, don't move.

Boom . . . boom . . . the door goes again.

I hear a man. "Hello?" It doesn't sound like Hazen, but I stay put, stay quiet, barely breathing, just in case. Pretend the room is empty, nobody's here.

The door swings open.

"It's time," he says. It's not Hazen. It's the man who works for the court, standing in the door. I can't remember his name. Names aren't sticking right now, don't know why. I remember his face, though. Know it's okay to go with him. Cindy introduced me to him when we came in and told me that he would take me to the courtroom.

It's time now, and all of a sudden I don't feel so good. I stand up, but I'm shaking, it's like I got the flu. I stand up, trying to look normal and walk to the door. I've got to remind my lungs to breathe, have to force my throat to let the air pass.

"I'm ready," I say. I'm trying to smile, but I don't know if it's working, feels like my stiff face is going to crack with the effort. Luckily, the man doesn't notice, he is already leading the way down the hall.

Hazen must be in there already. His guard isn't in his chair anymore. Hazen must already be in the courtroom.

My body is shaking. I can't stop it from shaking. It's shaking all over.

"You're safe," I say, walking down the hall. "You're safe . . . you're safe . . . you're safe. . . ."

•   •   •

They bring Gemma in. She's walking that hunched-down walk. That walk she does when she's trying to act invisible. And it's funny, brings back memories, makes Hazen smile. Makes him smile for the first time in this whole damned charade.

She's walking all scrunched up. Face pale, like all the color was vacuumed out. Pale, translucent, beautiful. Scared. He can tell. Eyes hurt, confused, vulnerable, violet shadows under them, like bruised flowers, must not be sleeping good. Must be worrying about him. About Hazen Wood, her man. Feeling bad, guilty about sticking him in prison. Probably didn't realize the consequences of telling, of opening her fat yap to the doctor. Got to teach her not to do that, when he gets out. Too dangerous, running off at the mouth like that. Got to teach her, let her know, for her own good. For her safety.

They futzed with her hair. Frou-froued it up. But that's okay. Looks good. Back to its normal color. Doesn't seem to be showing the pregnancy yet. Looks good enough to eat.

He tries to get her to look at him on her journey to the witness stand. Wants to smile at her, let her know there are no hard feelings, that he's okay, that he forgives her. Wants her to look at him. But she doesn't. Just follows the bailiff, looking down at her sneakers.

She raises her right hand, says the oath, voice barely above a whisper. Wouldn't know she was talking if he hadn't seen her lips moving. Had to lean forward, strain his ears to hear her, hear anything. Miss her voice, that soft, delicate voice she has, miss the soft hitch, the slide of it.

Her hand, the uplifted one for the oath, is trembling slightly. She looks terrified.

And Hazen, he feels this surge of outrage. That the police are putting her through this, the insensitive assholes! Using her, forcing her to testify, when it is obvious she doesn't want to be here. It is obvious that this is too much of a strain on her. The child is pregnant, for Chrissake, they should leave her alone!

He turns to Levy, because as much as he likes seeing her, he cares for her, for her good health even more. "Is there anyway to get her out of here?" Hazen whispers. "I don't know if the poor kid is up to it."

"Yeah . . . she looks bad . . . that's good," Levy whispers back. "This is your chance, Hazen. This is your best shot. If you can get her not to talk, do it. The ball's in your court. It's showtime."

"What?" Hazen whispers. "What are you saying? You want me to scare the kid?"

"Yeah, that's right. Scare the hell out of her. We've got to break her down in order to get you off. Have to discredit her. I'll have a better shot at it if you have her intimidated." And while Hazen's surprised that Levy would suggest such a thing, he's got to give him credit. It's a good idea. Might help. Because the prosecutors, they're putting a real messed-up spin on things, painting him as a monster. Doesn't know where they get off making up that crap. And he feels for Gemma and all, but this is war, and in times of war, a man's got to do what a man's got to do.

•　　•　　•

I can see him. I'm trying not to, but it's really hard. Whenever the DA moves, or shifts his weight, I can see a part of Hazen. A flash of him. It's way worse than seeing all of him at once and getting it over with. The DA's asking me questions, and I want to answer, but my mouth's not working, glued shut. Lockjaw. A wordless freak. A mummified sack of dry bones and dust. Fossilized. Everybody, looking at me, the whole courtroom, full, waiting. Got to, want to speak, do like we practiced. The DA, asking me questions, things I know the answers to, things we rehearsed over and over in his office, but everything's clenched shut, and all I seem to be able to do is shake my head, yes or no. Mouth won't talk. Body starts rocking, won't stop. We rehearsed this over and over, what I'm supposed to say, and now I'm messing up. I've let him down, the DA, I know it. His words are kind, gentle, but I can see the impatience, the frustration in his face, and that makes it worse. I want to speak. I do, but no words are coming out.

The DA walks back to his table, shaking his head like he's pissed, sits in his chair with a thump. Exhales hard. His hand slides under his glasses, massages the bridge of his nose, elbow on the table for support. My heart, so loud in my ears.

The other lawyer jumps up. Hazen's one. Firing off questions. But it's hard to hear him. Hard to focus on what exactly he's saying. He's not blocking Hazen from my view. He's not standing where the DA was standing, he's striding all over the place, and Hazen, he's sitting at a table right in front of me and a little to the side. There he is, can't miss him, no matter how hard I try. His lawyer pointing at him, gesturing at him, pounding the table with his fist right in front of where Hazen is sitting. Impossible not to look, even though Cindy said not to. Don't want to see him, but he's sitting right in front of me. Staring at me. Eyes fixated on me, like he's a dog and I'm a bone. Almost don't recognize him at first. His hair is cut short, clean, like a banker.

Looks different, but his eyes let me know it is him. The way he's looking at me. That's how I know for sure.

He's wearing a suit. I've never seen him in fancy clothes before. He's got a tie on too. Pale blue with small white triangles. I try to focus on that. Don't look up. Don't look at his eyes, because they are freaking me out. I can tell what he's thinking, and none of it's nice.

My whole body is shaking, trembling like a leaf. A leaf in a windstorm that's about to fall off. And I'm back in that trunk. That urine-soaked trunk. The smell, closing in on me, gagging up my throat. I'm back in that trunk, no clothes, tied up, unable to breathe.

And I'm scared. The way he is looking at me. My belly racing all out of control. Feel like I'm drowning all over again.

I'm trying to hang on, but I'm panicking, like that day, that time he found me in the Dumpster, hot and cold, heat and ice, running, rushing through me. I'm drowning. Drowning . . .

Hand rising to my throat, trying to clutch in air, and his lawyer, Mr. Levy, I think that's his name. He is asking me all kinds of questions. Dirty, filthy questions, and Hazen's looking like he likes it. Smirking at me. And Mr. Levy, he's talking about bad things. Things that I did. How I begged Hazen to have sex with me. And I did . . . I did do that, and I want to explain, that, yes, I said those words, those words that he quoted, but Hazen had a knife, he was making me say those things, beg for it or he would cut me! I want to explain about those things, get my mouth open, but Mr. Levy doesn't let me. Cuts me off, moves right on, on to the next subject. Says this is not a case of kidnapping. This is a case of mutual consent, granted I was underage, but I was a whore. That's what he says. That I was a whore. Making me out to be a cheap whore, saying I did it for money. That I was just a cheap, sex-driven nymphomaniac. Twisting my words, twisting the circumstances. Getting things, lies like that out before the DA has a chance to yell, "Objection!"

All those people looking at me. Like I'm a freak, an oddity in the zoo. Embarrassing. Humiliating for Joseph and Cindy to hear what I did. The things I did to survive. And Bonnie's here, and Dr. Fries. Even Ms. Lindstrom came and is hearing this. It feels real bad, because after our blowup, after I yelled at her, she was getting nicer, and I was starting to like her. And I know they must think all these lies this lawyer is saying are true, the real deal. I mean, why would they believe me? My side of the story? I'm just a kid. And here's this guy, this grown-up in a suit and shiny shoes, why would they believe me?

I'm crying. Don't want to, but I am. Can't help it. Everybody listening to these horrible things about me, and the worst part is, some of the things this lawyer is saying, some of them are true.

I feel like a squashed bug, being sucked down the toilet with all the other crap and the shit, and nobody cares. Good riddance, flush her down.

I'm drowning, hand scrabbling, tearing at my throat, trying to talk, to explain, trying to breathe. But when I manage to get any words out, Mr. Levy just twists them back in on themselves and crams them down my throat.

And I am done for. This is it. I'm well-and-truly dead, when I hear a noise, a throat clearing. Loud, pure like a bell. A church bell, calling me home, calling me to mass. And I follow that noise, that bell, that cough. I follow it to Cindy, all dressed in red, and she smiles at me. Doesn't look repulsed, disgusted by me and the things that I did. She smiles at me, face clear, like cool fresh water. And smiling at me, she lifts her right hand, and gently knocks on her heart, a gentle tap, like she's testing a watermelon. A love tap, a heart tap. And my sobs are still coming, but my throat loosens up, can let go, take my hand away from it now. My throat loosens up, and even though I'm crying, I know I will talk, for her, for me, for all the other girls out there, girls like us.

And Hazen, he's looking at me like he's still got that knife at my throat. Trying to force me to do as he wants. Bend me to his will. Control me, train me, like the good Gemma dog he had before.

He is trying with his look, to gag me again. Silence me. Bind and suffocate me with his stinky cut-up underwear. And I feel this rage swell up. A huge enormous wave of it, and I want to stand up and scream, bellow, "No!"

Want to roar it out.

But I don't. I settle myself in Cindy's face. Calm my heart to beat like hers. I don't bellow. I don't rage. But I do talk. I stop crying and I talk. I speak. I tell the truth. I don't let Mr. Levy stop me. I answer Judge Phillips's questions. And I tell him more. I tell him all the things the DA and I had talked about. I answer Hazen's attorney's questions. I don't let him twist my answers. I keep talking even when he tries to shut me up. I tell the truth. I try to keep the trembling out of my voice. I answer all of the questions. My voice seems so loud in the silent courtroom. Which has become so quiet, I can hear the buzzing of the overhead lights. And I feel like I'm yelling, but I guess I'm not, because the judge, Judge Phillips, keeps leaning forward, his hand cupped around his ear, "I'm sorry, Gemma, could you speak up, please?"

I tell my story. I tell it all, trying to talk loud, but my voice barely rasping above a whisper. And I can feel his rage. Hazen Wood. I can feel his rage crashing over me in waves.

But I keep swimming, I keep telling, I keep talking until I've finished. Until there is nothing left to tell. I keep on telling until I reach the shore.

And when I've finished talking, I know I've done well, because Cindy is smiling, nodding her head. And Joseph and Bonnie and Ms. Lindstrom, they're all smiling at me, and I try to smile back at them with my shaky lips.

I don't look at him. I never want to look at him again.

Judge Phillips says I am done, and he smiles at me too, not a big smile, just a tiny upturning of his lips. I almost didn't see it, didn't know it was a smile. His eyes clued me in, dark and compassionate.

The bailiff comes to get me, to take me out of the courtroom, and I'm glad I am done. I get up from my chair. Start to exit the witness stand, and that's when it hits me, the flu. Hits me like a ton of bricks falling on my head. Perfectly fine, and then bam! I have to hold the handrail for a second. Legs all wobbly. Vision blacking out, like a TV screen, shutting off in slow motion. First the outer edges go black, like a picture frame, and then it's like the blackness bleeds inward, until there is only a little pinprick of vision, of light left, and then that goes too.

"Are you all right?" the bailiff says. The one who was supposed to guide me out of the courtroom.

I nod, but I have to hold the handrail for a second more, until my vision comes back. And then I walk my wobbly, rubber legs out of the courtroom. I keep my back stiff. Don't look at him. Hazen. Don't look, even though I can feel him trying to make me. I don't look back. The big door swinging shut behind me.

And it's like the sound of the door closing makes the flu hit me even harder. The nausea. And it must be some terrible horror of a flu, some powerful, instantaneous flu, because I have to run fast to the bathroom. Am scared I won't make it, that I'll barf all over the fancy, shiny, hall floors.

When Cindy finds me, I'm crouched over, dry-heaving into the toilet, all vomited out, but my body won't stop trying to expel the poison. Clutching the toilet bowl for dear life.

Odd, the things that can be comforting, the smooth, cool, porcelain of a public toilet. Now who would ever think that would be a comfort? But it's true. There was something solid about it. Steady. Reliable.

And that's where Cindy finds me. On my knees clutching the toilet bowl, don't care how filthy, who peed in it. Don't care. Hunkered over it, trying to throw up, dislodge this horrible feeling in my throat, in my gut.

"Oh, honey," she says, as she kneels down beside me and helps me get up. She washes my face with cool wet towels. Paper towels soaked in water. My hands, my wrists, the back of my neck. "You did well, Gemma," she says. "You did real well."

"What's going to ha . . . happen?" I ask, even my voice wobbly. "What's going to happen now?" Can't let go of her arm, can't help it. "Are they going to . . ." I feel dizzy. I feel so dizzy. "Are they going to let . . . let him out?"

"We don't know yet," she says. "We'll have to wait and see. You did a good job."

She tilts my chin up, and I can see that she means it and she smiles at me, love in her eyes.

"We were so proud." She smooths back my hair, helps me get it out of my face. "So proud of you, Gemma."

When I feel well enough, we walk outside to the parking lot, the car. Street lamps, flicking on. It's not dark yet. But they're lighting up so they're prepared. Ready for the night.

The following organizations may be able to refer you to help if you (or others you know) are in an abusive situation.[1]

CHILD HELP USA
Hotline: 800-4-A-Child (800-422-4453)
National child abuse hotline

JUSTICE FOR CHILDREN
2600 Southwest Parkway, Suite 806
Houston, TX 77098
713-225-4357
Jfcadvocacy.org
Advocates for children's rights

NATIONAL ASSOCIATION TO PROTECT CHILDREN
123 Haywood Street, Suite 315

---

[1] Please note that inclusion here does not indicate endorsement of this novel on the part of the organizations listed.

Asheville, NC 28801
828-350-9350
www.protect.org

NATIONAL CENTER FOR MISSING & EXPLOITED CHILDREN
699 Prince Street
Alexandria, VA 22314
800-THE-LOST (800-843-5678)

NATIONAL RUNAWAY SWITCHBOARD
800-621-4000

NATIONAL SEXUAL VIOLENCE RESOURCE CENTER
123 North Enola Drive
Enola, PA 17025
877-739-3895
www.nsvrc.org

SIDRAN INSTITUTE
200 East Joppa Road, Suite 207
Towson, MD 21286
410-825-8888
Sidran.org
Nonprofit that supports people with traumatic stress conditions

1. The author wrote this novel from two perspectives; Gemma's voice is in first person, and Hazen's in a second first-person point of view. Why do you suppose the author chose to tell the story this way?

2. There is a lot of swearing in this book. Did you find it offensive? Did it feel correct for the situations and thoughts of the characters?

3. Gemma and Hazen have widely divergent ideas of what God is. Are your beliefs more closely aligned with one character? If so, which one and why? Or does neither point of view mesh with your understanding of a Higher Power?

4. Were you surprised when Gemma's mother said, "Don't tell them about Buddy?" How did you feel reading that? Were you, like Gemma, still holding out hope that maybe she meant something else or did you already know in your belly that Gemma's mother was aware, on some level, of what was going on?

5. How did you feel when Gemma's mother chose her boyfriend, Buddy, over her daughter? Do you think this is a common occurrence in homes where there is abuse (sexual or otherwise) or do you feel this was the exception to the rule? Why?

6. Did Hazen remind you of anybody you know? Did getting inside his thought process scare you, make you feel dirty somehow, like you needed to take a shower to wash him off, or did you find yourself reading his story in a more removed and analytical fashion? What about Gemma?

St. Martin's Griffin

7. Gemma was relieved when the police caught Hazen, but she also struggled with feelings of responsibility and guilt. Why do you think she had such mixed feelings? Would you?

8. Ms. Lindstrom asked Gemma, "But what I don't understand is why you didn't run away? There you were, out in public places, why didn't you just walk up to someone and ask for help?" Have you ever found yourself thinking those questions when you heard about abduction cases, like Elizabeth Smart, Shaun Hornbeck, or Jaycee Lee Dugard? After reading about the kind of abuse, control games, domination tactics, and challenges that Gemma endured at the hands of her perpetrator, do you feel you have a deeper understanding of this type of situation? Do you still feel judgmental?

9. Did you know that approximately 150 million girls and 73 million boys worldwide are subjected to sexual violence each year? The most extensive study on sexual abuse that was ever done in Canada showed that children make up 23% of the population, but account for 61% of the sexual assault victims, and that 53% of women and 31% of men in Canada were sexually assaulted as children. The U.S. justice department stated in 2002, that 1 in 3 girls and 1 in 7 boys are sexually assaulted before they reach the age of 18. Do these statistics shock you? When you think about the numbers, do you think about your own high school experiences and the people that you grew up with in a totally different way? A lot of them may have been hiding secrets. Does that surprise you?

10. Are you glad you read this book? Why or why not?

For more reading group suggestions, visit
www.readinggroupgold.com